CARRIED HOME

HEATHER MANNING

www.cleanreads.com

Carried Home is dedicated to everyone who helped me get here.

Thank you to God, because without Him, I'd be nowhere.

Thanks to my whole family, especially my sister, Cortney, for helping me edit my first draft (and drawing some pretty awesome sketches in the margins!), and my brother, Nathan, for helping me detect "teleporting pistols" in my next draft.

Thanks to my friends for putting up with me, especially Kira. (There may or may not be an orange velociraptor in this book. It's your job to find it.)

Thanks to my awesome publisher, Astraea Press (Clean Reads), for helping me get here. (You rock, Stephanie!)

And finally, thanks to my readers, because without you, my work would be meaningless.

CHAPTER 1

Near Port Royal, Jamaica
1696

"We simply cannot!" Lady Ivy Shaw panicked. She had spent far too much time away from her home in England; far too much time away from her family. Why, with her gone for such a time, something terrible could have happened to poor little William! Already, she could imagine him accidentally toddling out a window or into the street to his demise. Or coming down with a fever and having a hard time recovering. Or...

"I'm sorry, Lady Shaw, truly I am, but the ship needs to be careened. I assure you it is for our safety. Careening will make our voyage back to London faster and safer in the end. It will take more time, but it is necessary. Besides, I have some business to do here in the colonies before we go back home. Those duties and the work that needs to be done on the ship could take longer than a fortnight." Captain Matthew Emery offered her a sincere look.

Inside, she knew he was doing what was best. Why would he intentionally do something to prevent her and Aimee from returning home, especially when he was aware of Ivy's worry for her brother?

But she could not wait any longer. She wrung her hands, fixing her gaze on the floor. A soft scuffle sounded from behind her and she spun around to find Aimee joining them on the deck. Her golden blonde curls flew behind her in the warm, salty breeze.

"What's the matter, Ivy?" Aimee's concerned gaze morphed into a glare when she took note of Emery.

Ivy sighed. "We will have to wait for Captain Emery to careen the ship and do some business here in town before we return to London."

Her friend's brow furrowed. "How long will it take?"

"Possibly much longer than a fortnight, milady," Captain Emery answered. "There is nothing I can do to prevent it. I already avoided the task of careening before we left London in search of Lady Trenton. And I am in need of the sums business here will provide."

Ivy shook her head, trying to think of an alternate course that would get her home to her brother in less time. Nothing. There was no choice. She glanced out over the bow of the *Cross's Victory*. The sun was setting, casting a slight shadow over the turquoise waters of the Caribbean. Her gaze slid to the back of the ship, where another vessel sailed just behind them. Eden's husband had sent his friend, Captain Thompson, to follow them until they reached Port Royal to ensure their safety. Ivy may never understand why her best friend, Eden, had married a pirate captain, but at least she was happy.

"I am utterly shocked to admit this, but for once, I agree with Captain Emery. If the ship needs to be repaired, then we should see to it before we are stranded in the middle of the Atlantic. Goodness, I cannot imagine being stuck on this ship with this... company for so long."

Ivy jerked her gaze to Aimee.

"Ladies, we can discuss this further when we reach Port Royal. We are nearly there. Right now, I must see to my duties to get the ship to shore. Again, I truly apologize, Lady Shaw, but this delay is unavoidable." Captain Emery nodded before turning and striding towards the forecastle deck.

It looked as if her case was absolutely hopeless, but she had to keep thinking and praying. There must be some solution.

"Land ho!" A shout drifted down from the shrouds.

Captain Gage Thompson lifted a spyglass to his eye and immediately recognized the cliffs surrounding Kingston Bay a few hundred yards off their bow.

"Any orders, Cap'n?" the sailor commanding the helm asked.

Gage had to stop himself from looking around the deck for his previous captain, Caspian Archer. He still was not accustomed to holding the title for himself.

"Sail her true to port, men!" Gage glanced about the decks, where his entire crew moved about, some climbing into the rigging to tighten the sails. He only had ten men, all of whom came from Caspian's ship. To run the ship smoothly without exhausting everyone required a crew of thirty.

At Port Royal, he needed to sign on some men so he had a substantial number to sail the ship and go into battle if they needed to. Right now, almost all of the men were needed above deck at all times. With the little rest they managed to snatch, the tired crew would never be able to keep the ship in tip-top shape.

Gage twisted to view the ship he escorted to Port Royal. Caspian had asked him to see the *Cross's Victory* safe to land. Eden—Caspian's wife now—had encouraged that request because her two dear friends were aboard it, and Gage had obliged quite willingly. Since the day he had seen her he could not clear the image of Eden's redheaded friend from his mind. Lady Shaw, her name was. She was enchanting, and something about the look on her face had made him unable to forget her. There was something haunting, some deep sadness he sensed in the gray-blue depths of her eyes. He longed to at least properly introduce himself to the lady.

When both ships were anchored at the docks, he would talk to the women and make sure they had everything they needed before he headed his separate way. Perhaps he could even learn what made her so mournful.

Ivy stood on the docks, clutching Aimee's arm and watching the scene in front of her with interest. Behind her, Captain Emery's ship bobbed in the docks among dozens of others. As the ocean lapped against the wood, a playful breeze danced around Ivy, causing some locks of hair to escape their confinement. She batted them away from her face.

Before her lay a bustling little city. Men carrying boxes, crates, and sacks called to each other and scrambled about. Sailors and what Ivy could only assume were pirates ambled in and out of the countless taverns that lined the streets.

If one could ignore the ragged sailors, this city seemed more civilized than she had imagined from the stories she had been told of a wicked town, filled to the brim with sordid pirates and shameless women.

"Ladies!" A shout came from her left, but when Ivy turned, no one seemed to be looking at her or Aimee. She glanced back at her friend and shrugged her shoulders. Whoever it was must be summoning someone else.

"Ladies!" A head, covered in wavy brown hair popped into her view. A few seconds later, he was at her side—the pirate Eden had sent with them.

What was he doing here? A spark of fear set her belly on fire. What was he capable of doing to two women alone?

The pirate seemed to be a charming man, she had to give him that. His chocolate brown eyes sparkled, and the deep tan of his skin set off the glistening white of his smile. Dark stubble peppered his chin. He bowed before Aimee and Ivy, bringing their fingers to his lips briefly as he did so.

Ivy stared at him, unabashedly curious. In all her life, she had never met a real pirate. She did not know what to expect from a man like him.

"My ladies, C-Captain Gage Thompson, at your service."

His face had warmed to a slight shade of pink as he gazed at her. Ivy shifted and absently patted her hair.

Silence stretched for a few moments. Ivy glanced at Aimee, who gawked at the man as if he had just jumped out of the sea like a wild fish. Finally, Ivy chose to break the silence. "You are Eden's friend?"

"Aye, milady. I have sailed under h-her husband's flag since I was sixteen years old. He asked me to ensure you arrived in Port Royal safe and sound."

"Well, as we have done so, you may now take your leave, sir. I thank you deeply for travelling with us," Ivy answered. She regretted the curtness of her words, but she was eager to get away from his piercing dark gaze.

"I-I would, milady, but I have not had the privilege of being introduced to you two fine young women."

Ivy flinched. This man seemed nice enough, but his flattery was useless on two ladies of class. That was just the way society saw things. She peered back at the *Cross's Victory*, anxious for Captain Emery to return to them. The pirate may have been Eden's friend, but she had no idea what he was capable of doing to two females who were without the benefit of an escort.

He raised his eyebrows, a charming grin curving his mouth.

Ivy remained still. His look erased his words from her mind.

Aimee stepped forward, covering Ivy's sluggishness. She curtsied and said, "I am Lady Aimee Dawson, and this is Lady Ivy Shaw." She nodded towards Ivy.

Ivy dipped her head politely, and when she raised her eyes, the pirate's gaze had not left her. He winked. She fidgeted with the end of her sleeve, glaring at him. She wanted no part of this pirate and his charms. *Where is Captain Emery?*

"Ladies, is there any way I can help you? D-do you need anything while you are here in Port Royal? I will be leaving tomorrow at dawn, so if you would like anything, please just ask it of me." He flashed them a charming, perfect smile.

Ivy sighed and looked around, then down, anywhere but at his attractive physique. His perfectly polished black boots filled her gaze. A thought occurred to her, and she jerked her head back up to his face. She had no idea why she had not realized it sooner.

"Captain... Thompson, is it?"

He nodded.

"Where is it you are going when you leave tomorrow, sir?" she asked, studying him carefully.

"The Carolinas, milady."

Ivy furrowed her brow. "What business do you have in the Carolinas?" She shook her head, envisioning what type of business a pirate might attend to. "No, never mind, I probably don't want to know."

Aimee let out a little puff of air next to her.

A grin stretched across Captain Thompson's lips. "Miss, it is not what you may think." Why did the man not address her and Aimee by their proper title? He probably did not understand how to do so. "I have no intention of raiding the town or any other mischief. Nay, I go there to visit my sister, whose husband passed away recently."

"I'm sorry for her loss, sir." Ivy glanced down. She didn't wish such a tragedy on anyone. A wave of guilt washed over her. She had judged this man from the moment she saw him, but he seemed to be quite caring and his sister was in an unfortunate state. Really, she should apologize.

"Aye, well, he was a brute of a man. I'm not sorry for her loss in the least, if you can forgive me speaking ill of the dead." Captain Thompson's gaze latched onto Ivy's for a second, before quickly diverting to the wood planks of the dock below them.

⚓

"Oh. Well. I'm sorry, I suppose."

Gage nodded.

Lady Shaw, the enchanting redhead, stared at him unabashedly. He suddenly felt flustered since she had managed to not look him in the eye since she had caught him staring at her from the deck of his ship. With her in front of him, he scarcely noticed her friend next to her.

After a few moments of rather awkward silence, Lady Shaw opened her mouth as if to speak, stopped, opened it again, and then closed it yet again.

Finally, she took a short step closer to him.

"Sir?" she inquired, her eyes fixed on his boots.

"Yes, miss." Gage stooped down to look at her pink face. "What may I do for you? Name anything, and it shall be done. You are Eden's friend, so you are my friend as well."

"Well, sir, you said you are sailing to the Carolinas... May I ask how long that extra trip would take and where you plan to go afterward?" Lady Shaw said, stuttering a little. The blonde woman, Lady Dawson, reached out and clasped Ivy's arm the second she finished speaking.

Lady Shaw glanced at her friend for a second before pulling from her grasp and stepping closer to Gage.

He could not seem to move properly. Or speak properly. "I—well, I can't be saying for certain, miss; it could take up to a fortnight to get to her—"

"Would you consider sailing to London in all haste, once you have finished your business in the Carolinas?" Lady Shaw spoke rapidly, pleading with her stormy gray eyes.

"Ivy!" Her friend whispered, pulling the lady back yet again before spinning to face Gage. "Sir, if you will please excuse us for a moment, I would appreciate it greatly." She smiled at him with a flutter of her thick eyelashes. Gage barely noticed her pretty features because he was far too distracted by Lady Shaw. Why did this woman want him to sail to London in all haste? Well, no matter. With her crystal-gray eyes and fire-tinted hair, he was almost certain she would be getting whatever she wanted from him.

"Yes. Yes, of course, ladies." He stepped back a few paces and examined Kingston Bay while the women spoke in hushed tones.

§

"Ivy, what do you think you are doing? You cannot just run off with the nearest man who happens to own a function-

HEATHER MANNING

ing ship. Why, you don't even know this person! I thought *you* were the responsible one."

Ivy sighed, barely listening to her friend.

This was her chance. Her one chance to get home, to take care of her brother before something went wrong. She would not be able to bear it if something happened to her brother, or any member of her family, for that matter, while she was away from them.

"Ivy!"

She leaned to her friend, smiling apologetically. "I know, Aimee, but he is a friend of Eden's husband. Surely he is a gentleman."

"He is a *pirate!* Now, I trust Eden's decision in the man she married, but friend or not, this man is a pirate! You know what that means don't you? Do not tell me you haven't heard stories, because I know you have, Ivy. You are usually the one out of all three of us who thinks rationally." Aimee crossed her arms defiantly.

"Aimee, this is none of your affair." Guilt weighed down Ivy's heart at her snappy tone. There was no reason to take her turmoil out on her friend. "I need to get home to William before something terrible happens. Please, just let me do this." Ivy moved her eyes to the captain, who had turned away politely, seeming to ignore their conversation. His back leaned against a barrel and his legs and arms were crossed as he stared into the bay. "You could go with me, Aimee, and leave Captain Emery. I know you detest his company for some reason."

"I am not about to go on a voyage with a pirate! That's even worse than sailing with Captain Emery. But Ivy, I can't lose you. Eden already moved away with her pirate. What if something happens to you? Besides, I will be worrying about you nonstop until *I* get home. Don't put me through this again. You know what it was like when we didn't know if Eden was alive or dead." Aimee reached out, resting her hands on Ivy's elbows gently. Ivy leaned away, and Aimee was forced to strain her neck to see her downcast face.

12

"Aimee, you do not understand. You have no younger siblings; you don't know what it feels like! Do you remember how it is for me back home? With Mama sick most of the time, William depends on me. When I am not there, no one is really left to tend to him. Papa never knew what to do with children. Something horrible could happen without me there! I don't care who I sail with, but I have to get back home as soon as I can, and this man is leaving tomorrow at dawn. What else can I do?"

Ivy took a step backward, her hand to her aching forehead, and bumped into a crate behind her. She swung her arms to right herself, and then noticed they had attracted a small audience of men. They were a raggedy bunch, all staring at Aimee and herself.

"You are making a scene, Ivy!" Aimee leaned in close as she whispered.

Captain Thompson seemed to notice, because he stepped between the ladies and the men, standing tall and giving them a formidable look. The men grumbled, and bit by bit, scurried away back to their duties.

Finally, Captain Thompson faced Aimee and Ivy. "Are you all right, ladies?"

Aimee jabbed Ivy with her elbow, giving her one last pleading look. "Do *not* force me to be alone with *Captain Emery* on that long voyage."

CHAPTER 2

Eden watched silently from the armchair near the port-hole of the cabin as her husband Caspian read aloud to her and their son, Reed, from an enormous Bible. Behind her, the sky was lit only by the twinkling stars that reflected in the black, glassy ocean. She loved the sea at night, when everything was dark and the sky so clear.

Reed yawned and leaned back in his chair, his eyelids drooping. A curl of tawny hair drooped across his forehead, and Eden smiled. The child's hair was just as unruly as his father's dark locks.

After a quick prayer, Caspian closed the heavy book. He smiled lovingly at Eden, and her heart fluttered as it always did when her husband looked at her.

Slowly, Caspian stood and walked towards her, a grin on his strikingly handsome face. She closed the distance between them, leaning her face against the strength of his chest.

He kissed the top of her head and leaned down to peer in-to her face. "Are you sleepy, love?"

She nodded, snuggling against his warmth. They had been up early, awakened by a fierce storm. Caspian had told her it was the edge of a hurricane they had narrowly avoided.

Reed clambered up to them, resting his little head against Eden's hip. "Mama? Papa? Can I sleep in here with you to-night?"

Caspian sighed and looked down at Eden. She shrugged, smiling at her husband. Ever since Caspian had remodeled the innards of his ship so Reed had a separate room and the couple could sleep alone, Reed had been none too happy.

"Yes, Reed. Just tonight, though. You need to start sleeping in your new cabin. You are six years old now." Caspian ruffled the young boy's hair, while Eden kissed his cheek.

She leaned towards her husband, whispering in his ear, "Remember, darling, he has hardly spent a night in his life outside of this cabin. He just needs some time."

He groaned as Reed scurried off to sit on the bed. "Aye, but some nights alone with my new bride would be pleasant, as well."

Eden felt her face heat at his words and she leaned her forehead against his shoulder, breathing in his scent of wood and spice. She slowly rotated from her husband. "Did you wash your face, Reed? I asked you to do that every night before bed."

The sweet child sent her an impish smile before running to the water basin that sat on his father's desk.

Caspian chuckled. "I must say, woman, you bring much civility to this ship of ours." He offered her a wink and moved to sit in one of the two leather chairs in the far end of the cabin to pull off his tall boots.

Eden giggled and gazed out the glass porthole behind Caspian. She stared at the night sky, allowing her mind to wander as she watched the still darkness. What other ships were out there, she wondered. What other people, what other lives, were going on while she rested in this cabin, contented with her little family?

Caspian leaned forward, elbows on his knees, and brushed a lock of hair from her forehead. "Is something wrong, love?" he whispered, glancing over his shoulder at Reed, who knelt beside the bed, his blond head bowed in prayer.

"Oh, nothing, Caspian... I just... I'm worried about my brother, I suppose. Do you think he is alive?" Eden rose and moved to crouch in front of her husband. "I was just thinking, he could be out there somewhere, sailing on the very same sea we are in, and I could never know the difference."

🛆

Caspian gazed into his wife's eyes, entranced by how they stared back at him so sweetly.

He hated seeing the dear woman upset. With a gentle grip on her arm, he pulled her to stand before moving her onto his lap. She sighed and leaned back against his chest.

"Then I will begin searching for him, love." He kissed her neck, inhaling her sweet scent of coconut and vanilla. "I say we make port at every city and ask around about his whereabouts until we locate him."

"Oh, Caspian... thank you so much!" She threw arms around his neck.

"Aye, my sweet. It's a joy to make you happy. Now, it's time we get some rest." After a slow kiss cut short by Reed's giggling, Caspian released his wife and allowed her to move behind a screen to change into her nightgown.

Reed moved over to Caspian, tugging on the end of his father's shirt that had come untucked. "Father, why was Mama upset?" The little boy's bottom lip quivered.

Caspian leaned down, crouching so he was at eye level with his concerned son. "She is worried about her brother—we don't know where he is. We will find him, though."

Eden emerged from behind the screen, her coffee-colored curls now tumbling over her shoulders in waves against the creamy white of her lacy nightgown.

Caspian felt his body warm at the sight of his wife, who slowly walked over to him, hips swaying with each step. She offered him a wavering smile, and reached up to place her hand on his cheek. He moved to put his arms around her waist, but not before he noticed the slight frown marring her pretty features.

He had seen that frown too many times for his liking.

Caspian let out a long breath, sitting down on the bed and pulling her down with him. "Darling, we will find him. Do not worry."

"If he's still alive..."

Caspian cut off her fears with his lips. Reed climbed onto the bed and Eden's lap, snuggling against her. Caspian pulled away from his wife.

"Let's not worry about it any longer, sweetheart. We will begin searching first thing in the morning."

Eden nodded and laid her head back against his chest.

CHAPTER 3

Ivy shifted away from her friends. Her boot stuck in the muddy street, forcing her to lurch her foot upward to free it. With an elegant swish of her skirts, Aimee crossed over, avoiding the mud, and placed her hand on Ivy's arm.

Captain Thompson took a step towards them.

Ivy cast a pleading look at Aimee. "Please," she whispered. She needed more than anything to return home as quickly as possible. Obviously, Aimee was not happy with being left alone with Captain Emery, but the girl would live. The man was not a monster by any means. He had gone out of his way to save their best friend, Eden. In fact, he was studying to become a minister. But for some reason he and Aimee had never gotten along well.

Aimee sighed, and Ivy recognized that she was softening.

Ivy turned to the pirate captain. "Sir, I beg you to consider my proposal." She paused and patted her hair. "I don't have the benefit of a lot of money, but I will give you what I have for your services, and I can gather more once we arrive in London."

He bowed. "Thank you, milady, but I have no need for your money. I do not sail a passenger ship."

Ivy's heart tumbled to the ground, and she was unable to control the tears that flooded her eyes. "I—"

"However, I would be honored to escort you to England as my guest."

Ivy blinked, unsure if she had heard correctly. "Truly, sir?" She held her breath.

18

"Aye, miss, I would not lie about such a thing. Please, your presence would be no burden to me."

"Oh, thank you!" A warm wave of relief swept over Ivy. She would be home with William in no time at all, and all would be well. Besides, her family was short on funds right now and she had dreaded how much money he would demand for the voyage.

"Lady Shaw. Lady Dawson." Captain Emery's voice drifted from behind them.

Ivy spun around to see the man approaching from the docks. He waved, jogging to close the distance between them.

Aimee snorted in a rather unladylike manner and twisted in the other direction, a glare marring her pretty features. Ivy frowned. Her friend really needed to learn to be more civil to this poor man.

"Ah, Captain Emery!" Ivy began. "I have some happy news. Captain Thompson here has agreed to sail me back home in all haste."

"After a stop in the Carolinas," Captain Thompson interjected.

Ivy continued, pausing only slightly as Captain Thompson spoke, "We shall set sail tomorrow."

Concern darkened Captain Emery's eyes. "Are you certain you want to do this, Lady Shaw? I... I don't know this man, or his reputation... it is highly unsafe." He eyed the pirate captain.

Ivy paused. She had expected much more of a protest from Captain Emery, but the man didn't look like he would try to stop her.

Thank you, God.

"Yes, Captain Emery. I need to get home to William, and if this man can help me get there sooner, I need to sail with him. If he was Eden's friend, I can trust him. I am certain."

Captain Thompson shifted his stance, and Ivy realized he was staring at her again with his chocolate brown eyes. Surely he was made uncomfortable by her and Emery's discussion.

"Very well, then. May God be with you." Captain Emery nodded to her.

Aimee released a groan of frustration.

Captain Thompson grinned fetchingly and bowed to Ivy. "I will leave you a few hours to bid farewell to your friends here, milady, while I attend to some business in town. Later this evening, I can meet you at the docks."

"Sir." Captain Thompson nodded to Captain Emery. "Miss." He bowed to Aimee, and within seconds, he strode out of sight.

⚓

As Gage sipped his rum, he took in the setting of the tavern around him. Men lounged at the many rickety tables, slurping their rum and entertaining the wenches on their laps. He pitied the women and wondered what bitter turns in life had caused them to practice such a vile profession. Shouts and curses permeated the air, along with the occasional gunshot and the ever-present clinking of swords. Young men and women bustled from table to table, refilling mugs with rum in exchange for coins.

Gage rubbed his hand against his face, scraping against the stubble he had forgotten to shave. He had been too concerned—first, with preparing his ship for the lady he had somehow invited on board, and later with assembling a substantial crew in Port Royal for their voyage. So far he had gathered twenty men, most of them rather unruly, and many young and inexperienced in sailing. But they were the best he could find under the circumstances, and he would take what he could get.

Blast, what was wrong with him? First, he stuttered like a fool in front of Lady Shaw as if he had never seen a woman before, and then he welcomed her aboard his ship to sail to England. Why, he had no business in England at all, and he had even less business consorting with a beautiful lady like her!

But her eyes had been so filled with anxiety, like her life depended on returning to England immediately. How could he let her be so upset without doing something to help her?

He did not even know her. For some reason, Gage had always felt like he had to protect every woman within his sight.

Gage sighed and glanced up as a tall man stopped in front of him. He boasted fine attire for a sailor, and stood straight with confidence.

The man cleared his throat, and Gage , realized the man had addressed him. "How may I aid you, sir? Are you looking to enlist in my crew today?"

The man scratched his chin. Only then did Gage notice the distinct scars marring the right side of his face.

Gage struggled to control a wince. He had seen many men in this profession with physical deformities, caused either from an accident in battle, or previously acquired, causing the men to be shunned by society and forcing them into a pirate's life. What cruel misfortune had caused this man's deformation?

"Aye, milord." He bowed, and Gage detected a refined tone in the pirate's voice. "Adam Douglas, at your service."

Gage nodded. He forced himself to move his gaze from the man's scars because he did not want to make him uncomfortable. "I am Captain Gage Thompson. What experience do you have in sailing, sir?"

Mr. Douglas raised a dark blond eyebrow. "I have been sailing for almost ten years now, and I have previously worked as both quartermaster and first mate aboard my fair share of merchant, privateer, and pirate ships."

Gage grinned. If he got the rag-tag group of men he had just recruited to agree, a fine first mate stood before him. The man actually had more years of sailing behind him for one so young than Gage himself, who had begun sailing quite young with his adopted brother and closest friend, Caspian. Gage didn't estimate this man to be more than two or so years older than himself.

"Why do you no longer sail under your previous captain, may I ask, Mr. Douglas?"

"I grew tired of his cruelty and didn't have it in me to lead a mutiny, so I left the first chance I found. I heard you were previously Captain Archer's first mate, and the rumor is he's a fair captain, so I was hoping his tactics had rubbed off on you, perhaps." The man lifted his eyebrows.

"Well, sir, I can only hope to be as good of a captain as Archer, but I assure you I will try. If you sign my articles, you have a place on my ship, Mr. Douglas."

⚓

Guilt stabbed Ivy's heart when Aimee's misty green eyes met hers, filled with tears. They were back at the docks, near Captain Emery's ship, waiting for the time when Captain Thompson would be ready for her. Now Captain Emery remained a few yards back from them to make sure they were safe among the riff-raff of the uncivilized town. He seemed to be minding his own business, and yet Aimee sent him an untrusting glare before leaning against a nearby barrel.

"Are you sure you have to do this? What if something happens to you?"

The warm salted-sea breeze seemed to mock them in its cheerfulness as it toyed with Ivy's hair. "Aimee, believe me, I would not do this if I did not have to. But I will be perfectly safe. God is with me; I know that, so you have nothing at all to worry about. And Aimee," she added, making eye contact with her dear friend so she knew Ivy truly meant her next words.

"Yes?" Aimee sniffled.

"Please, do not act as if Captain Emery were the devil himself. He truly is a good man; you just have to treat him properly. Please, allow him another chance to be your friend. I do not want your voyage home to be a miserable one."

Aimee lifted her chin. "I'll try, Ivy, but not for him. Only for you. That man can rot in the bottom of his little ship in the center of the sea, for all I care, but I will try." She sent another feisty glare in the man's direction, but if he heard her, he didn't offer any indication.

Ivy smiled at her friend's pluck. She wished she knew exactly what had gone on between Aimee and Captain Emery to generate such strong hate between them. "That you will try at all pleases me, my dear friend."

Aimee placed her hand on Ivy's arm. "I will miss you so much." A sob choked her voice. "Please don't run off with some pirate like Eden did. What will I do all by myself?"

Ivy chuckled, pulling Aimee into a hug and not caring they were in a public setting. She patted her friend on the back as a horde of men paraded by, transporting the cargo of a nearby ship. "It will be all right, Aimee. I'm not going to get married to some uncivilized pirate. I am sure Eden has good reasons and knows what she is doing, but I would never do something like that. You have nothing to fear. I will be waiting for you when you return to London, and all will be well."

Brushing a tear from her cheek, Ivy leaned against her friend. Somewhere behind her, a throat cleared obtrusively. She twisted to find the handsome Captain Thompson grinning at her, his white teeth flashing in the afternoon sunlight.

"Good evening, ladies." He bowed slightly to each of them as Ivy pulled away from Aimee. The women nodded their heads in acknowledgement. "Captain." He offered Captain Emery a smile before turning back to Ivy. Emery quickly filled the space between the women and the pirate, but remained silent as Captain Thompson spoke.

"Are you prepared, milady? I planned to give you a tour of the ship and allow you to dine and sleep on it tonight, so you are accustomed to it before we begin the voyage, if that suits you. This way, if you have any second thoughts, you may change your mind and return to your friends here." He nodded to Aimee, who now stood next to Captain Emery, a glare darkening her face.

"Yes, milord, I am ready and must insist we leave as soon as we can on the morrow."

The captain beamed. "I will try my best, Lady Shaw."

Ivy turned to her friends to wish them farewell. Aimee sent her yet another pleading look, and Ivy blinked back tears when she saw her dear friend's sobbing face. She sighed and drew Aimee into a long embrace.

"Everything will be fine. I will get home safely to William, and you will get back, too. Don't worry. We will see each other in no time, my dear." Ivy whispered before pushing away and gripping Aimee by the shoulders at arm's length. "And remember your promise regarding Emery. Please."

She squeezed her friend one last time before turning to Captain Emery. "I thank you from the bottom of my heart for taking us to find Eden. There is no way Lady Dawson and I can ever repay you for your kindness."

He bowed to her, bringing her hand to his lips. "It is the least I can do, milady. I shall pray for your safe return home every day."

"I appreciate that greatly, Captain Emery. I will pray for you as well."

Captain Thompson stepped forward, touching her elbow briefly. "The day is slipping away from us, Lady Shaw. Shall we be going?"

Ivy jerked her arm from his touch—after all, a man of his low class should definitely not be touching her—and nodded, giving her friends one last sad smile before following Captain Thompson down the docks to a longboat.

⚓

Gage resisted the urge to bury his face in his hands as some members of his newly acquired crew rowed him and Lady Shaw to his newfound ship. What was he thinking, cordially inviting this woman to join his voyage? Any other time would probably have been all right. But he had only spent the last two weeks as a captain after his friend Caspian had given him the ship. He hardly had enough confidence in himself to run the ship without sinking it, much less in captaining the ship and protecting a lady like her. He risked a glance at her out of the side of his eye. The sun, which was beginning to set, cast a glinting glow off of her copper curls which remained in their tight confinement atop her head.

She faced him, brow wrinkled in a frown. "Which one is yours?" She gestured to the many ships docked in the bay.

He pointed to the *Siren's Call*, as he had renamed her, bobbing a few dozen yards to their right. Her masts stretched up, endeavoring to touch the clouds above them.

She glanced back at him. "How fast does she sail, Captain?"

He frowned, initially feeling uncomfortable but then realizing she only asked because she wanted to return to England as fast as possible.

"I believe we can get up to fifteen knots out of her, at our best."

She offered him a blank look. A pirate next to Gage chuckled as he leaned forward, rowing the boat.

Heat flooded Gage's face. He was probably speaking gibberish to the poor woman, even his crew could see that. What would a lady like her know about nautical terms?

"Milady, this ship can sail with exceptional speed when she has been freshly careened. Faster than Captain Archer's ship, actually. We shall reach our destination in all haste. Don't worry over it."

The bow of the *Siren's Call* loomed high over their heads, and Gage's men stopped their rowing. He assisted Lady Shaw to her feet and she stumbled as a swell roved across the water. She swung her arms about, and he grabbed her waist to steady her. Gage allowed his hands to remain on her middle for longer than what was needed for the woman to regain her balance. Heat flooded over him, and he quickly removed his hands. What was wrong with him, ogling over the poor woman so? Her face shifted to a light hue of purple, and she backed away from him.

He took a deep breath. A man behind him grunted. Gage stepped forward and gestured to the rope the crew already aboard ship had thrown down for him.

"Ladies first."

After letting out a puff of air, Lady Shaw grabbed the ropes and began her ascent. Gage made sure to follow right behind her, fearful that she would stumble. He wanted to be the one to catch her should she fall, rather than one of his crew members.

The trek up the side of the ship was slower than most he had witnessed, but Lady Shaw eventually reached the railing. Gage stretched an arm up to give her a boost over the bulwarks before landing on the deck behind her with a light thud.

He glanced around, noting the barrels lining the decks. The crew that had remained on the ship while he was at port recruiting more men lounged on the deck, some playing cards, others drinking from bottles of rum. When they took notice of the lady, they whistled and offered catcalls and lewd comments.

"Har, ye went for a crew, and brought us back a treat instead, didja, Cap'n?"

"All you could find was a lady to join yer crew?"

Gage frowned. For some reason, he had forgotten how uncivilized his peers could be. Lady Shaw's face became a dark shade of crimson and her eyes pleaded with him before she bowed her head low.

He cast her an apologetic look before announcing, "Lady Shaw is our guest, and you will treat her no less. I don't want anyone bothering her. Do you understand me, men?"

Grumbles drifted from the men, and Gage decided to leave the matter there.

"At least this one ain't a stowaway!" One man who had joined Gage from Caspian's ship shouted, and others chuckled.

They were referring to Captain Archer, and his stowaway-turned wife, Eden.

"Silence, men!" Gage tried his best to use the commanding tone that sent Captain Archer's men scrambling to do his bidding.

He would never be as great a leader as Caspian.

But his men did shut their mouths and went about preparing the ship to set sail at his bidding. Mayhap Gage wasn't a complete failure after all.

Ivy tried to steady herself against the swaying of the ship. She had taken her short moments back on land for granted, she feared. Captain Thompson placed a gentle hand on the small of her back but soon removed it. The man was behaving oddly, but what was to be expected of a pirate? He had no doubt never even met a real lady before his time spent with Eden. Ivy's father had taught her some men were simply born beneath others and there was nothing to do about it.

The rest of the ship's crew climbed up from the longboat and sauntered across the deck. Each thump of their boots sent shivers splintering down Ivy's spine. What was she getting herself into? At least on Matthew's merchant ship she knew she was safe. Here she was stuck with a group of uncivilized miscreants. Who would protect her from them should they attack?

Ivy cringed at her thought. She had no right to be so judgmental of the men, but what choice had they given her, really?

Captain Thompson cleared his throat. "Milady, may I escort you about the ship, now? Or do you wish to rest?"

"Nay, Captain, I'm afraid there will be plenty of time for rest on our voyage. Please, do show me about your vessel."

He beamed and offered her his arm. Ivy hesitated, considering her options. She didn't want the man to think she wanted to touch him, and yet she did not wish to offend him by not taking his arm. However, without holding onto him, there was a large chance of her toppling to the deck. She squeezed her eyes shut at the vision of her feet in the air, petticoats exposed. Nay, that was not an option.

Ivy let out a sigh and accepted his outstretched arm. He guided her about the main deck, pointing out the different masts and sails to her. They all passed through her mind without her noting any. She assumed she would never need to know the information, but listened to be polite.

She detected a certain pride in his voice as he led her about the vessel. Captain Thompson led her down a stairwell, lighting a lantern as they went. The light cast an eerie glow across the dark setting. They passed several doorways until the captain halted before one.

"This will be your cabin for the voyage. It is meant for some of my officials, but they have agreed to sleep with the rest of the men so you may have your privacy. Many ships don't have a separate cabin like this anyway unless they are a passenger vessel."

"Thank you very much, sir." Ivy pushed a lock of her hair from her eyes that had escaped her bun. Really, the man was quite kind, offering her a place on his ship and wanting nothing in return, and giving her a cabin for herself as well.

Captain Thompson nodded his response and moved down a hallway, his heavy boots thumping as he walked, but Ivy stopped in her tracks. Her blood chilled as realization struck her. Was the man being kind, or... or... could he want something—not monetary—in return? Only now thinking of what she had gotten herself into, she shuddered. She would have to discuss this with him later.

The captain halted, faced her, and raised a questioning brow. Ivy opened her mouth to speak but refrained. She did not want to give him any ideas if they had not yet occurred to him.

"Milady?"

She gave him a small smile and shrugged.

He cleared his throat and continued on their journey. His path led them down a narrow ladder.

Filthy smells assaulted Ivy's senses and she quickly pressed the back of her hand to her nose.

Captain Thompson glanced back at her and chuckled, the white of his teeth glimmering in the lantern light. "You'll grow accustomed to the stench in time, milady."

"I know, Captain, even though I was only off of Captain Emery's ship for a few hours, I suppose my nose was glad to be rid of it."

He smiled. "Well, milady, it's a long voyage ahead of us so the sooner you get used to it, the better."

"Over there is where the crew sleeps." He gestured towards another dark passageway that wound downward. "And down there is the hold where we keep the supplies, whatever treasure we may find, and any cargo."

The further they traveled into the bowels of the ship, the more Ivy felt like gagging. She didn't understand how someone would willingly choose to live on a ship like this their entire life.

She allowed her gaze to rove over the captain, who walked in the foul darkness with confidence. Although he was quite handsome, by the way he was dressed and how his hair was disheveled, he appeared to fit right in with this ship of his. But the second he grinned, she couldn't force herself to concentrate on the fact that he was a rogue.

She closed her eyes and focused on clearing her mind of such thoughts.

⚓

Once back on the main deck again, Gage shifted his weight between his feet as Lady Shaw moved to the starboard rail, gazing down at the water lapping beneath them. Seeing the woman on his ship shifted his thoughts to Addie.

The poor, sweet girl—young woman now, he supposed, but he knew he would always see his sister as a little girl—widowed at the age of seventeen. He had just received word from her that her husband had died, leaving her penniless in the Carolinas.

Gage was anxious to reach her and take her on his ship with him, where she would be protected. He hated the fact that she had been married off to a man he had not met. She was his sister, after all, and he had thought he should at least meet the man. But Gage had been away, sailing with Caspian at the time, and had not received word of the wedding until she had actually moved to the Carolinas.

His mind drifted to the years of their youth. The fact that he had never been able to provide for her on his own still haunted him. Gage had, after all, taken her with him to wander the streets after their mother had died. He still didn't know what exactly became of their father. The man had left when Gage's mother found out she was expecting another child, and had never returned.

Gage shuddered as he recalled the months spent running the streets of New Providence, terrified they would not survive to see the next day, wondering how they would find a meal and a dry place to sleep at night. Finally, they were taken in by Caspian's family—but those months had been the worst of their lives by far.

One day during that time, they stepped inside a store, trying to find a brief respite from the heat of the Caribbean summer. Before they were shooed out by the shopkeeper, seven-year-old Addie had pointed to a bolt of vibrant pink taffeta. Young Gage had taken one look at his sister's brown, tattered, filthy frock she was outgrowing by the minute and wished with all his heart that he could get the pretty fabric for her, but he did not even have enough money to find them something decent to eat.

Well, before he found Addie, he wanted to bring her some fabric for a new dress. It was probably a foolish notion, but he felt compelled to do it. However, he had no idea how to purchase fabric for a woman.

But luckily, Lady Shaw stood before him, dressed in a pleasant lilac-colored gown that he thought must be fashionable. She had to be a God-given gift, sent straight to him.

Gage cleared his throat, and the lady twirled around. She wrung her small hands together.

"Milady—"

"I—"

They spoke at the same moment before Lady Shaw interjected, "You first, Captain."

Gage paused for a moment, giving her a chance to speak if she wished to. When she stood there simply staring at him, he voiced his thoughts.

"Lady Shaw, I was... I beg of you to consider going back into the town with me, just for an hour or so."

Her eyebrows slowly rose, and Gage continued after studying her for a few moments. "I... I wish to purchase some fabric, and I wanted a female's opinion on which to choose. If you don't mind, I was hoping you could aid me..."

"Fabric? What would *you* need to purchase fabric for?" She furrowed her brow, still wringing her hands.

Gage felt heat rush to his cheeks. What a fool he was, rambling like an idiot in front of this woman. He stifled a groan.

"I-I'm sorry, my lady. I plan to present it to my sister so she may have a new dress, but I am afraid I am not familiar with ladies' fashions, so I was wondering if you could... would..."

The lady smiled, the first time he had ever seen her do so. Her face glowed pleasantly and Gage suddenly wished he could make her smile more often. They had a long voyage ahead of them for him to try.

"Yes, Captain, I will help you. I have always enjoyed shopping with my friends back home."

Gage grinned. At least she did not think him a complete fool.

CHAPTER 4

Ivy was grateful to steal another few hours on land before her long, torturous voyage back home. Remembering the seasickness that wreaked havoc on her appetite the first few weeks of her search for Eden, she stifled a groan. She prayed conditions would be far different this time.

But now she had a pirate captain to worry about in addition to her health. She studied the man as he ambled in front of her, his well-worked muscles moving as he did. His curly brown hair rustled beneath his tri-corn hat in the ever-present breeze.

The man led her through the town toward the shop from which he insisted they purchase fabric. She wondered exactly why he so desired to make this purchase. He certainly seemed to be an eccentric man.

The captain stopped suddenly and whirled around to face her. "Forgive my horrible manners, milady. I don't know what got into me." He offered her his arm, and she hesitated.

Ivy did not wish to be improper, allowing a pirate like him to escort her, but there was nothing else to do. She knew she was being completely foolish. No harm could come from accepting his arm; the sailor was no doubt attempting to be a gentleman.

She tucked her hand over his arm, and a grin illuminated his face. As they continued their stroll down the muddy streets, Ivy held her skirts up as modestly as possible both to keep up with the captain's fast stride and to avoid dirtying one of her only two gowns.

They passed farther into the town than she had been so far, and both the changing scenery and the darkening sky sent a shiver of fear down her spine. Taverns lined the streets, and drunken, raucous men flooded into them; women of questionable morals spilled from balconies and porches, displaying their wares.

Ivy inhaled a deep breath before looking away, but choked on the stench of rotten fish mingled with alcohol, urine, and filthy body odors.

Captain Thompson grinned at her. Did the man never stop grinning? "I suppose the smell here isn't much more pleasant than back on the—my ship. I apologize. Just be sure you stay close to me at all times. I don't want anything happening to you on my account."

She nodded. All the men's gazes who drifted her way sickened her. Some whistled and nudged their friends, chortling and offering lewd suggestions. A shiver iced down her spine.

Captain Thompson tightened his gentle grip on her arm, giving her a small, reassuring smile. He ignored the men and urged her forward.

"How old is your sister, Captain?" Ivy inquired, trying to make conversation as they journeyed to the store.

He didn't speak for a moment, and Ivy wondered if he would answer. But eventually, he said, "She is seventeen now. Blast, I cannot believe my baby girl is seventeen years old already."

Ivy held back a smile. She knew how the man felt; her brother was three years old but, to her, it felt like he had been born yesterday. "I understand."

The man winked at her, an action that betrayed the forlorn look of his face, and finally paused before a wide building. "Ladies first." He motioned for her to ascend the stairs to the porch.

She entered the building, which was a shop lined with fabrics of all shades and textures, strewn with ribbons, laces, threads, and sewing supplies. Aimee would love this place. Pretty things such as these fascinated the dear girl.

Captain Thompson entered behind her. His sailor's attire and masculine carriage made him appear utterly out of place in this frilly store. He strode across the room and paused before a table covered in heavy bolts of rich fabrics. "What do you think, Lady Shaw? Which is the best?"

Ivy laughed softly at his male point of view. "That depends on your tastes, Captain. I suppose I find this one exceptionally pretty." She pulled out floral-printed yellow linen.

Captain Thompson sighed and pushed the bolt back onto the table, dismissing it with a wave. "Aye, I suppose, milady, but Addie never liked yellow." Ivy studied him as he dug through the pile, an intent look tightening his handsome features. She grimaced. Had she again thought of the pirate as handsome? At least she had only said it in her head, but there must be something terribly wrong with her to think such a thing.

He pulled out a sage green fabric that was rather plain, even for Ivy's simple tastes. "It depends on what this sister of yours likes, sir. I don't know about that one."

His brow furrowed. "Nay, then it will not do. Show me another one you like, milady."

What did her opinion matter? Ivy stopped herself from inquiring. What an odd man he was...

Ivy shrugged her shoulders slightly and continued her search for a suitable material. She spotted a lavender lawn that peeked out from beneath a pile and tugged it out in front of Captain Thompson.

His face lit up. "That one. It's perfect. It makes me think of her just by looking at it." His eyes searched hers before Ivy finally looked down, uncomfortable at how she felt when she stared into those chocolate depths. She could not describe the strange, yet pleasant tremble that passed through her.

Ivy finally gave him a small smile, glad to have helped him.

After asking her how much of the material would be needed to create a decent-sized gown for a woman of Addie's size, he purchased the fabric, and they emerged from the store.

Darkness almost completely blanketed the sky, and the streets were lit merely by occasional torches and lanterns that twisted shadows across the buildings. The sounds of the city were more frightening now, and depraved laughter filtered through the buildings they walked near. Captain Thompson seemed to notice her discomfort and offered his arm. She gladly took it, relieved at the rush of safety she felt holding on to the strong stranger.

A loud, high-pitched cry emerged from beyond a corner, and Ivy felt herself stiffen once again in apprehension. She flinched and sought Captain Thompson.

"Just a babe, milady. Nothing to fret about."

They continued on their way, and rounded the corner. Ivy gasped when she spotted a young woman dropping a cloth-wrapped bundle on the front steps of a building. A squirming, cloth-wrapped bundle.

⚓

A baby.

Gage watched in horror as the young lady casually stalked away without one hesitant step or look back. Lady Shaw's fingernails dug into his skin until he wondered if she drew blood. It was just what he needed to get him moving.

"Miss! Stop this instant!" He squeezed Lady Shaw's hand reassuringly before letting it go and starting after the woman. Her curly blonde hair tumbled down her back. When she spun around he understood just what was happening. As he had feared.

The low-cut gown and garish makeup smeared on her face gave her profession and her predicament away as clear as the crow of a rooster. He grabbed onto her arm and she struggled against his grasp.

"What?" She tried to tug her arm away but he held her tight. "Hey, what do you want with me?"

Lady Shaw ran near them, halting at the door to the church. She picked up the wailing child and held the squirming bundle close to her chest.

Something hot and liquid slid down Gage's cheek and it took him a moment to realize the woman had spit on him. He quickly released her arm.

Lady Shaw approached, patting the child on the back. Its sobbing slowed and then ceased. It leaned its face against her chest. "Why would you abandon your *baby?* How could you do that?"

The woman let out an odd kind of growl. Gage found it hard to read her face underneath the layers of paint masking it.

"She's better off here than with me. Now let me be!" The woman hissed, then paused. "Do you work for the church?" She didn't give them a moment to answer before continuing, "Her name's Emma. I want her to have at least one part of her heritage, although 'tis a poor one."

"I—"

"How—"

Before either Gage or Lady Shaw could respond, the woman turned and fled into the darkness.

Gage shouted out, but there was no response.

🎼

Gage stared in disbelief from the gurgling child to the woman holding it in her arms. Her eyes pleaded with him. "We need to go after her. She can't simply leave her child."

After a moment of hesitation, Gage jolted forward in the direction the woman had sped away. "Miss! Please, we only wish to speak with you."

Lady Shaw's shoes pitter-pattered as she ran behind him. She followed rather fast for someone holding a little one. "Where did she go?"

"I'm not certain! Come on." He snagged her hand, hopefully making it easier for her to keep up with him as she balanced the tyke on her hip. The street ended in an alleyway, which they entered. "Miss!"

"I don't know if she went this way." Lady Shaw worried.

"There's no other way for her to go." Gage continued through the alley to another street. He tensed when he realized what part of town this was. No doubt they were directly on the woman's trail, but Gage was not about to let a lady walk in that direction. "Lady Shaw, I fear we have lost track of her. It would be best if we continued to the ship."

A man sauntered towards the building and planted a slobbery kiss on the neck of a woman standing on the corner. She sent him a hungry smile and pulled him into the establishment, her arm slung low around his waist.

There was no way Gage would allow Lady Shaw and the child close to this area of the town.

"But she could have gone in that building."

Gage ran a hand through his hair, thinking. "I don't think so, miss. We need to get back to my ship if you want to set sail for London on time."

Lady Shaw bit her lip as she scrambled to balance the child, who was throwing her weight around in the woman's arms. The woman did a decent job of handling her, though. Gage could tell she was accustomed to holding children. "I... I suppose we should head back then. I do not wish to delay us."

Gage nearly heaved a sigh of relief as he braced a hand against the lady's back, twisted her around, and guided her back to the street on which they had come upon the child.

"What shall we do with her, Captain?"

The sounds of the street faded to his ears, and all he could see was the baby in Lady Shaw's arms. The child turned her little head and reached a tiny hand out to him in a sweet gesture.

He knew at that moment he couldn't leave this little one out in the streets. What if someone had taken him and Addie in right away after they had been abandoned? He couldn't let this girl go through what he had when he was small. But what would he do with a *baby*?

"Captain, please. We cannot leave her here, for some stranger to take care of. *Her own mother abandoned her.* Sweet thing. We need to take her with us. I beg you."

Gage stifled a groan. Dash it all, the woman was thinking the same way he was. He had hoped she would have enough sense to persuade him to leave the child alone, so they could begin their journey as soon as she had wanted only hours earlier.

"Lady Shaw... exactly what are you going to do with a baby on board a pirate ship?" There, he forced the voice of reason out from his throat.

The child let out a small whimper, drawing Gage's attention. He had no idea how old the babe might be, but she was certainly not a newborn. Maybe she was a year and a half, or two years old? Gage could not guess for certain. Small copper ringlets of hair framed her face, and wide blue eyes blinked up at him. She again reached her tiny, open palm up toward him, and in that moment, his heart melted.

There was no way he could let reason make itself known in this matter.

⚓

Tears wetted Ivy's eyes as she moved her gaze to Captain Thompson. She would not be able to live peacefully knowing she had left this child behind on a doorstep, alone in the terrible night with no one to love her, no one to keep her safe or to take care of her. A shiver crawled down her spine as she imagined the possibility of something similar happening to poor, dear, William.

Captain Thompson was staring at the babe and she wondered if she actually caught a glint of moisture in his chocolate brown eyes. How tender and loving his gaze was.

"Lady Shaw..."

Ivy prepared herself to close her ears to another objection, but stilled immediately at his words.

"I... I don't know what we will do with her, but, yes... I agree we should take her."

CHAPTER 5

Eden woke that morning to find sunlight streaming in through the window of the cabin. She sat up to discover she was the only person in the room; Caspian and Reed had already risen for the day without waking her.

Startled, she gathered and donned her clothing before she gazed out the porthole. The sun was already quite high in the sky, reflecting on the churning of the turquoise ocean. Eden quickly headed out of the cabin, eager to find her husband and son.

The sea freshened the air and the sun warmed her face as she stepped onto the deck.

"I wondered when you'd wake, my darling." Caspian's voice sounded from behind her, and he chuckled, a deep and rich noise that made Eden's insides turn smooth.

Eden rotated around to grin at him. He wrapped both arms around her and pressed a kiss to her forehead. "Good morning, love."

"Good morning." She stood on her tiptoes to plant a kiss on his lips before turning away. "Where are we, Caspian?"

"We aren't too far from the Bahamas. Since we are so close, I plan to stop in New Providence to see if we can find information about your brother." Caspian pulled Eden back against his chest when the ship rocked over a swell.

"But, Caspian, I know he has been in Port Royal. We should search there. I should have thought of it when we were married there. I should have done something." Eden fidgeted with her dress.

Caspian squeezed her tight, stilling her hands. "Sweet-heart, we were thinking of other things during our visit in Port Royal, and rightly so. Now, just because your brother has been to Port Royal does not mean that is where we will find him. We are practically looking for a specific grain of sand in the bottom of the ocean, so it will take some searching. We can start at the island closest to us first."

Eden had to admit her husband was speaking sensibly. "Yes, Caspian, I think that's what we should do. I am sorry I'm so frantic about this. I just wonder if he is alive, or what he is doing. He never visited or wrote to me again, and I don't know why."

Her husband brushed a curl of hair from her eyes and offered her a tender smile. "Well, love, remember you told me he chose the life of sailing to get away from your father. Maybe he didn't want to be discovered and forced back home. I, for one, believe it is more taxing to sit in a parlor room, doing nothing but business every day."

Eden lowered her eyes, deep in thought. Everything Caspian said was true, but would her brother really let her think him dead just to escape a boring life? Maybe the price of freedom was worth it to her brother. She had run off from home to be free herself, very much like he had.

$$\text{\$}$$

Agreeing to allow a woman to join him on his ship was one thing, and Gage certainly would be teased enough by his crew for permitting that. But a *babe?*

However, Gage knew even if Lady Shaw were not with him, he probably would have taken the little girl on his voyage anyway. He hated to see the poor thing abandoned by her own mother. Families were meant to love and take care of a child, not leave them on the cold doorstep of a church.

Gage knew all too well the effects of an unloving family.

"Captain Thompson, for how long do you think you will stop in the Carolinas?"

Gage spun to see Lady Shaw still cradling the little child, Emma, in her arms. By the loving way she held the baby, Gage could tell she was familiar with little ones. Of that he was glad, because other than growing up with his sister a few years behind him, Gage knew nothing about children. He supposed he had taken a part in raising Reed, Caspian's son, but the boy had been raised by his mother until he was a little older. Gage had simply been guessing when he had taken care of the little guy.

He wondered if he would ever settle down to find a wife and have a child of his own. Gage certainly liked children, but he doubted a decent woman would ever want to marry a privateer like him. One glance at Lady Shaw made him wish even more for a wife of his own. She was so beautiful and she cared so much about the abandoned child that he had no doubt she would make a great...

"Mr. Thompson," a soft voice interrupted his musings.

Lady Shaw peered up at him, patting her tightly wound orange tresses with a petite hand. Her legs moved rapidly to keep up with his pace.

He slowed a bit. "What is it, milady?"

She blinked. "I asked you how long you intended to stop in the Carolinas?"

"Oh. Please accept my apology, Lady Shaw. I suppose I was thinking of... other things. I'm unsure how long it will take. I will need to find Addie and see she has everything she needs, get her some money or a way to make a living. Mayhap a week? If that does not succeed, I would be happy to take her with me on my voyage. Then we would take less time."

Lady Shaw nodded slowly as they continued walking. "Sir, you said your sister is only seventeen years old, and she is already a widow? Why, she's younger than I am, and I've barely considered marriage yet!"

Gage averted his gaze, not wanting her to see the anger in his eyes. "Yes, well, I would not say I approved of the marriage. I am not certain she did either. Our... our adopted father practically sold her off to the highest bidder. This highest bidder was a brute of a man who moved her away to the Carolinas. I am afraid to say I have not seen her since before her wedding. She wrote to me expressing her disdain for him, and I recently received a letter telling me of his death."

§

Ivy knew this man's—and his sister's—private lives were absolutely none of her business, but she was intrigued by this woman who was so young a widow. With a glance at Captain Thompson, who seemed inclined to make the rest of their walk a silent one, Ivy repositioned Emma on her hip.

What on earth was she going to do with a baby once she got back home?

Oh well, there was nothing she could do about it. She refused to see this poor little girl abandoned. Emma gurgled and reached a hand out to slap Ivy in the face. The impact stung a little, but the baby was only playing with her. Ivy stifled a giggle. She already loved this little darling.

§

The moment Lady Shaw stepped on the deck, right ahead of him, the crew started laughing. Gage barely held back a grimace. Well, if the men had not thought him soft for bringing a woman on board, surely they would now that he had found a woman *and a baby*.

It would be more of a struggle now to command like a true captain while his crew laughed at him.

"Cap'n, a woman and a baby?"

"Why, Cap'n Thompson's a real family man now!"

Gage tried to block the men's comments out of his mind as they continued to tease him. He knew he was doing the right thing by taking the child with him. Why, it was easy to tell Lady Shaw was going to be a good mother to her.

The woman backed up against him when one of his sailors stepped too close to her, peering at the babe before leering at the lady. Gage grabbed her by the waist and moved her behind him. He stepped forward and nudged the man back.

"I will hear none of your complaints, men. This child was abandoned by her mother. It was only the Christian thing to do to take her in with us. Lady Shaw will help care for her."

The men grunted and grumbled.

"If a woman's bad luck on a ship, then a woman with a girl-child ain't a good thing, neither! Especially a woman with red hair." Rogers, a man with a hard face stepped forward, pointing a grimy finger at Lady Shaw.

"I demand you put an end to your foolishness this instant. Lady Shaw and Emma are here to stay."

Adam Douglas, the man whom Gage had met at the port and hired as his first mate, nudged Rogers back. "What, are you all truly frightened of a little tyke? What kind of men are you? And you know the saying of a woman on board being bad luck is pure falsehood. I've sailed on a ship with the captain's wife on board and no harm came to us."

Rogers glared at Adam, and then moved his glare to Lady Shaw and the babe.

Gage grunted in agreement and stepped forward. "Rogers, you weren't sailing with us when we were with Captain Archer, but we had a woman stowaway on board then. No bad luck plagued us. In fact, I gained this ship and Captain Archer gained a wife."

Some of the men snickered at that. "Fine then, Cap'n. We shall see." Rogers whirled around and disappeared into the crowd of men on the main deck.

Gage stilled for a moment before speaking to the rest of the men. "I'll hear no more complaints. Return to your stations and prepare to set sail. I want to leave this port in all haste, men."

"Aye, Cap'n!" A chorus of men shouted.

Gage turned to Mr. Douglas, who had remained by his side. "Please oversee the crew while I take Lady Shaw down to her cabin."

Adam bowed slightly. "Of course, Captain."

Lady Shaw stepped forward, her eyes wide as she bounced Emma on her hip. The child reached her open hand out toward Gage, her fingers spread apart wide. He touched her tiny fingers and chuckled.

"Follow me, Lady Shaw, and I will escort you to your cabin."

Ivy took the captain's proffered arm and followed him down the stairs he called the companionway. He passed a few doors before stopping at one at the end of the hallway. The man opened the door and motioned her inside with a grand gesture.

It was an odd sight to see a man of such low class acting in such a gentlemanly manner. He grinned at her, his eyes twinkling. "I hope you enjoy your voyage, Lady Shaw. I know the cot is not a comfortable place to bed, but it is all I have to offer you. Please, milady, just tell me or my first mate, Mr. Douglas, if you need anything."

He walked into the room after her and held the door open.

"Will we still be departing tonight, then, Captain Thompson?"

"Aye, miss. I want to reach my sister in the Carolinas in all haste. I do not know where she is living or what she is doing, but I do know her wretched husband left her with a hefty debt. Even though she is a tough little thing, I don't want her fending for herself for too long." A bright, fond look spread across Captain Thompson's face as he spoke of his younger sibling. The man truly seemed like a great brother.

"I understand, Captain. I hope she's all right."

Captain Thompson chuckled. "Although I want to make sure she is well, I know how strong a young woman she has become. She should be all right. Thank you, milady. Are you sure there is nothing you need before I go back on the main deck?"

Ivy bounced Emma on her hip. "Yes, Captain Thompson, I am certain. Thank you very much." She glanced at the child in her arms, who appeared far too thin for such a young age. "Well, I think it would be good for Emma to eat something before bedtime. Is there some fruit your men could spare for her? It's probably too much to ask for you to find some milk. Or perhaps something for me to eat, as well?"

"I will see what I can do, milady. We can't let either of you fine ladies go hungry, now can we?" He tweaked the child on the chin. "I will leave you two to get settled, Lady Shaw. I hope you rest well."

After a bearded man brought in a banana for Emma and a biscuit for Ivy, Ivy settled herself and the child on the cot in her cabin and took a moment to observe her surroundings. The cot took up most of the room. A tiny table was pushed between the bulkhead and the cot, and a wooden, straight-backed chair rested nearby. The far end of the cabin—if it could be called the far end, because it was not far away—was graced with a little, round porthole. All in all, the room felt quite cramped. Ivy would be lucky if she could cross it in any direction with more than two or three strides.

Ivy balanced Emma between the bulkhead and her hip as she peeled the banana. She plucked off a section of the fruit and offered it to the child, who was babbling nonsensical words and waving her hands. Emma reached for the piece of food and devoured it within seconds. It appeared the poor dear was hungry. And, well she should be. Who knew when she had last eaten?

Ivy's own stomach growled. Now that she thought of it, she had not eaten in some time either. She broke a piece off the biscuit the man had also given them and moved it toward her mouth, but little Emma eagerly held her hand out for it. Letting out a giggle, Ivy offered the piece to the child, who gobbled it down. Apparently Ivy would be waiting to eat until tomorrow, but that didn't matter. It was best the growing child ate to her fill first.

Gage settled himself on his armchair and closed his eyes. They had finally set sail, and he was beginning to discover that captaining a ship was much harder work than Caspian had ever made it appear. He rubbed his forehead, where a nagging headache had begun to form. Not only did he have to deal with gaining the men's respect, but now he had to care for a woman and a baby. And that was no one's fault but his.

A night's rest would do him good.

He opened up his Bible to get a bit of reading done by lamplight before he retired for the night, but a shrill scream interrupted him. Every muscle in his body tightened. Was Lady Shaw being harmed?

Gage leapt to his feet, grabbed a pistol, and headed out of the cabin, intent on saving the lady. A child's wail followed the woman's scream. He skidded to a stop in front of Lady Shaw's door and barely avoided a collision with Mr. Douglas.

"What's going on, Captain?"

Gage ignored his first mate and pounded his fist on the door. "Lady Shaw?"

The woman didn't answer and Gage didn't give her much time to, either. He shoved the door open and peered inside, pistol at the ready. Adam trailed behind him, cutlass in hand.

A shrieking gasp met Gage's ears. The moonlight flickered through the porthole and illuminated the cabin. Lady Shaw sat upright on the cot, clutching a wriggling Emma to her chest. Emma released a heart-wrenching wail and Lady Shaw's eyes widened.

Gage glanced about the room, but saw no immediate threat, so he entered. The woman must have been dreaming, because no one was in her room to cause her to scream. He faced Adam once more. "I think I can handle this, Mr. Douglas. You may go back to your station. Thank you."

Adam bowed and left the companionway. Gage closed the door behind him. He fumbled around in the dark for a moment before he finally lit a lantern that rested on the tiny table. Lady Shaw began to scramble to her feet, but Gage laid a hand on her shoulder to stop her. Emma shrieked and reached her little arms out to Gage.

"No, milady, there's no need to get up. I-I just came to check on you because I heard you cry out." He stretched out his arms. "Could I hold Emma? Perhaps she would calm down and you can get some sleep."

"Please do, Captain Thompson. I suppose I woke her up and now she just won't settle down." Lady Shaw swung her legs over the side of the bed as she handed the girl off to him.

Gage hefted the babe up in his arms and bounced her against his chest. The child's wails morphed into giggles and squeals of delight. He could not resist a chuckle himself. After a couple moments, he swung her back to his chest and snuggled her face against him. Lady Shaw flashed him a smile as she gazed at the baby.

Rocking the girl back and forth, Gage nodded to the woman. "What made you scream, milady?"

Gage dragged over the small, wood-framed chair and positioned it next to her.

The lady drew her coverlet up to her chin, and only then did Gage realize he had barged into a woman's bedchamber while she slept. And the lady wore only a nightgown. He felt his face heat at the realization.

"I'm sorry to have disturbed you, Captain. I simply had a nightmare. I am truly sorry; I have had that nightmare before, and I don't doubt I will again." Lady Shaw pushed at a long strand of orange-red hair that had escaped its braid.

"No, no, miss, it was no trouble at all." Gage bounced Emma on his lap and brushed his fingers across the little girl's face. *My, but this baby was sweet.* She giggled and grabbed his finger, then stuck it in her mouth. He grinned and observed Lady Shaw, who stared at him. "What was your nightmare about, miss? My mother used to tell me if I talked about whatever bad dream I had, it would go away."

⚓

Ivy could not move her gaze from the rough-looking privateer captain who gently held a baby girl. It was such an endearing sight that she wanted to hug the man. Besides, he had made

Emma happy within a matter of seconds when she had been wailing at the top of her little lungs just a moment before!

Her mind drifted back to the question he had addressed to her. She blinked. "Oh, it's just a nightmare I've been having... about something happening to my little brother. That's why I'm so anxious to get back to him. I don't want anything bad to happen while I'm gone."

Captain Thompson tickled Emma and glanced up at Ivy. Her breath caught in her throat when he looked at her in that manner. What on earth was wrong with her? This man was a privateer. She should not be enjoying his company. Ivy stood, still clutching the coverlet from the cot against her chest.

"Captain, I know this is your ship, but it is really improper for you to be in here with me at night. If anyone from back home in England found out about this, my reputation would no doubt be in shreds."

"Now, now, I only came in here to fend off some unknown danger. I will leave the second I get this child to fall asleep. There's no reason you should be stuck awake all night waiting for her to doze off. I agreed to take her with us just as much as you did, sweetheart." He presented her a grin so beautiful, her breath stopped in her throat and her face heated. Not only was this man incredibly handsome, but he was so caring. *Had he just called her sweetheart?*

She needed to stay away from him. A man so confusing was not something she wanted to bother with. All she needed to do was get home to William before something terrible happened to him. There was no need to worry herself about some pirate like Captain Thompson.

"Very well, sir." Ivy settled back down on the edge of the cot and tried to ignore the presence of this man in her cabin.

The man rocked Emma back and forth, murmuring soothing words. The girl's eyes slowly drooped shut.

"Wherever did you learn to care for a baby, Captain Thompson? Do you have children of your own?"

"Oh, no, miss, I'm afraid I do not have any children to call my own. I suppose I have simply always enjoyed spending time with young ones, and they tend to enjoy the time they spend with me." He winked at her.

"I see. I love my brother like he is my own child. I've practically been a mother to him starting a couple of weeks after he was born and my mother got sick." She wrung her hands in her lap.

"Sorry to hear about your mother's misfortune, Lady Shaw." Captain Thompson kissed Emma on the forehead. The child was snoring quietly, her little head resting in the crook of the man's arm. Her short copper ringlets hung in disarray, some strands randomly sticking out. When Ivy glanced at the captain, she noticed his hair stuck out in much the same manner. She stifled a giggle. The man gazed at her with somber eyes for a moment before she remembered his statement.

"Oh, my mother is all right. She just... retires to bed most of the time, and, well..."

"I understand, milady." He gazed down at Emma and a sweet smile quirked his lips. "Well, I believe our little one is fast asleep. I suppose I shall leave and let the both of you get some rest." Captain Thompson stood and gently transferred the baby to her arms. His arms brushed against hers for a moment and Ivy felt heat creep up her neck to her face. Finally, she settled Emma in her arms.

Captain Thompson offered her another breathtaking grin. Was the charming captain ever without a smile or wink?

"Good-night, milady. I hope you sleep well."

CHAPTER 6

Addie Thompson Poole's mouth watered when she noticed the apple perched on a stand in the center of the market place. The midday sun only enhanced its ruby color. She could already imagine the crunch of biting into it, the sweet juice dripping down her chin.

Years had passed since her life on the streets, years since her brother had been forced to break the law simply to keep them both alive. And now, she didn't have Gage. All she had was an empty brocade bag. Nothing at all left from Jacob Poole. *Worthless man.*

Addie had sold everything they once owned, even the grand home in which they resided in the most opulent neighborhood of Charles Towne. But she still could not pay all of the gambling debts Jacob had owed. The debts she had never even heard of until after the man had died.

She gazed at the apple longingly.

Her stomach grumbled.

It was a very tempting idea to take the fruit and run. No one was watching. She could get away with it. Her belly ached for the opulent food her husband had gotten her used to dining on every day over the last year. Now she had nothing. *Worthless man.*

Aimee squeezed her eyes shut, stopped a moment, and then continued on her way. Had her letter reached Gage yet? Would he come for her? As of now, she was unable to send post to him to tell him how low her money supply had sunk because she could not afford to send him anything. She hated to be dependent on any man, but Gage was the exception. Her brother had been there for her through everything, good and bad. Besides, she had no honorable way to make a living for herself. The men who her husband was indebted to let her go after she had sold all she could. Now she survived without the help of any man.

It had been weeks since she'd dined on a full meal. The last several days she had been lucky to acquire even a few bites of food. She did not wish to be reduced to begging. Hot rays of sun bore down on her, causing a steady stream of sweat to slide down her back. Her vision swirled.

Although Addie thought herself a strong woman, she felt like she would faint if she did not get out of this awful late summer sun, and quickly. But she had nowhere to go. She had no home, and no one would want to take in a homeless widow. And who could blame them?

Addie stumbled across the street and spotted a large, ornate door. A church.

The Archers, the family who had adopted her and Gage, had been a churchgoing family, but Addie had not stepped foot in such a building since she had married Jacob. Jacob had scoffed at her when she suggested attending church the first Sunday of their marriage.

Addie opened the heavy door and cool, refreshing air greeted her. Surely whoever was here would have something for her to fill her belly with before she had to resort to begging or stealing. Maybe they would let her work for her food.

⚓

Adam Douglas stared at the horizon where dark storm clouds billowed, as cool gusts of air slapped against face. He ran a hand through his hair to push it out of his view. The *Siren's Call* bobbed in the deep water and rose back up again. Sea mist washed over Adam's face.

The sky continued to darken, and a wave of worry washed over him. A storm was brewing, but how violent was it? Memories flooded back to him of another ship, another terrible storm, only about a year ago. He clenched his fists and tried to rid his mind of the memory. He could still see James's young face, hear his pleas for help. There was nothing Adam could have done. There was nothing anyone could have done to help him.

He cringed at the distinct memory of a *splash* that had met his ears, despite all of the howls of wind and battering of rain. No, this splash was James's body meeting the ocean. Adam had tried to follow after James, but he was attached to a lifeline that cut his reach short. The other men told him James was a goner for sure, and in a tempest so strong there was nothing to be done. They would lose a dozen other lives just to save a single one. But that didn't help Adam. James's face, his eyes wide, a scream tearing out of his throat, still haunted Adam's vision.

James had gone under the surf immediately, never to be seen again. Moisture dampened Adam's eyes. James had been a young man, but he had a wife and a baby at home. And now they were alone. Alone, with no one to care for them. James had saved Adam years before. And this was how he was repaid. Adam had been sent below after the event, when the crew saw he was not thinking correctly. Sent below at a time when the entire crew's presence was demanded. He still could not forgive himself.

He did not think he ever would.

Adam scratched his chin and shook his head, trying to forget the horrifying memory. The ever-darkening skies held no comfort for him. Besides James's death that night, many other men had come close to losing their lives, Adam included. The ship had almost capsized. By the grace of God, they had survived the night.

Wind whipped against his face. A droplet of rain landed on his sleeve.

Many other ships had not faired quite so well. A feeling of dread clenched his stomach, threatening to tear it in two. He took a deep breath. Right now, he needed to stop thinking of such things.

A masculine grunt sounded behind him. Adam twisted to see his new captain, Gage Thompson. The man's face scrunched together in thought. He faced Adam.

"Are you all right, Mr. Douglas?"

Adam flinched at the sound of his name. "Yes, Captain Thompson. Please forgive me. I seem to have simply been... lost in my thoughts. Was there something you needed?"

"No, Adam. I was just wondering what you thought of the storm approaching. Some sailors back at Port Royal warned me that there may be a hurricane in my path and I fear I may have heard correctly." The captain clasped his hands together behind his back.

Adam squeezed his eyes shut for a moment to try to forget the pain and ignore the fact they had sailed straight into what seemed to be a vicious storm. "It does look much like a hurricane, Captain. Aye, I fear that is what we approach. To me, our best choice would be to turn around and wait out the tempest back at the port. We would risk many lives to continue. I believe we could beat the brunt of the storm if we stopped and sailed straight back now. "

Captain Thompson rubbed his face with his hands. "I'll go see what the crew thinks about the issue. I do not wish to put anyone in unnecessary danger."

⚓

Ivy rubbed her sleep-crusted eyes and gazed down at the sleeping baby nestled in her arms. It was not so uncommon to awaken with a child cradled in her arms, due to the many times she had comforted William after a nightmare. But this little tyke was new.

Ivy smiled slightly as she studied Emma, who was snuggled in her embrace, still fast asleep. Dark copper eyelashes fluttered with each exhale. She made sweet, child-like noises that made Ivy miss William all the more. Ivy pressed a kiss on the baby's forehead. What was she going to do with this little one? Of course, she could keep her, and would be happy to, but that would not be good for either of their reputations. She had no idea what would become of them when she got home, but there was no way she would allow the child to be abandoned.

A knock sounded on the door, startling Ivy. She glanced at the porthole, where no light streamed through. The skies were black. Who would knock on her door at this time of night? She yawned, then sat up, making certain not to jostle Emma.

"Who is it?" she called softly.

"Captain Thompson, miss. I'd like to talk to you immediately, if you are decent." The man's booming voice woke Emma. She whimpered until Ivy scooped her up into her arms.

"Hold on just a moment, Captain, if you please." Ivy yanked the coverlet off the bed and wrapped it around her body to cover her nightdress. She had not thought to pack a dressing gown in the satchel she had taken from England in search of Eden, and she had purchased nothing since.

She rushed to open the door. Why on earth would the captain be visiting her at this time of night?

Captain Thompson entered and closed the door behind him. He sat in the wooden chair next to her sleeping cot. The man studied her from head to toe and sucked in a breath. "I didn't know you were not awake yet, Lady Shaw. Please forgive me for disturbing you."

"Why, Captain, I only rise in the morning. It's the middle of the night!" Ivy bounced Emma in her arms.

Captain Thompson frowned. "It is the middle of the morning, miss."

Ivy glanced back at the porthole.

He frowned for a moment. "Ah, the sky is dark because of a storm. That is why I came to speak with you."

Ivy's face flooded with heat. She never overslept. A second look at the window told her the sky was indeed smothered by a mass of dark, angry clouds. A shiver iced down her back. "Why do you want to speak to me of a storm, Captain?"

"Well, milady, I wished to inform you we are approaching a hurricane."

Ivy gulped. She had heard of hurricanes at sea, terrible storms that swept sailors away, never to be seen again.

"What about the hurricane?" Shouldn't he be talking to his crew about the storm, not her? She knew nothing of sailing.

"Well, milady, the crew and I understand how violent storms like this can become. My men want to turn back for the port to wait out the storm. That would mean waiting a couple of days, perhaps even a week, delaying our trip." His lips quirked upward in a sad, halfhearted smile.

Ivy's stomach sank. The voyage was already going to be delayed by their stop in the Carolinas to visit Captain Thompson's sister. She didn't know how long she could wait before she had William safe in her arms again. They could not be delayed.

Emma's head sank down on Ivy's shoulder, asleep again. Ivy laid her on the bed, bunching blankets around her little body to keep her in place as she slept.

Ivy turned back to Captain Thompson, fury replacing the fear that was churning inside of her belly. There was no way she would let another day go by with her sailing *away* from her little brother. She trusted no one but herself with the boy's safety. "Please, Captain, do not turn back. I cannot wait any longer to see William. We are already making a stop to find your sister in the Carolinas. Please, I could not bear it if we turned around and lost last night's travel. I *cannot* sit in some port, waiting for a storm to pass, while I do not know what condition my brother is in."

Captain Thompson's grin vanished. His chocolate-brown eyes grew large. "Milady, I did not think you would object to this. The safety of my crew is obviously important—"

"What about the safety of my little brother, Captain? I have no idea how he fares. He could be ill. Don't you understand? I would think you could, since you have a little sister of your own." Ivy tried to steady her voice, but it shook with emotion. She needed to get to her brother. "Don't you want to get to your sister as soon as you can, as well?"

§

Gage ran a hand through his hair and then rested his elbows on his knees, his chin cradled in his hands. The woman had a point. He did long to return to Addie, to make sure she was safe, to get her home with him so she didn't need to worry about a way to support herself. But what about his crew? Surely he could persuade some of them to agree to continue on. Some of them would be cocky enough to agree.

He had heard of men who had sailed through hurricanes and survived. One captain had kept his whole ship intact and his crew alive after braving a violent storm. But how could Gage manage that? He had next to no experience as a captain, and he certainly had never sailed through a storm with a ship in his command. Could he do it? And how would he live with himself if something did happen to one of his men, on his account?

He didn't want to know how it would feel to be responsible for someone's death, someone who was under his command. Suddenly the role of captain was much more difficult than he had imagined when serving under his best friend, Caspian.

"What do you think, Captain? Would you please attempt to sail through it, for my sake? If we start on our way and conditions grow too poor, we could turn around and rest in a port to wait out the storm, could we not?" Lady Shaw sat down on the edge of the cot and rested a hand on his arm.

She had soft hands. Very soft hands. He laid his hand on top of hers, enjoying how her ivory skin contrasted with his deep tan. Her eyes met his and his breath stopped in his throat. Gage suddenly forgot about the storm, forgot he had a decision to make that could put the fate of his men in jeopardy. And the fate of this beautiful woman before him.

Stormy gray eyes, almost the color of the clouds overhead, searched his. A stubborn lock of orange hair had escaped from the braided coil at the base of her neck. Gage's fingers itched to tuck it behind her ear, but he felt the act would be too familiar of him.

He clutched his hands together in his lap and forced his eyes from hers. When she looked at him so sweetly, and her pleasing scent of lemon tickled his nose, it was hard to just sit there and be close to her. Gage pulled farther away from her and took a deep breath. She seemed oblivious to her effect on him.

"Please, Captain Thompson." The lady made eye contact with him and he swallowed.

How on earth was he expected to resist her?

"It is highly unsafe. Do you not want to make it back to your brother in one piece, with a whole crew?"

Lady Shaw wrung her hands together. "Captain, please. I understand the risk, yet it is of utmost importance that I reach William as soon as I can. As I have told you many times before, I am truly worried about his safety. I don't know what he will do being without me for so long." The woman's voice rose slightly, disturbing Emma. The child whimpered and shifted restlessly.

Gage leaned forward and took the babe from her arms. He kissed the little girl on the cheek. She stared up at him with wide blue eyes. Lady Shaw stared at him in a much similar way, her beautiful eyes looking deep in his. How on earth could he upset such a wonderful woman? It wasn't as if she were asking him to sail through a hurricane out of selfish reasons. No, she wanted to get back to her poor defenseless brother. There was no way he could deny her that. Besides, he wanted to get to his sister soon. Surely his crew could handle sailing through this storm.

He leaned his forehead against the baby's and shut his eyes. "I will try, miss. I will try."

⚓

"All hands on deck!"

Gage stood on the main deck of the *Siren's Call*, his fists planted on his hips. He grimaced as he gazed at the horizon. The stormy sea mist drenched him. What was he doing, sailing through what promised to be such a violent storm? To begin with, he was concerned about whether or not he had the strength in him to command a crew all the way across the Atlantic Ocean. Now, he was making himself responsible for the safety of his entire crew, and a lady. And a baby.

He had only been in several storms at sea before, and none had been as severe as a hurricane. So now, Gage silently petitioned his Heavenly Father for the strength to get him through the coming hardship. Lightning cracked the black backdrop of sky. A moment later thunder groaned from above, shaking the ship.

Boots scuffled on the deck, and some men grunted. Gage whirled around to find most of his crew gathered on the main deck, as he had requested moments ago.

Adam nudged his way to the front of the crowd and spoke for them. "Captain, what is it you called us up here for?" He cast a nervous glance over Gage's shoulder at the dark storm clouds.

Gage grinned, hoping it would either have a calming effect on the crew or himself. It did not seem to succeed either way. He took a deep, steady breath. "We are approaching a violent storm, possibly a hurricane, as you can obviously see." He scanned the men's faces, but gauged no reaction. "I see no adequate option but to sail through it."

A few men grumbled, but no one made any grand protest as Gage had feared they might. His stomach fluttered. He'd thought maybe, if the men complained enough, he would not have to do it. But whenever he closed his eyes, he could see Lady Shaw's eyes pleading with him.

Rain showered down on them, and a wave crashed over the rail. The ship rocked from side to side. Gage forced a smile on his face before they could see through to the seed of fear growing inside him.

CHAPTER 7

Captain Caspian Archer kept an arm around Eden's waist in a possessive gesture and held Reed's hand in his other one as they strolled down the streets of Nassau. Both Eden and Reed flinched at what they saw as they walked through town. Scantily clad women draped themselves over balconies and porches, their faces painted unnaturally. Although Caspian and his family walked under the full light of day, almost every building they passed reeked of alcohol and foul body odors. A man leered at Eden, and she tucked herself tighter against Caspian's side.

Port Royal had been a rather vile town, especially for Eden, who had grown accustomed to the quant cities of England, but Nassau was practically overrun by pirates and privateers. This was no place at all for a lady. Or a child. Caspian squeezed his wife tight and willed Reed to ignore the prostitutes and violence around him. Why again was he taking his innocent family here?

Because as long as he could protect them, Eden's happiness was worth it. If she wanted to find her long-lost brother, then he would go to the ends of the earth to help her do so.

Eden nudged him, shock evident in her eyes at what she witnessed. Only months ago, there may have been unbridled fear in her eyes, but today there was a quiet strength. Caspian leaned forward and planted a kiss on her forehead as they continued to walk. Reed tugged on Caspian's arm.

"Papa, I'm tired."

Caspian glanced down at his son's drooping eyelids and chuckled. Yes, the poor boy truly was tired. He leaned down and hefted Reed in his arms. The boy leaned his head against his father's chest and closed his eyes. Eden reached over and brushed a lock of hair from the child's face.

"Darling, how far away is this tavern you thought could help us? We have been walking for quite a while now." Eden scrunched her nose up in thought.

Caspian chuckled. "Do you suppose I should carry you too, my wife?"

Eden playfully hit his arm. "You know I didn't mean that."

"It is close now. Just a street or so further. I know a man who works there and sees a lot of the men who come through this town. Hopefully he will be able to remember if he has seen your brother pass through."

⚓

As the ship plunged over another wave, Ivy pressed a hand to her stomach. She had hoped she had gotten over her seasickness, but in the midst of this storm, there was no hope for her. She squeezed her eyes tight and lay back against the cot. Oh, but she hoped this tempest would be over quickly! Emma, who sat curled in a ball on the other side of the bed, wailed.

Ivy sat up to retrieve the child just as the ship dipped deeply to the left. Ivy was sent flailing through the air, only to land with a loud thump on the wood deck.

Emma cried out again, this time stretching her short arms out above her head. Ivy scooped her into her arms, murmuring into the baby's soft hair. "Shush, now, love. Everything is going to be all right, sweetheart. Shush, shush, shush."

The baby's face was contorted with fear, but after a couple of seconds held tight in Ivy's arms, she seemed to calm down to some degree. Ivy took a deep breath. How long was this awful tempest going to last?

Ivy stood and braced herself against another wave as she rose to settle herself back on the bed. She braced her feet at the foot of the bed and held Emma close, since she did not wish to be sent flying again.

A knock on the door broke through the crash of the storm. "Who is it?" Although she shouted the words, she could hardly even hear herself through the din of wind and rushing water.

"Adam Douglas, milady. The *Siren's Call's* first mate. Captain Thompson asked me to check on you."

Ivy felt a wrinkle form on her forehead as she staggered towards the door and opened it the tiniest crack. Goodness, when would this storm stop from tilting the deck to and fro?

Mr. Douglas seemed decent, and spoke almost like a gentleman, but could she trust him alone in her bedchamber? He had a look about him that was almost frightening, especially with the large scar that sliced his face in half.

Rain poured down relentlessly, seeming to come in all directions, despite the overhead coverings of the companionway. The poor first mate was drenched. She widened the door and stepped aside, allowing him entrance. He bowed slightly and made his way inside. Rain poured off him in sheets, soaking the floor of her cabin. Ivy noted a large coil of rope gathered in his hands.

The ship plunged over a swell, causing Ivy to crash forward into Mr. Douglas, who threw his arms out to brace her. "This is exactly why I came, milady." He held up the rope in his hands. "Captain Thompson told me you and the babe must be tied to something stationary during the storm for your safety."

Ivy frowned. She had never heard of such a thing before. Then again, she had never been in a storm at sea. "Must I, Mr. Douglas? I would hate to be so immobilized and helpless." The deck teetered under her feet, and she wobbled. Mr. Douglas's hand reached out to steady her.

"Well, milady, Captain Thompson told me it was for your safety and the child's. Should the storm become too violent, if the both of you are tied down, you won't be tossed to and fro. I know of men who stayed below during a storm and got their bones crushed."

Ivy clutched Emma to her chest as the ship plunged downward, and then surged back up. Would the storm truly grow so fierce that the movement could break their bones? A shiver of fear etched across her back. Surely Captain Thompson would turn back towards the port if conditions became too violent.

"But... what if I get stuck down here and need to leave?"

Mr. Douglas briefly laid a reassuring hand on her arm. "You will be all right, Lady Shaw. I have not sailed with Captain Thompson before, but I am confident he is a good captain. He will do his best to keep everyone on his ship safe, and if anything should happen, he will send a trustworthy man down to help you."

"But what if something happens before someone comes to retrieve us, Mr. Douglas? I don't want to annoy you, but I cannot be tied up with Emma relying on me."

The man glanced at the door, a frown darkening his face. He could be handsome, except for the side of his face marred by blurry scars. It almost looked as if part of it had melted like wax. Light brown hair curled tightly around his face, and his eyes were a dark forest green. After a moment, he pulled out an object from his waistband.

The light of the single candle in the room glistened on the metal blade of a knife. Ivy almost allowed a gasp to escape her lips. This man, although he was a sailor on this... pirate ship, had acted in no way but honorably towards her. Surely there was nothing to fear from him.

A smile brightened his face, making him more attractive. He held out the knife innocently; handle first, with the blade in his hand. "I will give you this knife to keep you safe. If you find you absolutely need to escape, you may cut the ropes with it. All right?"

CHAPTER 8

If the ship inclined to the side once more, Ivy was certain they would capsize. She hugged Emma to her chest. "Oh, Emma. We need to pray that we survive this storm. I was not sure it was so bad earlier, but if we need to be tied to the bed to be safe, then perhaps it is something to worry about."

Emma tugged on a piece of her hair. "Mama."

Shock hit Ivy like a slap of seawater. "Oh, sweetheart, I'm not your Mama."

"Mama, Mama, Mama."

"If only I was your mama." A vision of Ivy strolling through London with little Emma in her arms surprised Ivy. Oh, how she wished she was this child's mother. But would it be right to raise the child alone? Surely the little one needed a father to help take care of her. Sadly, Ivy saw no father in Emma's near future.

"If only you had a papa as well."

The ship dipped deeply into the ocean. The ropes cut into Ivy, but held her in place. Their pressure against her skin panicked her. What if they capsized? Her hand reached the knife that Mr. Douglas had offered her.

"Papa?"

"Yes, a papa." Ivy loosened her grip on the blade. "A papa would help take care of you. He would protect us. But you do have a Papa, my dear. God loves you because you are his child. Just like I am and... and Captain Thompson..." Ivy's insides tingled at the thought of Captain Thompson also being a child of God. She had always been taught that she, a lady was far above those of more lowly birth. And yet she went to church with commoners. Everyone was welcome in their Father's arms.

Emma leaned against Ivy's chest and smiled. "Mama."

"Oh, my darling."

Shouts hailed down from the main deck. How long would the men need to struggle against this storm?

The ship plunged to the side once more, further than it had before.

They were going to capsize. There was no doubt of that. And Ivy would not allow Emma to be caught down here below the waterline when the ship capsized.

Ivy fingered the knife before she struggled against the binding ropes.

⚓

Please, Dear God. Some help would be much appreciated. Gage pried the soaked hat off his head for a moment, shook the water off, and then repositioned it back on his head. He raised his eyes to the skies. They continued to dump water on his ship. The waves and wind buffeted them around and around, up, down, and sideways. Sometimes the deck tilted so far to one side, Gage feared they would capsize.

Although the men grumbled about their condition, they obeyed his orders faithfully. It seemed as though they understood how serious a situation they faced. Many a man had died in such a storm at sea.

Lightning cut across the black sky. Only a second later, thunder rumbled.

Despite the situation, a cold resolve enveloped over Gage. He confidently barked orders to his men, and they obeyed, tying the sails back up and doing whatever needed to be done in the effort to save their ship.

Adam had returned to the main deck and was assisting both Gage and the crew, repeating and carrying out orders. He had said in a few words that Lady Shaw and Emma were safe in their cabin below, fastened to the cot. A wave of nausea slapped Gage at the realization of what he was putting them through. A lady of her stature should not be subjected to a storm so violent, but there was nothing to do. If he sailed through this successfully, they would arrive at their destination all the sooner and Lady Shaw would be reunited with the brother who was so precious to her. Besides, the further they entered the storm, the sooner Gage would be able to find Addie and protect her from all the dangers of the world. He understood where Lady Shaw's way of thinking came from.

The deck tilted violently to the right. Gage was forced to grab onto the foremast to keep from tumbling over. They continued to tilt until the deck lay nearly perpendicular to the churning sea. Finally, the ship righted and Gage could breathe again.

Adam, his face a greenish hue beneath his scars, stumbled towards Gage. He stared in horror at the rising sea around them. The last thing Gage needed was for one of his men to freeze on him. He needed his first mate. This man appeared to be well experienced with life at sea. So why was he behaving so?

Gage grasped the man by the shoulders. "What's wrong, Mr. Douglas? Are you all right?"

Adam blinked, wiped droplets of rain off his forehead with his wrist, and looked down. "I am fine, Captain. Don't worry about me."

Gage frowned but released him. It would do no good to slow down any member of his crew. A moment after Adam vanished from sight, a soft hand landed on Gage's arm. He spun around. Lady Shaw stood behind him. She had Emma wrapped around her waist with a sheet. Lady Shaw's bronze curls were soaked with rain. The woman stumbled as the ship plunged over a wave, but righted herself after a moment.

Fury kicked Gage with full force after a moment. What on earth was she doing up here? Adam had told him she was safely tied to her bedpost. Gage held her arm and immediately led her back towards the companionway. He would not allow himself to be responsible if anything happened to her or the babe.

The ship plunged to the side, causing Lady Shaw to jolt forward. She landed hard against him and he could not help but throw his arms around her. To steady her, of course.

Her sweet citrus scent mingled with the salty rain and ocean water as she strained against his arms. By the time she disentangled herself, her face was a bright shade of cherry red.

"What on earth are you doing up here, woman? I clearly asked Mr. Douglas to make certain you stayed safe below."

"I..." She inhaled and wiped some of the wetness out of her face. It did no good. The constant shower of rain replaced what she had wiped off in an instant. "I was a little... frightened down below. I didn't feel safe tied down there, so I cut us free with the knife Mr. Douglas gave me."

Thunder cracked and Gage noticed her attempt to hide a shiver. She hugged the baby close to her body. The ship teetered yet again, and Gage could not stop himself from gathering the woman and child in his arms. When the lady protested, he explained, "I will not have you falling on my account." He squeezed his eyes shut tight for a moment, enjoying the feel of having a woman in his arms for once. "Now, I need you to go back down to your cabin. I will send someone to help you tie yourself to the bedpost again. My men have already attached lifelines for themselves to the mast, so they will have to cut themselves free to help you."

She shifted her eyes to his. They were the color the sky had been right before they'd sailed into this wretched hurricane. Emma let out a screech almost as loud as the howling wind. Gage pried the baby from Lady Shaw's arms and rocked her until she settled down again.

After a second, he returned the child to the woman. She did not appear to be going anywhere in a hurry. He clenched his jaw. It was a terrible feeling to be harsh with her, but he needed to so she could be safe. Before speaking, he inhaled a deep breath. "Go back to your cabin. I will not ask you again."

A frown creased her forehead, but she moved to leave at last.

She whirled back around. "Captain Thompson..." Rain dripped off her nose as she hesitated. "Stay safe, sir."

⚓

Ivy exhaled deeply.

Rope cut into her arms as the cabin pitched to the side, but she remained in place. Emma squirmed against Ivy's chest.

Captain Thompson had seen to it that Mr. Douglas had followed them back to the cabin and made sure they were securely tied to the bed. To make matters worse, he had taken her knife because he did not trust her to remain in place.

And now, although she hated feeling helpless, Ivy had to admit she was glad to be kept stationary in this cabin that was constantly pitching from side to side. She knew she would have been injured by now if she had not followed the captain's orders. Well, maybe he was not so bad after all. He obviously had only hers and the child's best interests at heart.

That still did not stop Ivy's stomach from tumbling.

The ship pitched to the side. Ivy lurched, but the rope held her in place. Rain continuously poured down, smacking the deck above, forming a demented kind of music. Now, she was glad she was down below, safe from the effects of the tempest.

But what of the poor crew above? They were soaked to the bone, beaten and battered. All on her account. *Lord, I am so sorry for my selfishness. Please see us safely out of this storm. Don't let any harm come to Captain Thompson or his men.*

A great crack sounded from above, followed by an ear-splitting thump. Men's shouts and heavy footsteps rent the air. Emma shrieked. Ivy whispered comfortingly to the girl and squeezed her eyes shut tight. What on earth was that awful noise? She prayed Captain Thompson would send someone down to her soon, if only to keep her informed of what was happening up there.

Besides, she had been kept in the cabin all night. How long would it take to be free of this storm?

Ivy stared out the window, which revealed nothing but inky blackness. Perhaps they would never return to safe waters.

Gage shoved a lock of hair from his face. Fierce wind whipped it right back into his eyes. He groaned. They had been sailing in this tempest for hours now, and his entire body ached from fighting the storm beside his crew. His men were just as exhausted as he felt, if not more.

Now, he stared at the fallen mizzenmast. There was no way they would make it out of this hurricane safely. With the mizzenmast down, if they did survive, then it would be hard to get to land safely to repair the ship.

Their survival seemed unlikely. A wave of emotion swept through Gage. He had put everyone on this ship at risk, and for what? To make some foolish little lady who wanted nothing to do with him happy. No, this was *his entire* fault. He had wanted to sail through this hurricane to get to Addie, as well. What an imbecile he was. Now, Lady Shaw would drown, along with poor, sweet little Emma, and all of his crew. Addie would lose her protector and Lady Shaw's brother would lose the one person who devoted her life to caring for him. What on earth was wrong with him?

A gust of wind slapped salty water against his first mate, Adam, who wobbled to maintain his balance. His clothes were soaked through, and his face ashen. The gray hue made his scars a pale white. He stared dully at the floor, seeming to ignore everything around him. A wave swept a chunk of the fallen mizzenmast and thumped it into Adam's shoulder. The man did not seem to notice.

Gage worked his way over to Adam. His first mate clearly needed a reprieve, before he went mad. "Mr. Douglas?"

Adam froze for a moment. Finally, he tipped his head up. "Yes, Captain?" A wave crashed over them, soaking Gage to the bone—as if he were not already drenched enough.

"I would appreciate it if you could—"A gust of wind tore Gage's hat off his head, but he caught it before it was swept into the swirling abyss of ocean. "—go below for a moment—I need you to check on Lady Shaw to make sure she is still all right."

Adam blinked and wiped an arm across his forehead, batting away some of the water.

"Go and stay with her for a while." Gage braced himself against the mizzenmast as he made his way toward Adam. "Perhaps it'll clear your mind." His voice strained in an effort to be heard above the din of the hurricane.

Finally, the man walked away, wobbling as the ship teetered underneath his feet. What on earth was going on in that man's mind? When Gage had recruited him in his crew, he had not expected such an able-bodied man to freeze in the face of a storm.

Gage's stomach sank as he brought his gaze back to reality. What were they going to do if their ship incurred any more damage? Besides the felled mizzenmast, punctures damaged the hull. A group of men were bailing and pumping out accumulated water, or they probably would have gone under already. Not that their chances of remaining above the surface were large, with the massive surges they faced.

While the men milled about frantically, obeying his shouted orders, Gage bowed his head and prayed. There was no chance but a miracle for them to make it out of this hurricane alive.

CHAPTER 9

It will be a miracle if we escape this alive, thought Adam as he gave a warning knock on the lady's door. Her muffled whimper sounded in reply, so he opened the door and let himself in. A wave of water followed him, saturating the deck of the cabin. Lady Shaw and the child were huddled on the bed, obediently tied to the bed post. Her vibrantly orange hair reminded him of someone else he had known years ago. Against his will, a smile curved his lips at the thought of the home he rarely missed.

A crack of thunder reverberated overhead, sending an icy shiver down Adam's spine and shaking the thought from his head. Although he was below decks, relatively dry and away from the drama, he could still sense everything going on above, and he felt all the more like a deserter.

He knew Captain Thompson had been able to observe his cowardice with one look. And a coward he was, through and through. Still, he could not erase the image of James's face from his mind.

"What is going on, Mr. Douglas? Is everything all right? We heard an absolutely dreadful noise a few moments ago. Is anyone hurt?"

Adam struggled to maintain his balance on the teetering deck. Finally, he sat down on a small, wooden chair. "Well, a few men have been injured, but I don't believe it was anything life-threatening." He sighed. They were lucky for that, at least. "The ship, on the other hand, has taken far too many blows. I don't want to frighten you, but some men are pumping water out of the hold, and we have lost the mizzenmast."

Lady Shaw's face tightened. "What is the mizzenmast, Mr. Douglas?"

"It is the second tallest mast on the ship. We need it to be able to sail anywhere successfully."

"Oh, my!"

"Yes, but hopefully Captain Thompson knows what he is doing. I have never sailed under his name before, but I hear he was trained by the best." Adam ran his fingers through his hair. He could not stop his hand from shaking. *Goodness, when would he ever get over his irrational fear? They were not going to lose another man in this storm. Besides, being down here, he would not witness anything that might happen. Yet why did he still worry?*

"Are you all right, sir?"

The lady must have noticed.

"Yes, milady... I am fine. I... I should be going now. I am sure the men need me up there. I will see to it that Captain Thompson sends someone down here to keep you informed. Stay safe, milady."

⚓

Ivy stared at the door Mr. Douglas shut behind him. The second he had opened it, water had gushed in, soaking the floorboards. A loud crash sounded from above now, making Ivy cringe. Was she imagining, or did she hear a man's agonized scream follow it? An icy shiver raced down her spine. Emma whimpered, and babbled something Ivy could not quite understand. The child had spoken a limited vocabulary for her age, causing Ivy to fear her poor first few years of life had taken the words away from her. Ivy rocked the poor child. What good had she done, taking in this little baby to supposedly save her, when now she was in danger of sinking to the ocean floor.

Now she had brought the poor darling on a treacherous ship to sail her to her doom. *Please, God, please let us be safe. Please don't let us drown. For little Emma's sake, if nothing else.*

Thunder rumbled as lightning cracked across the sky in response, almost directly on top of each other. Would it ever stop? Surely they had been in this tempest for hours upon hours. She had never experienced a hurricane before, only heard about them in wild tales retold by the sailing merchantmen who attended her church.

Church. Oh, how she missed church. So many friends and loved ones back home probably missed her as much as she did them. Now she may never hear their voices again, at least until they were all reunited in heaven.

The ship dipped violently to the side, and then the tossing stopped for a moment. Thunder crashed again, and they wobbled on a wave, but it seemed more subdued than the last few. Exhaustion weighed down Ivy's eyelids, until she finally gave in to the heaviness. Her head nodded against her chest. Tortured dreams kept her in a restless slumber.

Someone pounded on her door. Ivy jerked awake. "Yes?" The gentle rolling of the sea beneath her caused her to nod off in sleep once again, if only for a moment.

A man's voice woke her again. "May I come in, miss? I trust you are all right?"

Ivy blinked rapidly and moved to sit up. Oh. She couldn't. She was bound to the bedpost. Panic swept through her to wake up so immobilized, but after a moment her memories returned. The hurricane. The terrifying noises. Being tied to the bedpost for her safety.

"Yes, sir... please do enter."

The door opened and Captain Thompson strode in, water dripping off his coat in rivulets.

A charming grin lit his handsome face.

What was going on? Hopefully something pleasant, guessing by the expression of mirth on his face. Then again, the man always seemed to have a smile on his face so that might not be the best expression by which to judge his feelings. Finally, he spoke, his grin never wavering. "Were you sleeping, milady?"

That was not exactly what she had expected him to say. Her face flushed and she suddenly felt self-conscious of her still-sleepy eyes. Was her hair mussed? She raised a hand to fix it, but found her arms still bound. A groan escaped her throat. Emma's weight pressed against her chest. "Yes, I'm afraid I did nod off, sir." She noticed how calm the ship felt. No pitching back and forth, no thunder, no lightning, no constantly pounding rain or sailor's boots above her. "Will you please free me, Captain? Mr. Douglas took my knife away, and it is absolutely dreadful to be chained up like this."

He winked at her. "Why, of course, milady, I will rescue the fair maiden." The man pulled a knife from his pocket and, in a flash, slashed the ropes that bound her. Ivy sighed and rolled her shoulders. Emma stirred, but still slept, which Ivy was grateful for. She loved the girl, but was not really in the mood to handle a fit from her.

"Thank you, sir. I appreciate it. Now, will you please tell me why you are here?" Ivy shoved the loose bits of hair that dangled around her neck back into her bun. She blushed when she realized how out of order she must appear in front of this pirate.

He bowed low before her and took her hand in his, kissing it as he did so. Her heart fluttered. What on earth was he doing?

"I just came here to inform you that we are free from the storm, miss. I hope you and the babe are well?" He raised an eyebrow at Emma, who fidgeted around in Ivy's arms. The child whined. She was waking. Suddenly Ivy's arms felt quite weak from holding the little one for so long. After a moment, she shifted Emma around and patted her on the back.

"Yes, sir, we are well. But how fares your crew? I heard so many men cry out, and the storm became so violent... Is everyone all right?" Ivy could not stop herself from wringing her hands together in fright of his anticipated answer.

"Well, miss, some men were injured doing various duties, but none are in serious condition, the surgeon says. We should be all right. Unfortunately, I cannot say the same for my ship."

Ivy's eyebrows knitted together in a frown. What was wrong with the ship? Were they going to sink now, after all they had endured? Surely that would not be fair. "What, Captain Thompson?"

He flung his hands together behind his back. "I'm afraid the storm really did not agree with her. We lost the mizzenmast, and then to top that off, some of our sails are ruined. There is also a fair amount of damage to our hull. Without the proper care, we could easily sink."

Ivy gasped. "What are you going to do about it, sir? That sounds terrible."

"We will have to stop somewhere and repair her. I know of an inlet not far from where we are, and we can get there safely to careen her to make the necessary repairs."

Ivy's heart seemed to sink to the bottom of the ocean. That meant even more time before she saw William. Too long. "How long would it take you to... to careen the ship, Captain? Surely it would not take too much time."

"It would probably take us seven days to successfully repair the ship to make her ready to sail you home. Milady, it would not be safe to take any less time."

No. No, no, no!

"Are you sure it will take so long? I... I understand you need to fix your ship, but do you think your crew could work a little faster? I need to get to William as quickly as is possible."

"I apologize, miss. There is nothing else I can do to speed the process or avoid it entirely. I will ask the men to work as quickly as possible, and we may be able to cut back one day, perhaps two. But other than that, we need to make sure this ship is safe. There is no way I am sailing you all the way to the Carolinas in a ship that might sink at any moment. Besides, if we sail into any enemy territory by chance or if we would happen to get caught by any pirates, we cannot be sailing a ship that is deteriorating. There would be no way to outrun or outperform them if we left the ship in this condition. I could not keep you and Emma safe."

Fire flashed through Ivy. "What about William's safety?" Her voice cracked. She held back a sob. It would be too unladylike to cry in front of a man for no valid reason, especially a pirate. She sucked in a deep breath, but guilt and shame swept through her in a fresh wave of tears. Emma was just as important as William.

Captain Thompson seemed to notice her state anyway, and concern and pity softened his gaze. "I am sorry, miss. There's no other way I know."

"Well, then you aren't so intelligent then, are you, sir?" Ivy snapped.

🎼

Gage frowned at the woman's statement. She had always seemed like a polite, well-spoken lady, but right now she was acting a vixen. Why must she hate him for maintaining her safety? He had done nothing wrong.

He glanced at the little girl in her arms, who was staring up at him. Her eyes, the color of the Caribbean Sea, were absolutely gorgeous. With her looks and sweet nature, this girl would probably have little boys fawning over her in a number of years.

The babe's chin suddenly wobbled, and then her loud cry rent the air as she stretched her chubby little arms out towards him. Gage leaned forward. "Can I hold her, miss?"

She nodded tersely.

He wrapped his arms around the tyke, and his arm brushed against the woman. His breath halted for a second. Her eyes met his. There was no longer anger or pain in them. Instead, he saw wonder and curiosity and something else there. A little gasp escaped her pink lips, drawing Gage's eyes to them. Oh, but she was a pretty little thing.

Gage leaned forward an inch more, but Emma launched herself between their faces. He leaned backward to balance her weight in his arms, and the moment between him and the lady ended. He sighed a long breath. Lady Shaw rubbed her hands against her cheeks, which were now a dark shade of pink.

Blast, was she an attractive woman. And he would have none of her. She was a proper young lady and he a pirate. Although everything had ended well for Eden and Caspian, a stowaway and Gage's former captain, things were not guaranteed in any sense with Gage and a refined aristocrat. He had no right getting himself involved with her. No right at all.

Emma bounced herself in his arms. She played with the curls around his neck and giggled as she scratched her cheek against his stubbly jaw. Gage leaned his forehead against hers and sighed. What would it be like to have a little girl of his own?

Children had always gotten along well with him.

He had always adored children.

This little one was so loving and defenseless. Gage felt a need to care for her as if she were his own. He glanced over at Lady Shaw. *Their own.* From what he had seen, the lady felt a much similar bond to the baby as he did.

But he had no prospects at finding a wife anytime soon, so there was no reason to hope or wish such a thing that would take Emma from Ivy. He had to get his head out of the clouds before he got his hopes crushed.

Emma bounced up and down in his arms. Gage beamed and bounced her harder, throwing her up into the air but keeping a good grip on her so she didn't plummet to the deck. Ivy rose and moved closer to him.

"Now, that is enough excitement for her. She was awake for so long during the storm that she really should be taking a nap now, Captain." The lady stood with her hands on her slender hips.

"Nay, milady. If she is tired, she will be tired. Right now she seems excited. Let her have some fun. Heaven knows, she has not had enough during her short life."

Lady Shaw crossed her arms across her chest but made no further objections. Instead, she stood and observed him and the baby.

He felt bad for the woman; he truly did. It seemed as if every turn of events conspired to keep her in the Caribbean and never let her return to London. There was nothing he could do, though. The ship needed to be careened for a safe voyage. In fact, he was a bit worried about their ability to even safely make it to the inlet in the island he knew. In these waters, they faced the threat of pirates popping up at any moment without notice. His heart sickened at the thought of those animals getting a hold of Lady Shaw or Emma.

Emma rested her head on Gage's shoulder and he held the baby tighter in his arms at the thought, and peeked at the lady. She was staring straight ahead, but when he made eye contact with her she did not seem to notice.

He rocked the little girl in his arms. Really, he needed to make these ladies' time at sea more enjoyable. Maybe he should invite Lady Shaw to dinner with him this evening before they made land. He could invite his crew, as well, and they could develop some more respect for him as a captain if they knew him better. Yes, that might be a good choice.

Suddenly, the woman sniffled. He leaned in to get a better look. Her eyes were red and a sheen of wetness covered her pale cheeks. She was crying.

"Oh, no, miss, no. Lady Shaw, please don't cry. Shhh, please." He rocked Emma in his arms and walked towards Lady Shaw, who had sunk back down onto the cot, her face in her hands.

"Please, Lady Shaw, everything's all right. There's no need to cry."

She let out an even louder sob.

He sank down onto the cot next to her.

What else was he to do? He released Emma from his arms and rested her between them before wrapping his arms around Lady Shaw. At first she pulled away, but he held tight, and after a moment she fell against his chest with a light sigh. She continued to cry, and Gage realized there was no point in begging her to stop. He was not certain she could.

Instead, Gage patted her on the back and ran a hand through her tangled copper hair. Some pins fell loose onto the coverlet. She twined her arms around his waist and moaned. After a few minutes, the sobs slowed. Gage felt it was safe to talk, hopefully without triggering another river of tears. "Lady

Shaw, what is wrong? Are you really that upset about your little brother?"

She sucked in a deep breath. "It-it is that, Captain, but not only that. I mean, I am so worried about him, and I fear I will not return in time to save him from some terrible tragedy. I know my fears sound irrational. However, I have these terrible nightmares about my poor little William. It seems like everything that happens prevents me from returning to him. It's almost like... God doesn't care if I get back to my baby brother. First, we could not find Eden, and when we finally did find her, Captain Emery told me he would have to careen *his* ship. I thought I would never get back in time, but then you offered to help me. Then, I found out about your sister and the extra trip we would need to make before I got home. And now, this storm, which made me doubt I would *ever* see William again in this life." The woman let out another sob, but composed herself after a moment. "And yet another obstacle gets in my way because we have to stop to fix the boat."

Gage cringed at her repeated use of the word *boat*. He owned a ship, thank you very much. But nonetheless, he understood Lady Shaw. He feared for his little sister's safety each and every day, and he would until he saw her safely under his own care.

"Miss, I can assure you God *does* care about your worries, and the safety of your baby brother. But you know something else? He instructs us not to worry about those matters. He wants you to trust in Him when you fear the worst and be confident in his care for William. That is all I can tell you, miss."

She looked up for a moment and a frown creased her forehead. Finally, she shrugged and untangled herself from him. "I suppose you are correct, sir." She brushed dust off her skirt. "I understand what you are staying, but I am afraid I will still struggle with my fears every day until I see William again."

CHAPTER 10

Addie Thompson exited the church with a smile on her face. She had met a kind lady, the minister's wife, who had taken her under her wing and fed her and given her fresh clothing. It was the first time in weeks she had walked away from anywhere with her belly full. The nice woman had offered for Addie to spend the night there with her and the minister, but Addie had refused. She had already received far too much charity, and she could not rightly accept an ounce more. She would need to find someplace to live and some way to make an honest living for herself. But where should she go?

She prayed Gage had received her letter and was coming to her aid. She did not enjoy accepting the help of men, since many of those who she had encountered in her lifetime had turned out to be rather useless, but Gage was her brother.

As she walked down the street, she bumped into a young man who growled at her with a twisted look of anger on his face. His wealthy frippery gave away that perhaps he was from the same area of town where her late husband had moved her. A moment after his gaze took her in, the anger changed to lust. She shivered. He grabbed her arm as if to steady her but kept his hand there for far longer than he needed.

Addie jerked her body away from him and continued on her way. The look he had sent her made her think of the only profession in which she had a good chance at making money. The meal she had just dined on disagreed with her stomach now and threatened to spill all over the sidewalk. She would never resort to something like that. She would die first.

Addie continued on her way, past all the shops lining Main Street. Which alleyway would be her home for the night? On her walk, she noted a sign in the window of one of the shops: "Hiring Seamstresses."

Now, this may be exactly what she needed.

⚓

Adam Douglas braced himself as the *Siren's Call* plunged over a swell. He glanced across the ship. Goodness, she looked completely and utterly broken. He had never seen such a thing—missing the mizzenmast, the sails tattered, rubble cluttering the decks.

His legs were restless and his body exhausted, but he thanked God they had survived the hurricane without losing any men. A few had been injured, but all were alive and recovering. Perhaps his nightmares would cease now that he had lived through this storm without losing another crewmate.

Captain Thompson caught his attention and moved over to him. "Hello, my good man. I would appreciate it if you could do me a favor."

Adam blinked. "Yes, sir. Anything you would like."

The captain's hands fidgeted in front of him. "Would you please visit Lady Shaw's cabin, Mr. Douglas? I would like you to invite her to dinner with us in my cabin, if you please."

"Yes, Captain, of course."

Adam spun on his heel and made his way towards the cabin. It would be pleasant to have the woman join their motley group for dinner. Although he hated life in England, he did miss the refinement of the ladies there, and Lady Shaw was like a taste of home to him.

⚓

Ivy rested her head against the pillow on her cot. She had finally gotten Emma back to sleep after Captain Thompson had woken her, and now she was simply exhausted.

Just as her eyes slid closed, a knock jarred her from her longed-for rest. Ivy suppressed a groan. "Who is it?"

"Mr. Douglas, milady. Grant me entrance, I beg of you. I am delivering a message from Captain Thompson."

Ivy's heart fluttered. A message from Captain Thompson? She scolded herself for getting so excited about a chance of a word from that man. For heaven's sake, she had recently gotten into an argument with him! But then, she had just been in his arms, as well...

She needed to stop thinking about such things. What she needed to do was concentrate on Emma and getting back to her brother. Otherwise, she would lose focus and not care as much or pray as hard for their safety.

Ivy rose from her position on the bed, careful not to disturb Emma, and opened the door. Mr. Douglas nodded to her and moved inside the doorway.

"What message did Captain Thompson have for me, sir?" Ivy folded her hands in front of her.

"Well, milady, he is going to serve dinner in his cabin this evening as celebration for surviving the storm, and he wanted me to ask if you would do him the pleasure of attending. I will be there, as well as a few others of the ship's officers. He said he would come here when everything is ready and escort you if you wish to join him." Mr. Douglas furrowed his brow as he spoke and observed her.

Ivy fidgeted under his attention and felt her cheeks heat. The captain wanted her to dine with him? Why would he want that, and what would come of it? Surely he just wanted her to join in the festivities and that was all. Another thought occurred to her: would there be drinking? There was nothing Ivy despised more than men drinking recklessly.

But the captain had invited her, and it would be rude to decline his request, so she would attend whether she felt comfortable or not. "Yes, Mr. Douglas, I will join Captain Thompson this evening for dinner. Thank you for coming here to ask me."

Mr. Douglas smiled slightly and bowed. "My pleasure, milady. I do hope you enjoy your day."

Once the man left the room, Ivy rushed to the tiny bit of mirror Captain Thompson had left on the desk for her. Oh my, her hair was completely out of place. She frantically shoved strands back into her bun and smoothed her dress down, but her efforts did nothing to soothe the wrinkles.

What was she doing, making sure she looked pleasant for a pirate captain? She had never really cared about such things before, and simply made herself look only just presentable before going out in public. So why was this man any different to her?

Ivy had to admit she enjoyed his company, but that was all it could ever be.

⚓

Gage ran his fingers through his short-cropped hair, trying to force some smoothness back into it. What he wouldn't give for a decent comb right now. After shaving his face this afternoon to make himself more presentable, he thought his hair should match up with the rest of him. He wanted to look like a real gentleman tonight, one Lady Shaw could be proud of, one she could... like. Appreciate. Respect.

He told himself that was all he wanted from her, but he knew it was not true. There was no sense in lying to himself, but it might be for the best that he did so anyway. A sophisticated lady like her would never want anything to do with him. In fact, he had no idea how to act around her. She was probably mortified he had extended an invitation to dinner with him. But she had accepted.

Gage pressed his hair down a final time, straightened his waistcoat—one that had seen some better days but was made of a rich chocolate brown silk, so it was his finest—and headed out the door. His bed was pushed aside and replaced with a table, large enough for five or so people to sit comfortably. He had invited Mr. Douglas, Rogers, his master gunner, and two other men from the crew, who held high positions in the group and had previously been in Captain Archer's crew. They were all seated already.

Hopefully the men he had chosen would behave decently around the lady.

Gage rounded the corner and ran his fingers through his hair once again. Adam bounded up the stairs at the same time and almost rammed into him. He took one look at Gage and chuckled. "Ready for your dinner with the lady tonight, Captain? Nice outfit. I'm sure she'll appreciate it."

Gage's face burned. "Am I that obvious?"

Mr. Douglas shrugged. "She got quite pink in the face at the mention of your name, sir. I suspect you aren't the only one who feels that way."

"We shall see about that," Gage laughed. "I will join you in a few moments then, Mr. Douglas."

Gage continued a few steps and knocked on the lady's door. He heard movement in the cabin before her sweet voice called out, "Who is it?"

"'Tis Captain Thompson, miss."

"Oh! I'll be there in just a moment."

Gage felt a grin forming on his face already, despite the nervousness that roiled in his stomach. This woman was so sweet and caring. He admired how she was so protective of her brother and Emma. After a minute, she opened the door and peered up at him. Her copper colored ringlets were pulled back into an elegant coiffure at the top of her head—for once not strained in a confining bun at the nape of her neck. It was rather becoming on her, Gage had to admit. Her gray-blue eyes were accentuated by the fresh blue dress she wore. He had never seen that one on her before. She inhaled a sharp breath as she gazed up at him.

"You," Gage cleared his throat, "you look absolutely lovely, Lady Shaw."

"Thank you, Captain Thompson. You look handsome yourself." Her face flushed to a bright pink.

Gage grinned at her. "Thanks miss. I am touched that you think so. Now, shall I escort you to dinner?"

"Thank you, sir, but what about Emma? Shall I bring her with me?"

Gage stepped back. He had almost forgotten about the sweet little girl. Hmmm... what to do with her? "If it is all right with you, milady, we can bring her with us to my cabin and let her rest on my bed while we dine. She looks rather sleepy, so perhaps she will be happy taking a nap in a few minutes."

Lady Shaw brightened. "Oh, that sounds wonderful, Captain. She sleeps much more than my little William did when he was her age. Thank you very much."

"You do not have to thank me, miss. I think the child should be as much of my responsibility as yours. Now, shall we go off to my cabin?" Gage offered her his elbow.

She accepted it without hesitation, much to his delight.

He patted her hand where it rested on his arm. Oh, how delightful it felt to walk arm-in-arm with such a beautiful, kind young lady. Why, if he was back home right now, he would be the envy of New Providence. Then again, if any of the other men on this ship saw him with her, they would be more than jealous. Gage could not hold back a grin.

CHAPTER 11

Ivy's cheeks heated as Captain Thompson beamed at her. He was ridiculously handsome, and he was acting so gentlemanly. She felt almost as if she were back home in London. Why, from what she had been told by society, it was not possible for men like him to act like he was! And that made him even more intriguing.

Ivy unabashedly soaked in his image. His wavy brown hair curled neatly just below his ears. It was slicked back nicely, rather than bouncing about rampantly as it normally did. The thick stubble on his chin and cheeks was shaved neatly as well, leaving his face smooth and clear. And quite good-looking. He wore a nice waistcoat of rich brown silk—a color that complemented his eyes perfectly. There was no denying it. He was positively handsome.

Captain Thompson caught her gaze and smiled widely at her. The man had a grin that could cause even the sturdiest of women to fall into his arms if she was not careful.

Ivy's face burned. She should not be staring at the man so. "I-I'm very sorry for gawking at you, sir, I simply... forgot my manners. Please forgive me." Ivy balanced Emma on her hip. The child leaned her head against Ivy's shoulder, her eyes drooping sleepily.

Captain Thompson winked. "No need to apologize, my dear. If it could be considered polite, I would find myself staring at you too long as well. You are quite... pretty."

Ivy tried to gently pry herself away from him, but he held tight to her hand and moved her towards his cabin. Was her face bright red now? "You speak too highly of me, sir."

He opened the door to his cabin and motioned for her to enter first. "Now, you must know that is not true, miss."

"What isn't true, Captain?" Adam Douglas rose from where he sat at the table and bowed slightly, offering Ivy a courteous smile.

Captain Thompson grunted.

Ivy blushed.

The captain waited until the rest of the men in the room stood—three men whom Ivy had briefly met earlier in the voyage, all with cuts and bruises on their faces, likely from the storm. Captain Thompson pulled the chair at his right out, and offered for her to sit.

She took the seat, and Captain Thompson pushed it in for her. His hands rested on her shoulders for a fraction of a second, long enough to cause heat to spread through her body, but quick enough so the rest of the men in the room did not notice. Had the man taken a... liking to her? The thought did hold some appeal.

To be honest, it held a lot of appeal. But he was a pirate, a sailor. Society expected her to marry well, to join her life with that of a gentleman, a wealthy man who would provide for her and not go away to sea on a whim. Her family would be shocked if she chose someone like Gage... Captain Thompson. That choice would be out of the question. It would be an embarrassment to her family. It might even hurt little William's chances of marrying well in the future. And for that reason, nothing could happen between her and the captain. She would not harm her baby brother on her journey to save him.

Captain Thompson turned to her side, and wrapped his arms around Emma. Ivy's face heated. She had almost forgotten she was holding the sweet child. Emma raised her arms, catching the man around the neck. She giggled sleepily. The captain chuckled, lifted the girl from Ivy's lap, and rocked her as he moved her over to his bed in the corner.

The three men guffawed.

"The cap'n's a blasted nursemaid!" said one.

Captain Thompson's jaw clenched, and his grip visibly tightened on Emma.

Ivy bit back a gasp. Surely he would not let one of his men talk to him that way.

⚓

A groan escaped Gage's throat. Surely he should not let his men talk about him so blatantly, especially in front of Lady Shaw. Why, what would the woman think of him?

Gage laid Emma down on his bed and bunched up the coverlet around her to prevent her from rolling off the side if she tossed around. Then he faced the man who had taunted him. Rogers. The same man who had pitched a fit when he found out a woman and child would be joining him on his voyage. Gage should have known better than to invite him to dinner in his cabin, but he had hoped the meal would create some more respect. It seemed to be having the opposite effect.

"Rogers, I suggest you learn to shut your mouth before it gets you in places you don't want to be. Taking care of an orphaned child is nothing to mock. Maybe you should learn things like that before you go about belittling your captain."

"No, sir, there's nothing wrong with bein' a nursemaid... Especially since we know you're barely a man." Some of the other men in the room chuckled.

Gage stiffened. He didn't bother a glance at Lady Shaw, for surely she was ashamed of him by now. "What do you mean by that, Rogers?"

"I should think ya know what I mean, cap'n! What kind of man finds a pretty morsel like this lady right here and keeps her in her own cabin? Now, it's bad luck to have a woman on board, and that's proven by the hurricane we endured, but how could a man not have a little fun with someone as pretty as her around? Why, I should take her for meself, and show her what a real man is. Besides, I bet it wouldn't be too hard to do. What kind of *lady* would travel alone on a ship full of pirates?"

Gage's blood boiled. Not out of pride at the insult to his manhood, but at the insinuations Rogers was making about Lady Shaw. One glance at Ivy told Gage she was positively mortified. He fisted his hands. "You will take that back immediately, Rogers, or regret you ever said it. I expect you to apologize to the *lady.*"

Rogers reached across the table and laid a hand on Ivy's arm. A hand that wandered, brushing against the lady's throat and upper chest. Ivy's eyes widened in horror and fear. Fury bubbled up inside Gage. A growl met his ears, and Gage realized it was his. He flicked the weasel's arm away, and rested his hands on Ivy's shoulders, squeezing them to offer some comfort.

Rogers continued. "Why should I apologize for somethin' that's true? Lady Shaw, would ya like to come join me this evenin' t' show ya what you've been missing out on?"

Ivy inhaled a sharp breath and trembled under Gage's hands.

"Rogers, I must insist you leave my cabin. You are not welcome here if you intend to treat a respectable lady in such a manner." Gage brought himself up to his full height and glared down at Rogers. The man was a few inches shorter than him, but met his eyes with a similar glare. This sailor was too ornery for Gage to want on his crew. He regretted ever signing him on.

"That's all right by me. I don't enjoy taking my dinners with two women and a little girl-child anyways."

The man all but ran from the room.

Gage groaned inwardly. He had wanted the respect of his crew, like Caspian had, but things were not turning out in his favor.

He glanced at Ivy. Her face was a deep red and her eyes watery.

"Lady Shaw—"

"Don't listen to Rogers, milady." Adam stepped up and moved closer to Gage and the woman.

Her bottom lip trembled. She abruptly rose and dashed to the door. "I-I'm sorry, gentlemen, but I'm afraid I have lost my appetite. If you will please e-excuse me."

Before they had any chance to respond, she rushed out the door.

Gage glanced between the door that was still swinging open and the members of his crew who remained in his cabin. He needed to find her quickly. It would not do to have her running about outside while Rogers had just gone in that direction. "Adam, please keep an eye on Emma and enjoy your dinner with everyone. I'm afraid I lost my appetite as well."

"Yes, sir."

Gage bounded out the door and almost ran over Ivy in his search for her. She sat, hunched up, in the companionway, her head pressed against her knees. A sob escaped her throat. Her shoulders shook.

"Ivy..." Gage sank down to the floorboards beside her and placed an arm around her shoulders.

She jumped. "Sorry, I... I did not realize you were there, Captain."

Gage moved away from her. "I didn't intend to frighten you, Ivy." He stood and offered her his hand. "Come with me. Let's go back to your cabin, my dear."

Her face pinked, and she frowned, but she did get up and let him lead her to the cabin. Once she was inside, he closed the door behind her and felt his heart sink at the tears streaming down her cheeks.

He had caused her these tears. It was his fault. And he felt terrible.

She wobbled on her feet.

Gage surged forward to steady her in his arms. She leaned towards him, her head pressed against his chest as he propped his forehead against her soft copper hair. He told himself he held her only to comfort her, but he knew that was not so. No, there was no way he could resist the chance to hold this precious woman.

"Shush, Ivy, it's all right. Don't listen to a word the imbecile says. You are a true lady if I ever saw one."

She exhaled a shuddering breath before sobbing again. Gage rubbed her back in slow, circular motions. Finally, she made a light hiccup noise and pulled away. He allowed her to move, but did not release his hold on her. It was too soon to stop touching her.

"I-I'm sorry for my... outburst, Captain. I'm not sure what came over me. I'm so sorry that man said such terrible things about you. I know they're not true. You're a gentleman. I admire you." She frantically wiped the tears from her cheeks, her stormy gray eyes still liquefied.

Gage pulled her back against his chest, warmed by her sweet words. "There is no need to apologize, darling. Nothing Rogers said or did was your fault. It is I who should apologize for allowing him to make those rude insinuations, and to touch you like he did." Gage glanced down and realized with the way he was holding her, he was touching just as much or more of her as Rogers had. He pulled away, disgusted with himself. While he intended to comfort her, he may be upsetting her further with such closeness after she was accosted by the vile man. "Forgive me. I should not touch you so. It is not my place." Gage averted his eyes, feeling heat brightening his face.

Her pretty face shone pink. "I do not mind you touching me, Captain."

Gage could not resist a grin. He repositioned his arms around her. "Will you please call me Gage?"

"Yes, Gage... I do not mind you touching me at all." She leaned her forehead against his chest sweetly. "And I don't mind you calling me Ivy, either."

"Now, darling Ivy, please do tell me you will forget everything that imbecile said."

"I can try to, Gage, but I worry about what he will do if he finds me alone."

"I have control of him and all the other men on this ship. Do not worry." Gage smoothed some hair out of her face. "I'll let you get settled here now, and leave you alone."

"What about Emma?" Ivy rose in a rush. "How could I have left her up there all alone like that? Oh, how awful of me." She patted her hair back in its place and moved back to the entrance of the cabin.

"You don't need to fret about Emma. Mr. Douglas is watching her right now, and I can keep her with me for the rest of the evening. It's about time I took care of her for once instead of forcing you to." Gage stood and tugged his brown waistcoat back into place.

Ivy wrung her hands. "No, she will be missing me. I don't want her to be all alone, even if it isn't for a very long time. I know she is quite young, but I think she sometimes has nightmares... either from the time spent with her mother, or from being abandoned. She might not do well with someone new."

"Don't worry about her, Lady Shaw. We will do just fine." He shoved his hands in his pockets and leaned backwards, studying her.

Ivy bit her lip. "Well, maybe I would get lonely without Emma here with me. I've gotten used to having her cheerful little face around. It would be... strange in this cabin without her, even for only a night. Please just bring her back, or send Adam with her. If I cannot take care of William while I am out here in the middle of the sea, then I would at least feel useful taking care of Emma."

Gage blinked. "Oh, well, you should have said that sooner, milady. If I had known that, I would have brought her back here right away. Just give me a moment, and I will be right back."

CHAPTER 12

The salt-laden breeze slapped Gage in the face as he trudged up the companionway on his way to his cabin. He reached a hand up to shove the hair that the wind had whipped into his face out of his eyes. Somewhere in the distance, an exotic bird squawked. He grinned. If there was a bird like that within hearing distance, then they were nearing the inlet to the island on which he would careen the ship. Even though Lady Shaw was unhappy about the decision, they desperately needed the reprieve and repairs this stop would provide after the violent hurricane they had just endured.

He raised a hand against his forehead to shield his eyes from the glaring sun. How amazing it was that the sun could shine so brightly and cheerfully after the black storm they had endured just hours before. Gage squinted at the horizon. Was that the green of a mountain he saw in the far distance?

After a moment, he shrugged and entered his cabin.

All of his men had dined and left except for Adam, who held Emma in one arm while he stacked dishes with his other. He bounced Emma on his hip. The tot giggled.

Gage grinned at the child's enthusiasm. He reached to take Emma from Adam, but the girl leaned back against Adam's shoulder. "Want Uncle Adam." She stuck her thumb in her mouth and closed her eyes.

Gage cocked his head. "Where'd she learn to call you that? I've barely heard her speak a word since we found her." The man was awkward with the little one, but she seemed to appreciate him well enough.

Adam cast him a sheepish look. "I've been talking to her while you were down with Lady Shaw. She actually knows a couple words—" he struggled to balance the squirming child in his arms "—don't you, Emmie?"

Emma chattered and wiggled her fingers at Gage.

"And why is she calling you *Uncle* Adam?"

"I don't know. It just seemed right." He bounced the girl in his arms once more and then set her down on the chair beside him. She crawled up the side of the chair and tugged on Adam's ear. His face scrunched up in pain as he gently pried her hand away from his head.

Gage shook his head and chuckled. Ivy probably would not be happy the man had gotten Emma to call him by such a fond name. Gage had no idea what was going to become of Emma once they reached England again, but he doubted she would live the rest of her life on this ship with Gage and his men. A privateer ship was no place at all for a little girl-child to grow up. Gage frowned. What *would* become of Emma when they reached England? When they had taken her in, all Gage had truly thought about was the girl's immediate future. Surely Ivy could not take her in with her. It would be highly improper, and foolish people would probably assume that, with her sudden, long departure, the child was truly hers. They even shared the same hair color.

And if they discovered the true origins of the baby, they would shun both the baby and everyone involved with her. Lady Shaw's reputation would be in shreds. She would have no prospects for a respectable marriage, and she would have no hope of a future. What would become of them after that?

Gage shoved the thought aside. He had no time to worry about that now.

"I need to take Emma back to Lady Shaw. She misses her, or I would keep the baby here for the evening."

Adam smiled sadly. "It's time to go back to Lady Shaw, sweetheart. You miss her?" He looked quite awkward with the little tyke, but she seemed happy with him.

Emma nodded groggily. Her eyelids drooped with sleepiness.

"You can go with Mr. Gage and he will take you to her, all right, sweetheart?"

"Otay, Uncle Adam." The child stretched her arms out to Gage. "Papa!"

Gage's face flushed to what he was certain was a deep red. He bit back a grin.

Adam chuckled. "If I'm her uncle and you're her papa, does that make us brothers, or brothers-in-law, Captain?" His eyes twinkled in amusement.

Gage bumped him with his elbow. "Shush. She is a baby. She doesn't know any better."

Adam sent him a lazy salute as Gage scooped Emma up in his arms and went on his way.

However, on his walk down to the cabin, Gage could not help but wonder if Emma called Lady Shaw "Mama."

He bounced the child in his arms. "You having fun on our voyage, sweetie?"

She babbled nonsense back at him, smiling like he had just bought her the world.

Gage leaned his forehead against hers. She smelled good. Fresh. Unpolluted by the cold outside world.

They arrived at Lady Shaw's cabin. He knocked on the door, and the woman opened it almost before his fingers even made contact with the wood.

"I heard you coming. You took longer than I thought you would, so I was just about to come up and check on you. But I see she's all right. Thank you for bringing her to me." Lady Shaw tried to grab the baby from his arms, but he held her back.

"Can I come in, or are you refusing to let me in your cabin now? I didn't know I had done anything to make you cross with me." Emma made a fussy noise so Gage shifted her in his arms and patted her on the head. He was positive her copper curls had grown longer since the day they had found her on the streets of Port Royal.

"Oh, I am sorry, Captain. I did not mean to be rude to you. I suppose you are welcome anywhere on this ship. After all, it *is* yours, isn't it?" Ivy stepped backwards into her cabin and rested on the edge of the cot that took up half of her space.

Gage entered the cabin and lowered himself into the tiny wooden chair adjacent to the bed. He patted the baby on the back and studied Ivy. Her hair was mussed, almost halfway out of the neat up-do she had confined it to before she had joined him for dinner. The deep-blue dress she wore hung wrinkled on her frame, but somehow she looked beautiful in it. Its lace trim withered limply. Now that he thought about it, he had only seen her wearing two different gowns. She probably had not packed more than that to go on her voyage to find her friend. Her stormy eyes stared at Emma with such a mournful attitude that Gage had to pry his gaze back to the floor.

The poor woman missed her brother terribly. And it was mostly his fault she was not well on her way to being with him again. He inhaled. "I'm sorry, Ivy."

"What? Oh no, it's all right. I was just worried Emma wasn't safe, but I see she is now. Thank you for bringing her." Ivy straightened her back and shoved some loose strands of hair behind her ears.

"No, milady, I meant to apologize for not getting you to your brother as quickly as you had hoped. I feel terrible to be keeping you from him."

⚓

Ivy remained silent as she stared at the peculiar captain. The man's wavy brown hair curled into his face, tickling his eyebrows. His large frame dwarfed the tiny chair he sat upon. Eyes the color of sweetened coffee peered back at her. For once, the ever-present grin was absent from his face. He held an expression of complete sincerity, which made Ivy bite her lip.

In all her life, it had been rare for someone to be so honestly concerned about how she felt. And this man, this barbaric pirate, cared more about her happiness than anyone back home in London. The thought warmed her heart to the core. "Th-thank you, sir."

"I hope to make our visit to the inlet and then the Carolinas as brief as I can. I want you to be happy." Captain Thompson leaned forward and encircled her hand in his.

Ivy's breath caught in her throat. She blinked. What was wrong with her, responding to the touch of a common man like this? What on earth would her mother and father think of her? Why, they expected her to marry a wealthy man, a lord, and here she was obsessing over the touch of a common pirate.

She needed to do something about this. No matter how chivalrous he was, she could not get herself attached to this man. In fact, she had every reason to distance herself from him as much as possible. Ivy prayed that would be easy to do over the next two weeks.

⚓

Adam Douglas stood beside Lady Shaw on the main deck of the *Siren's Call*, staring at the bay in front of them. Lush green plants infested the majority of the inlet, after the line of pure white sand stopped. Mountains towered in the distance. In only fifteen minutes or so, the *Siren's Call* would be careened on that shore. The land was certainly a welcome sight after the hurricane the crew had endured.

"How long do you think it will take us once we reach the island?" Lady Shaw took a step forward and shielded her eyes against the sun.

"Oh, I cannot be certain. All I know is Captain Thompson will push the men as hard as they can go so we can be finished more quickly. I have never attended a careening before."

Lady Shaw's face tightened, drawing together the lines of freckles on her forehead and nose.

"I'm sorry, milady."

"No, no, no. There's no need to apologize." The woman tucked a piece of copper hair behind her ear. Adam smiled sadly. He had only ever met one other person with hair such a vibrant hue. A young girl back home, from the days of his childhood. Back in the days before the side of his face was so grotesquely disfigured. "What's wrong, sir?"

"Oh, no. Nothing is wrong, milady. I was just remembering something from before... from another time." He brushed a swatch of hair back behind his ear.

The woman studied him for a moment, then finally looked away.

"After we careen the *Siren's Call*, it shouldn't take us longer than a fortnight to reach the Carolinas, and just a day or so to find the captain's sister. Then, we sail straight back to London in all haste. You'll be back with your brother before you know it." Adam gazed across the sea wistfully. Lady Shaw and Captain Thompson were both on missions to find and help their younger siblings. What was *his own* little sister doing without him, back in London? Sometimes he missed her so terribly the pain forced him to stop and catch his breath. But he had left that life behind when he had chosen his profession, and there was nothing he could change. He would never see her again.

Lady Shaw laid her hand on his arm, drawing him from his thoughts. "Are you all right, Mr. Douglas?"

He blinked. "Oh, yes I am. I'm sorry."

She frowned. "You seem agitated." Adam had nearly forgotten what it was like to have a woman near. They were so caring and intuitive.

"Iv-Lady Shaw?"

Adam spun around. The captain stood behind him, arms crossed. His face lit up with a boyish grin when his gaze landed on Lady Shaw.

"Yes, Captain Thompson?"

Gage didn't seem to notice Adam standing before him. "Oh, I had... wanted to talk to you, miss. It's not anything important; I was just hoping..."

CHAPTER 13

"Ouch." Addie bit her tongue as the needle sliced through her skin. How clumsy could she be? Surely sewing a patch on a shirt should not be this difficult. She had been shocked that the tailor who had hired her did not care she'd come with so little sewing experience. He had thought she was being modest about her abilities, but she had never sewn more than a button before in her life.

She glanced at the heaping pile of clothes in the basket beside her. It seemed to double in size daily, yet she struggled to complete more than one piece in a day. Mr. Faulke had kindly offered for her to sleep upstairs in the shop—and encouraged her to take her work up there with her since she was falling behind on orders so rapidly. There was nothing she could do about it, though. The work was so small and tedious. She would much rather be outside tending a garden with larger tools, where her work actually produced something.

What would become of her? Would she spend the rest of her life in the Carolinas, repairing other people's clothing, working for some man? The last thing she had wanted with her life was to work for a man, after what she had dealt with being married to her husband, but there was nothing she could do about it. She needed money to live, and this was the only reputable job she could find.

The needle poked into her skin once again, and she cringed. Goodness, she did hope Gage would get here soon.

☙

"I need to go check our course. Good day, milady. Captain." Adam strolled away.

"What is it you wanted, Gage?"

"Never you mind it." Gage eyed the ever-approaching island. They were only minutes away from the shore.

"But you acted as though you wanted to say something important. Are you certain?" Ivy fidgeted with her hands, wringing them around. She was moving them so much Gage wanted to take them in his own and hold them until they went still.

"I'm sure." Gage had intended to discuss little Emma's future with Ivy, but he couldn't bear to think about it, much less speak of it. He did not want to force Ivy to care for her on her own, but there was no way he could see her given to some stranger to raise.

Ivy hesitantly reached out a hand and rested it on his arm. "Thank you for being so kind about taking care of Emma." Could she read his mind? "It's rare to find a man who would be so tender with a stranger's child. Or his own child, for that matter." Her expression darkened.

Gage's face heated as he chuckled in response. "I love that little girl. She is no burden to me at all."

"Awaiting orders to make land!" A voice from the shrouds forced Gage to take his eyes off of the beautiful woman in front of him.

As he inspected the island, Gage whispered to Lady Shaw, "Why don't you go back down to your cabin with Emma, and send Mr. Douglas back up here? I will send for you when we are ready to exit the ship."

☙

"I know, sweetheart, I know. It's all right..." Ivy cringed. Emma screeched particularly loudly when the longboat they sat in plunged over a swell. She patted the girl on the back. A warm, strong hand rested on the back of Ivy's neck and toyed with a lock of her hair, out of the view of the others. Startled, she glanced over her shoulder to find Captain Thompson grinning down at her. Rather than make her uncomfortable, his touch made her feel safe.

Emma wailed yet again.

"If your lady doesn't quiet the babe, I will, Captain."

Ivy's stomach dropped when she realized the comment was from Rogers. The man was purely a monster. His dark eyes leered at her and he leaned closer to her from his position across the longboat.

Captain Thompson's hand stiffened on the back of her neck. "You will do no such thing. If I hear another word from you, I will maroon you on this island."

Rogers grunted and leveled a hard glare on Ivy. A shiver coursed through her body. She had been safe on board the ship, where she could lock herself in her cabin, but now? Now, she had no protection but the captain sitting next to her.

Please keep me safe, God. She tugged Emma closer to her chest, but the girl would not be quieted. Captain Thompson looped his arm around Ivy's shoulder and leaned close. His lips almost brushed her ear as he whispered, "May I take her?"

Ivy studied him. His chocolate brown eyes gazed down at her and the child with tenderness. She resisted a smile. This man would make a good father someday, and a good husband. Too bad he would never be *hers*.

When Captain Thompson nudged her in the side, she realized she had been staring. Heat rushed to her face as she pressed a kiss to Emma's forehead and settled the child on the captain's lap. He leaned her back against his waist and wrapped an arm around her. After a moment, her sobbing quieted. Ivy's lips quirked upward in a smile. What was it about this man that always calmed the child?

The tiny boat halted abruptly. Ivy blinked up through bright sunshine to find they were at a sandbar, mere feet from the body of the island. Captain Thompson rose and leapt from the boat onto the sandbar with Emma in tow. He held out his hand with a flourish, as an indication for Ivy to join him on land.

She glanced behind her, where Rogers still pierced her with his glare. Ivy placed her hand in Captain Thompson's and allowed him to assist her out of the longboat. His hand remained on the small of her back as the rest of the men filed off the boat.

Gage leaned down onto the sand with a groan. It had been a grueling day. Careening was hardly his favorite part of sailing. He had worked with the men all day, and now the labor was catching up to him. Besides the physical work, he now had the responsibility of making decisions and keeping everyone working.

He closed his eyes and let the inky blackness of nighttime on the island sweep over him. Every once in a while, it was nice to rest on stable earth, rather than to be plagued by the nonstop rocking of a ship. Just as sleep had begun to take over his body, a small hand patted his knee. A giggle followed. Gage sprang into a sitting position and blinked, struggling to adjust his eyes to the darkness. The embers of the fire barely illuminated the little face of Emma beside him. A smile split across Gage's face. He leaned forward and snuggled the child close to him.

Careful not to wake his crew, he whispered to the little one, "Now, what are you doing up?" She wound her arms around his neck.

Gage's gaze drifted to the other side of the fire, where Ivy slept soundly. He had been wary of allowing the woman to sleep out in the open on the beach with the rest of the crew a couple paces away, but there was nothing he could do about it. The ship lay tilted on its side, so there was no way she nor the crew could reside there. And the nearby jungle was not a safe location in which to sleep. Instead, Gage had ensured that Lady Shaw and Emma were positioned well away from the other men—half the length of the inlet. Plus, any man who wanted to harm her would have to get past Gage *and* the camp's fire.

Gage rocked the child. "Why are you away from Lady Shaw, huh, sweetie?" He pressed a kiss to her temple.

"Papa!" Emma squealed.

He chuckled. "Hush now. We can't have you waking the men up. Now, let's get you back to Lady Shaw. She could wake up and get worried if you're not there."

Gage carefully rose and tiptoed his path around the fire. When he reached Lady Shaw, he stopped and could not keep himself from staring for a moment. She was so sweet when she slept. Red hair tumbled over her shoulder, and she pillowed her cheek with her hand. He crept close and planned to deposit Emma on the sand beside her, but Emma cried and squirmed in his arms. The noise startled Ivy, who immediately sprang to a sitting position. Gage repositioned his hold on Emma in order to press a finger to his lips, urging the woman to remain silent.

She blinked rapidly. Her gray eyes almost appeared black in the moonlight. Confusion washed over her features. The last thing Gage wanted to do was frighten her, so he slouched down into a crouch so as to avoid intimidating her. A gasp escaped her throat.

"It's me. Captain Thompson," he quickly supplied.

She rubbed her neck. "Oh. What... what are you doing here? It's late. This is... indecent."

"I realize that, milady, and I don't want to tarnish your good reputation. However, none of the men are awake." Gage shot a glance over his shoulder to ensure that statement was true.

"That's no excuse..." Her face was drawn tight with something Gage couldn't identify. "You shouldn't be here at this time of night. We are alone."

He felt a grin stretch across his face at her needless fretting. "Milady, I only came here because Emma wandered off. It was dangerous, really. She could have stumbled into the fire."

Lady Shaw seemed to jerk into a state of full awareness. She swung around, patting the sand in search of Emma. Gage chuckled. "She's right here with me, my dear." Relief washed over her face and she stretched out her arms. After a moment of reluctance, Gage handed the child over. He pressed a kiss to the top of Emma's head. Her fuzzy hair tickled his nose. "You two sleep well, all right?"

Gage offered a smile for Lady Shaw and rose. He should spend the least time possible near this woman. It would not do to have a crew member finding them and jumping to the wrong conclusions. Just as he moved away from the two, Emma whimpered, "Papa!"

He swung around, ready to save the woman and the child from some unknown intruder. But no one was there. Instead, Emma rested in Lady Shaw's lap, her arms stretched out towards him. Gage paused. Lady Shaw's jaw clenched and her delicate brow furrowed. After a moment, her face flushed. "Emma, he is *not* your papa." Her hushed voice held a sharp tone. She met Gage's gaze. "I'm so sorry, sir. I have no idea why she would—"

⚓

Ivy bit her lip and squeezed Emma closer to herself as heat continued to stain her cheeks. She hoped Captain Thompson had never heard Emma refer to her as *Mama.*

"What's wrong, miss? She can call me 'Papa' if she so wishes." He crouched down on the sand, his face nearly level with hers. Ivy squeezed her eyes shut. This was mortifying. If Emma had said either in public back in London, her reputation would be in shreds.

"No, she may not. People will think... oh, never mind. It is simply wrong. We do not want her to get confused."

Captain Thompson's eyes remained on Ivy. Emma broke the silence by launching herself towards the man. Ivy had no choice but to release the tyke, or she would have tumbled on top of him as well. The captain chuckled and caught Emma in an embrace. Something tugged on Ivy's heart as she gazed upon the two. He truly was a good man, and they looked so sweet together. A sigh escaped from her lips. "If she wants to sleep by you, then that's all right with me." Ivy stifled a yawn.

Captain Thompson grinned. The moonlight made his teeth shine. Was the man ever without his charming smile?

"Goodnight then, milady." Just as he rose, Emma shrieked once more.

Ivy cringed as she heard some of the men on the other side of the beach grumble. Heaven knows what they would do to her if Emma disrupted their sleep more than once. Oh, what had she been thinking, dragging a baby along with her on a ship like this? She *hadn't* been thinking.

Captain Thompson whispered soothing nonsense to the girl, who pointed down at Ivy. "What is it? What do you want, sweetheart?" He lowered himself to kneel next to Ivy once again.

"Sleep here."

Ivy gasped. Emma had barely ever said more than one word the entire time she'd been caring for her, much less words that made sense together.

"You want to sleep by your ma—Lady Shaw?" Captain Thompson's brow furrowed.

"You sleep too."

Ivy squeezed her eyes shut in horror.

"Oh... well... I..." Captain Thompson let out a long breath before Ivy finally opened her eyes. His face shone bright red, even in the moonlight. "I can't... sleep here too, darling. It wouldn't be right."

Emma's tiny face crumpled. Ivy sucked in a deep breath. The poor girl. After everything that had happened to her—*abandoned* by her own mother—Ivy hurt to see her upset. Would it be so hard to grant her one request? Ivy met Captain Thompson's gaze. He stared at her in bewilderment. "If it's all right with you, Captain, you may stay... nearby so Emma can fall asleep happily. I would hate to deprive her of something so simple."

"Sleep... here? By you?"

"Yes, sir. I know it isn't proper, but neither is sleeping on a beach filled with forty men. I do not think allowing one to sleep a few feet closer to me—separated by a babe—will harm me overmuch."

He ran his fingers through his hair. "You're certain?"

"Aye, sir."

Ivy scooted over and reclined on the sand, leaving plenty of room for Captain Thompson. Just because he slept *near* her did not mean he had to sleep *next* to her. Slowly, the man also stretched himself out and positioned Emma between them and rotated his back to her. "Goodnight then, milady."

Ivy's lips tugged upwards in a small smile. "Goodnight, Captain."

CHAPTER 14

"Well now that ya mention it, I do remember a lad answering by the name visiting here nigh on a month ago. But I don't recall his last name bein' Trenton. No, it was somethin' else... blast it, me old mind don't remember things like that anymore!" The man who owned the tavern—Blakeley, Caspian had called him—leaned heavily to the right, looking over Caspian's shoulder. Eden followed his gaze to find two men brawling. "Ay, you stop it! I'll have no fighting in me tavern! Outside to the back wit' ya!" The two men paused for only a second then scurried out the door. A wave of other customers followed to view the fight. Eden leaned against her husband's shoulder, eagerness for news of her brother overwhelming her. This was their fourth stop at a port in an effort to find him, and she prayed this one would be successful. Caspian's arm wound around her waist, and his hand tangled with hers.

The tavern owner turned back to them, his face apologetic. "Now, what was I sayin', Archer? Oh yes, I remember the man. Have no way of knowin' if he's yours or not, but I did hear him talkin' about looking for a crew to sail with. He was in search of a new captain—from what I understand, the last one was a beast."

Caspian ran a hand through his hair. "That's the only clue I've found so far in the search for my man, Blakely. I don't think it could hurt us to take it. Do you know, by chance, if he ended up signing on with anyone?"

Blakely scratched his chin, which was scruffy with a gray beard. "I don't believe he did. I think he said somethin' about headin' back to... Port Royal. But I don't know if this is your man. I don't want to send ya searchin' all over the Caribbean for someone who just shares the first name of this sailor you're searchin' fer."

When a pirate ambled too near, Reed backed up, closer to Eden. She placed her hand on his shoulder. It seemed as though she had no hope for finding her brother. Well, maybe everything was better off this way. She had a new family here, one she was very happy about. But she would be much happier knowing if her brother was alive. Eden craned her neck to peer up at her husband. Her voice a low whisper, she said, "What should we do?"

Caspian pressed a kiss to her forehead. "We are going to Port Royal."

§

Gage awoke before the rays of dawn had fully shed their light on the beach. Something soft moved under his arm. He blinked sleep-blurred eyes against the glint of the sun. The ocean was beautiful in the morning. Colors—lavender, turquoise, and even a pale yellow—danced across the water as the waves lapped gently against the beach.

Memories flooded back to him as he gazed at the most beautiful part of the beach—the woman who slept with her head on his arm, and the baby who nestled against him. He could not stifle a grin. This made him feel like a family man. Ivy shifted closer to him. Her copper curls wound over her shoulder and tumbled onto the sand. When so close to her, with her face peacefully drawn in sleep, Gage noticed a smattering of light freckles on her cheeks. They were as charming as her and practically begged for his lips to touch them.

After his slumber almost two feet apart from Ivy and separated from her by Emma, he had ended up awfully close to the woman by morning. The feelings running through his heart concerned him. When had he grown so attached to this lady? It was not his place. He was... her ferry home. That was all. He was meant to carry her home to London, and nothing more. Misery tightened in his gut. If he was wise, he would push these feelings away. But apparently he was not wise, because he could not brush away the longing jabbing at him to press a kiss to her forehead.

A blow to his stomach knocked the thought right from his head. Gage glanced down at Emma, whose leg had kicked him in her sleep. He chuckled quietly and drew her closer to him with the arm that was not around Ivy's waist. The thought was pleasant, and led his mind down some dangerous avenues.

Just as Gage was about to rise and move away from the woman, a gasp met his ears. Ivy had woken, her stormy gray eyes wide. "Captain Thompson."

"Aye, that is my name. Although I still would much prefer it if you would call me Gage."

She frowned. Finally, her gaze found Emma and realization crossed her face. "Well. We'd best get up, before... before someone sees us like this."

Gage could not resist the opportunity. He leaned forward to hug her, with Emma cradled between them. Her sweet scent of citrus teased his nose as her soft curls tickled his cheek. She was so soft... so lovely. After a second, her arms wrapped around his waist and Gage let out a sigh of contentment. It would be easy to get used to having someone as sweet as her to embrace every day.

"Blast it all, look what we have here! The captain actually *does* know how to touch a lady."

Gage jerked away from Ivy and squinted up at the crew member who had invaded their privacy. Jennings.

Peterson—a man who could typically be found shadowing Rogers—chimed in, "I don't think he does. I know I'd be doin' a whole lot more than simply *touchin'* that lady."

Gage stiffened his jaw. The audacity of these men. A soft hand wrapped around his fist. When had he clenched his fists? He relaxed his hand and allowed his fingers to entwine with Ivy's. He cast her a sidelong glance. She stared at him with a look of inner strength, strength he hadn't always been aware she possessed.

Gage faced his men. "I will not have you talking to me like this. I don't want to hear another word from my crew about Lady Shaw. Our affairs are not yours."

The men jeered, but walked away. Gage extracted his hand from Ivy's, before she could feel it tremble. What was wrong with him? He was not cut out to be a leader, a captain. So why did he go on pretending like he was born for this position? *It's what you've always aspired to be.* But what did that matter, anyway? He was useless, doomed to forever be under someone else's command.

Ivy's hand rested on his elbow and she tugged him to face her. Her gray eyes searched his in concern. "Are you all right, Gage? Don't listen to those... monsters. I think... I think you're a wonderful, strong man. A much better man than any of them could ever hope to be."

Gage's heart soared at her complement, but his pride cried out. She could tell he wasn't confident in his abilities as captain? Could the rest of his crew tell as well?

"Did I say something to upset you?" Ivy shifted Emma in her arms. The child still slept.

"No, milady, you said nothing. I just... forgive me. I must go." Gage spun on his heel and exited the woman's area of the camp. He needed to distance himself from the lady, and he might as well begin sooner rather than later.

⚓

Ivy crossed her arms across her chest and watched as Gage's men cleaned the ship and repaired the broken wood. They worked quickly, but this was their third day spent on the beach. Ivy had begun to wonder if they would ever finish the job. How badly had the hurricane damaged the ship?

She was also beginning to wonder what she had done wrong. Hurt spread through her like ice despite their tropical setting as she gazed at Gage—well, she really ought to call him

Captain Thompson. The man had seemed to keep himself quite busy since the first morning they had spent on this island. Even during the nights, when Emma had cried herself to sleep, he avoided them and spent the majority of the time pacing across the beach. Well, it was better this way. It was better to discover what a cruel person he was before she grew even further attached to him.

And yet Ivy found it hard to tear her eyes from the sight of him. With one hand pressed against his brow, squinting against the dark clouds that dotted the sky, he stood waist-deep in water. Ivy's face heated as she caught a glimpse of his bare chest. He had begun to shed his shirt while they worked on this island. His chestnut-brown hair damply curled around his ears due to the humidity in the air.

He shouted orders to his men, who scurried down the side of the ship, scraping off all the excess crust that had accumulated on the *Siren's Call*. His gaze caught hers and held it for a moment as he turned. She frowned and glanced away, bouncing Emma in her arms.

Captain Thompson had all but ignored Emma because of all of his work, as well, and Ivy could tell the child had been affected by it. What a monster.

A hand briefly tapped on Ivy's elbow, garnering her attention. She whipped around, prepared to fend off one of Captain Thompson's men. Mr. Douglas smiled down at her and nodded to Emma. She backed away a step. Douglas had been nothing but a gentleman to her, but how could she rightly trust him? He was employed on this pirate ship. Now they were in the expansive setting of this wild island, would he take that as an opportunity to harm her or Emma? "You might want to hold the babe a little less tightly—it would do her good to breathe."

Ivy glanced down at Emma. She practically had the poor girl in a stranglehold. Quickly, she loosened her grip on the child and laughed nervously. Surely Mr. Douglas would never hurt either of them.

"Are you all right, milady? Something seems to have upset you."

"Oh, don't worry about me, Mr. Douglas. I just... I just thought you were someone else." Ivy smoothed a copper curl out of Emma's face.

"May I... hold her?" Mr. Douglas indicated to the child.

"Oh." The man had watched Emma for her and Gage before, so surely she would be safe if he held her for a moment. She handed the little one over.

Adam looked quite awkward trying to balance the moving child, but after a few moments she seemed to grow accustomed to him.

"How have you been doing? I know a lady like you has not slept on the sand much in her life." Mr. Douglas tickled Emma, eliciting a giggle. He seemed relieved to have made the child happy.

"I actually much prefer it to the constant rocking of the ship," Ivy replied with a rueful chuckle.

Lightning cracked across the sky. Emma sobbed, and Ivy restrained a whimper of her own as dark clouds rolled across the sky. Mr. Douglas's brow furrowed kindly. It was a pity the side of the man's face was scarred so badly. He really would have been handsome otherwise, and he had such a generous heart.

"Don't you worry about the storm, milady. It should just be a little rain—it won't harm us a bit."

"Oh, good, sir. I did not enjoy the storm in any way, and I'm afraid Emma did not either."

Adam bounced the baby in his arms. She grabbed his chin in her hands and shoved it side to side. "I must get to work, milady, but it was nice to speak with you." He handed Emma back to her and jogged to stand next to the captain.

Ivy sank down onto the sand. She couldn't help but watch Gage as he bantered back and forth with his crew, as if he had all the confidence in the world. His men might not realize that, but she knew it was not true. She had seen the hurt, the fear in his eyes when his men accused him of not being a true man. Ivy found it endearing, really, and she wanted to help him build up his confidence. But he had refrained from speaking to her the past few days, and despite her attempts to speak with him, he had barely responded. Well, no matter how he acted to her, it was still hard to tear her eyes from him. She rocked Emma against her chest, hoping the little one would distract her from the strange feelings she was developing toward Gage.

A man somewhere behind her chuckled. She glanced back and dread clenched around her heart. The sailor leisurely leaned his back against a nearby palm tree. She knew the man, but could not quite place his name. Either way, she was not too fond of him from the way he had treated Gage. He was speaking in murmurs—loud murmurs to another man... Rogers?

She leaned backwards to hear more of their conversation. "What a fool he is... leaving a... thing like her like that. He needs to learn how to be a man... someone else will take her." The man glanced at her and made eye contact. A shiver crept through her body. Rogers replied to him, but she could not make out his words. Gooseflesh popped up on her skin and she hugged Emma close.

These men would drive her mad with distraction. Ivy had to admit, she also felt some fear in their presence. Heaven knew what they were capable of. She needed to get away from them at once to get some peace and quiet.

The lush green of the jungle behind her beckoned her to join it, offering her a reprieve from the nonstop stares and leers from the ship's men. Biting her lip, Ivy flashed a glance at Gage, who did not seem to be paying any attention to her actions. Well, that was all the better. She did not need him following her. Not that he would, though. He didn't seem to care if she was well or not as of late, so why should he bother to keep her safe in the jungle?

Ivy tore into the greenery, and a blast of warm humidity hit her face. She stepped farther inside the jungle, whipping branches out of her way. Somewhere in the distance, an exotic bird called. Emma clung to Ivy's waist with all her might.

Ivy continued her trek through the jungle at a rapid pace—she needed to get far away from the men of that horrid ship, and she needed distance right now. After a few minutes she finally slowed and spun in a leisurely circle, pushing loose strands of hair off of her neck. Sweat dripped down her neckline, but at least her surroundings were quiet. Peaceful. Everywhere she moved, green met her eyes. Off in the distance, a growl rumbled through the trees and shrubbery. Ivy gasped and spun around. Panic filled her. Maybe it would be best to turn back to the camp. Which... which direction had she come from?

"Oh, Emma, what have I done?" Ivy nudged the tyke closer and buried her face in the short curls, inhaling their sweet scent. What had she been thinking, charging aimlessly into a wild jungle with a baby?

Something rustled in the trees behind her and it was all she could do not to scream. Thunder crashed, and in a second, rain was pouring through the jungle's canopy. Emma giggled and pointed at the water pouring down on them. Ivy spun around. From which direction had she come? They needed to get back before something dreadful happened.

The branches in one direction were disturbed, like she had come from that area. A shiver iced down her spine. It seemed better to go somewhere than to stay here waiting for some monster to pounce and eat both of them, so hopefully it wouldn't hurt to go that way. After one glance over her shoulder, she hurried down the somewhat visible path. Emma's weight seemed to grow heavier by the second. Ivy's shoulders ached. Water toppled down on them from the branches above, and before Ivy knew it, the soaked fabric of her dress chafed her skin with each step she took.

It seemed like she had been walking for hours. Surely she had not wandered this far from the beach. Dread flooded her body, paralyzing her for a moment. Surely she was going in the wrong direction. She had just journeyed even farther away from the beach. "I'm sorry, Emma."

Thunder shook the entire island and Emma wailed. Ivy stopped in her tracks and cuddled the girl close to her body. "It's okay, sweetie, we are all right. Shush."

Something howled in the distance. She launched herself forward and let out a cry of her own.

Her breath left her body.

Something tugged at her skirt. A branch. Ivy tore free and continued on at a rapid pace. Emma began to slip from her arms, but Ivy held onto her steadfastly.

Ivy ran faster than she ever had before. Whatever was in this jungle with her, she would protect Emma with everything she had. Tears streamed down her cheeks. If something happened to her—out of her own stupidity, nonetheless—William would be entirely on his own.

Oh God, please help me find my way back to the camp. Please. For Emma's and William's safety.

Smash. Her body collided with something tall and hard. A tree. She collapsed to the muddy ground.

Ivy gulped in air and tried to calm herself. Her limbs were too weak to rise. Rain continued to pour down on her, unforgiving. Strong arms wrapped around her waist, pulling her up to a sitting position. Strong arms? She blinked at the image before her. Gage. What?

"I—I didn't see you... I didn't know you were there. I—"

"Be silent, woman. Take a moment to catch your breath." Captain Thompson's arms moved her so her head rested in his lap. He pried Emma from her arms and set her at his side, with her back resting against him. Sweat mingled with the rainwater. Ivy drank in air. How long had she been running?

Captain Thompson brushed the hair out of her face as she tried to regain her composure. His hand rested on her shoulder, gripping it in a gentle, reassuring way. After a few silent moments where only the sounds of her panting and the rain bouncing off of the leaves filled the air, the man spoke. "What on earth were you doing?"

CHAPTER 15

Gage shook his head at the sight before him. Ivy's hair was a tangled mass of orange, pouring onto his lap like a stream of water. Her face was red from exertion, and sweat and rain dampened her dress. Still, she was probably one of the most beautiful things he had ever seen.

While his men rested for a short break, Gage had returned to the beach ready to talk to Ivy again. Of course, he had avoided her for the past few days out of embarrassment for their encounter, but he had to make things right between them. When he realized she was nowhere in sight, he had questioned all of his men. Jennings had seen her slip away into the jungle and thought she was going for a short stroll—obviously not the case. And when Gage heard the shrill scream of a woman and the wail of a child, he had suspected the worst. He muttered a prayer of thanks under his breath that both the woman and the child seemed unharmed. The rain slowed down to a trickle.

He reached into the mass of copper curls and began to untangle them, gently massaging her scalp as he did so. Ivy's eyes slid closed. "That feels good."

Gage chuckled. "What were you doing, milady?" He shifted his weight. The muddy floor of an island jungle was not the most ideal place to have a conversation with a pretty young woman, but he did not want to head back to the beach yet. The privacy out here was much welcome.

"I just... I just wanted to get away. From the men. From everyone. They were talking about... things... when they thought I wasn't listening, and I just wanted some peace and quiet. The jungle appeared inviting..." Ivy's breath seemed to be almost even now.

Gage ran a hand along the line of her jaw. Emma leaned against him, yawning sleepily. When he had heard their cries... oh, he did not want to think about it. "Why did you scream, Ivy? What happened?" She had been running at full speed when she had collided with him.

She stared up at him, her eyes the exact color of the stormy sky. "I... I don't know. I kept hearing things, and I thought there was some ravenous animal after me. The creature probably left, or it was just my imagination. I'm not sure what it was. It just frightened me and I wanted to stay safe. I could not let Emma get hurt."

Gage brushed his thumb across her cheek. "You probably heard an innocent animal in the jungle. But you were smart to stay safe like you did. I'm just glad you're all right."

Ivy sat up, but swayed. Her face had drained back from bright red to creamy white. She leaned back against his chest. Emma nodded off to sleep against his knee, and he grinned.

The rain started up again. Ivy sighed and snuggled her head against him.

"Please don't ever run off somewhere like that again without even telling me first." He was so close to her, her ear tickled his lips as he spoke. Warmth radiated from her body. Rain trickled between them. His gaze traveled to her lips and stayed there. Some color stained her cheeks, and her lips, her pretty lips parted slightly.

Before he knew it, he had lowered his mouth to hers. She stopped moving for a few moments, but then she wound her arms around his neck and joined in the kiss wholeheartedly. Gage groaned in delight and ran his fingers through her curls. She made a sweet noise in the back of her throat.

Rainwater gushed down in a torrent, clearing his head from some of the heated thoughts churning through it. He tore away from the woman, but not before he noticed her swollen lips and flushed cheeks. Egad, but she was beautiful. He squeezed his eyes shut for a moment to gain his composure.

If they intended to make it back to camp any time in the near future, he needed to stop looking at her. She reached out a hand and touched his cheek. Self-consciousness began to plague him. He hadn't shaved in a few days. Was his face too prickly for her? Had it hurt her skin? What did she think of him? Surely he did not look his best after traipsing through the jungle on his way to find her. He probably smelled terribly as well. What did he think he was doing; he had no right to kiss such a lady...

She pulled his face towards him and kissed him of her own will. Gage inhaled through his nose and angled his head to deepen the kiss. He pulled away for a second. "You are beautiful, Lady Ivy Shaw." She resumed the kiss before falling against him once more.

"So are you, Captain Gage Thompson." She let out a breathy laugh. "Emma!" Suddenly, she jerked away from him and frantically searched around.

Gage blinked. What...?

He glanced down to find Emma sleeping peacefully on the floor of the jungle. She must have gotten jostled away from Gage while he was... doing other things.

Gage scooped the child up in his arms and reluctantly glanced at Ivy. "I suppose we should get back, then. Adam was quite concerned when I left."

♪

Caspian pressed a kiss to his wife's ear as the bartender—a young man in his mid-teens—spoke to them. Unlike the last town, he was unfamiliar with this tavern and its inhabitants, but he had a reputation in the Caribbean, especially in Port Royal, and he was lucky the lad had heard of him and was willing to help.

"Well, have you met the man?" Eden crossed her arms across her chest. The young man's face reddened when his gaze took in Eden. Caspian could not help but bristle. He pulled his wife closer and tucked her against the side. There would be no mistaking she was his.

"Aye, I remember 'im. He had a strange look about 'im, that fellow. 'E was looking to sail under a new captain. Didn't talk much, but I've seen 'im around the city a few times, I 'ave. I believe 'e was 'ere for the earthquake a couple years back."

"Did he find a new captain to sail under?" Caspian rested his hand on Reed's shoulder. The child leaned his head back against him.

The young man fidgeted with his sleeves, which were too long for his short frame. "I 'eard 'e signed on with a man who was practically recruiting an entire crew. I can't remember the man's name... I'd never 'eard of 'im before."

Caspian frowned. He knew a man in such need of a crew. Perhaps it was too insane to be actually be true, but perhaps... Caspian could find him and they would know.

⚓

Addie sighed as she gazed down at her latest work. The two pieces of fabric didn't quite meet up with each other perfectly, but it was close. Much closer than she had managed last week. The stitches could almost be called even. Quite an improvement. She smiled and hugged the fabric close to her chest. Of course, she probably looked insane to the city dwellers who strolled below her window, but she did not care.

She had actually done something right. Mr. Faulke might be pleased with her for once, and she could actually get caught up on mending the basket of clothing beside her chair. Maybe for once in her life she could actually work to gain her share of food. When she had lived with the Archers, she had been allowed to garden and that was all. Then her husband had kept her inside without much contact with anyone or anything besides him. Now, she could actually earn her own living. There was no greater feeling in the world.

⚓

Adam felt sure he had never experienced any worse feeling in the world. Ever since they had boarded the ship once more, he had been riddled with nightmares. James's face still haunted him. Sometimes, when he closed his eyes, he could see the agony. *God, please help me.*

Why on earth should Adam have been spared that night and not James? James had a wife. A baby. Adam had no one, save the family he had left behind and not seen in years. God help him, he got fighting mad when he thought of it. It was not fair. He had made sure all of James's belongings—and his last share of money—were sent to his wife when they had reached port. Yet for some reason, the man's death continued to plague him.

Adam squeezed his eyes shut and flung himself over onto his other side in the hammock. He needed sleep. Sleep would do him a world of good, and perhaps help him forget about his nightmares.

⚓

Ivy's face heated as Captain Thompson—Gage—held her hand beneath the surface of the table in his cabin. She was not sure why he continued to invite her to dine in his cabin when the men there persecuted him in front of her, but she had to admit she enjoyed the time spent with him. He met her gaze and flashed a grin at her, his brown eyes sparkling.

One by one, Gage's leading crew members exited the cabin, leaving only Gage, Adam, and Ivy. The men had pestered Gage today as usual, but their comments were few and far between. Maybe they had realized how rude their remarks were, or had gotten tired of repeating the same accusations. She smiled as Gage rubbed his thumb across the side of her hand, but Ivy could not shake the feeling that she should not be allowing him to touch her. Surely there would be no future for them. After all, Ivy had promised Aimee she would not return home attached to a pirate.

Adam rose and stepped around the table. He caught a glimpse of Ivy and Gage's hands under the surface and flashed them a knowing look. Ivy quickly removed her hand from the captain's grasp and twisted her head the other way. Gage's chuckle was a low rumble in her left ear.

Gage stood and retrieved Emma from where she slept on his bed. Ivy quickly forgot her embarrassment and took the child in her arms. Oh, how she loved this little one. Gage leaned over her to press a kiss to Emma's forehead.

A deafening crack blasted from somewhere in the distance. Ivy froze. Something splashed in the ocean.

Ivy latched her wide gaze to Gage, who seemed unable to move. After a moment, he inhaled deeply and grabbed Ivy's hand. Adam stepped closer to the both of them.

The cabin door burst open.

CHAPTER 16

"What is going on, Peters?" Gage glanced at Ivy, who rocked Emma against her chest. Adam stood next to her, staring at his captain. "Stay with Ivy and the child, Mr. Douglas."

Gage stepped outside and shut the door behind himself. Peters fidgeted with his hands before speaking. "There's been a ship spotted off our bow. A pirate ship. We didn't recognize her colors, but we certainly recognized the meaning of the skull and crossbones."

A frown tensed the muscles in Gage's face. "She fired on us."

"Aye, and we didn't take that t' be friendly. We thought you should know."

Gage ran a hand through his hair. *Why now, Lord? I'm not ready for this. Especially with a woman and a babe on board to care for. Why?*

"You should decide if we run or fight." Peters started up the stairs and toward the main deck. Gage followed him.

"I know what I should do, Peters." Gage immediately regretted the sharp tone of his voice. He had to admit, he had only snapped because he also doubted his abilities as a captain. However true it may be, Gage did not like to think about the subject. Why, he had hardly been successful in his few weeks as captain, and he fretted about every future decision.

Including the one that loomed directly in front of him when he walked up onto the main deck. His entire crew, minus Adam, stood facing him. Above their heads, the distant mast of a ship rose from the sea. Pirates.

God help us.

$

"What's happening?"

Adam spun around from the window to face Lady Shaw. She balanced Emma on her hip with one arm and tugged on a piece of her bronze-colored hair with the other. The woman's and the babe's hair were almost identical shades of orange. They really could pass for mother and daughter if Lady Shaw would ever want to claim her.

Adam reluctantly glanced back out at the window. Bits of the captain's conversation had filtered through the door and he had seen a ship off their bow from the porthole—he could piece together what was happening. From the shouts on the deck, he could also guess what would happen next. Although he longed to be with the rest of the crew as first mate, he did not want to leave Lady Shaw and the child alone while something could happen to them, and his captain had commanded him to stay. He glanced back at the woman and remembered her query. "We've run across the path of a pirate ship, milady."

Her eyebrows scrunched together and her face paled. "I-I've never been near actual pirates, not counting your men."

"We are privateers, milady, or at least we will be official privateers after your—Captain Thompson gets some paperwork done."

"But what is going to happen now?"

"Don't worry, milady. We will most likely confront them, but I have no idea how that will fare."

She pressed her face against the little girl's head. "If we get captured, what will happen to Emma?"

Adam smiled inwardly. It was sweet of her to worry about the baby's fate, and not her own. The smile vanished when he realized what they *would* likely do to the woman and the child if they were discovered. He had to tuck them safely away in such an event.

"Well, milady, let's hope that event will never come. Now, follow me. We should get you somewhere more secure."

§

Ivy gasped when Mr. Douglas opened the door at the same time as Captain Thompson. They almost collided. Ivy studied him with hopeful eyes but was disappointed at the sight before her: his face was several shades paler than normal, his hair was mussed, and he wrung his hands. If ever he was a man with no confidence, it was right now.

"Are you all right, Gage?" Ivy stepped forward and laid a hand on his arm. He blinked, petted her hand absently, and let his arm drop.

"Yes, yes, I'm fine. I just came here to say I need Adam to come up on the main deck with me, and I need you to take Emma and go to your cabin." His voice quavered as he spoke and even more color drained from his face. What was going on?

"Are you sure you are fine?" Ivy quirked an eyebrow as she rearranged Emma on her hip.

"Yes." His voice was raspy, and he averted his eyes as he spoke.

A cannon shot off in the distance.

"You need to get in your cabin, for your protection and Emma's."

Splash.

"I will. Please be careful, Gage." Ivy held his gaze for a few moments and searched their chocolate depths. She noted fear. *God, please help us.*

§

Ivy cringed as another disturbing crack rent the air. They had been hit. Again. Although she hated to admit it, she was afraid to look out the porthole to see what was going on around her. The action could cause her to panic, and she did not need that. So she had stayed perched on the cot with an unusually quiet Emma in her lap for the last thirty minutes. The little tyke had fallen asleep moments ago.

It really would have been more pleasant if Emma was awake to keep her company, but she supposed it was all for the best. The child had been frightened by the noises of the battle, so it was a blessing when she had finally drifted to sleep. Ivy's arms ached from supporting her, so Ivy reclined on the cot, propped her back up on the pillows, and closed her eyes.

The sounds above were frightening, honestly, and they were bringing on a pounding headache. Ivy rubbed her temple and groaned. The ship lurched over a swell, and nausea crept into her throat. A roar of men's voices caused Ivy's eyes to snap open. Their voices were cheerful, yet angry. Bloodthirsty. *God, please end this quickly. Please do not let too many lives be lost, either.*

Ivy pressed Emma against her chest and inhaled her sweet scent. The roars of the men seemed to double. She strained her ears—was that the crew of the other ship she heard as well? They seemed too close. Terribly close.

Loud thumps pounded on the deck above her. Fresh roars rained down. Curses spewed. Metallic clinks and gunshots tore the air. *Oh, no.* Were the pirates boarding the ship? What would happen now?

She squeezed Emma against her chest. "We need to stay calm, little one." The words were meant more for herself than for the sleeping baby.

Please keep the men safe; even Rogers. I don't want anyone to die.

⚓

As Adam forced his way against the horde of enemy pirates, the metallic tang of blood tainted the air. The crew of the *Siren's Call* was near to finally pushing the miscreants back. Half an hour ago, the others had been ahead of them and were almost forcing them off of their own ship. But Captain Thompson had led them forward and they almost had an advantage now.

The man had significantly taken over command of the crew and his strategies in this battle were working well to their advantage. A man lunged at Adam's side, slashing with his sword. Adam managed to avoid the strike and parry back until another pirate distracted him and Adam could slip away.

Adam stepped forward and eyed the men around them. "Captain!"

Gage was far ahead now, separated from his crew. A feeling of dread stuck in Adam's stomach. It was not good to be surrounded by the enemy, away from one's crew. "Captain!"

But it seemed as though the captain could not hear him, and it was too difficult to reach him.

⚓

Gage thrust his sword forward, matching the enemy's blow. He wiped the sweat from his forehead as he retreated. Another sailor distracted the man, giving Gage a chance to catch his breath. Egad, what was wrong with him? He had not been able to outrun the pirates, and now his men fought the wretches hand-to-hand. And it was *completely his fault.*

A balding man's cutlass swung down at Gage's head, but he managed to parry his blow and slice at him with his knife. He couldn't help but wonder how Ivy and Emma were faring in the cabin below. A barely audible prayer for their safety escaped his lips. At least they were still beyond the reach of these men. Gage grunted, and shoved two men back with his blows and a volley of metallic clangs.

Gage ran a hand through his sweaty hair, forcing it back from his face in an attempt to clear his sight of vision. If he *did* survive this battle, he would need to clean up before he went to see Ivy. He must look—and smell—a fright.

Clunk.

Pain reverberated through his shoulder.

He spun around to view his attacker. A burly man braced a pistol in one hand and a sword in the other. A twisted grin spread across his face.

Gage blinked. He felt his hand move as an instinct.

Too late. He saw the sword slide through his side.

He didn't feel it, but he noted blood gliding down his waist.

Gage drove his knife at the man's shoulder, but he knocked it from his grasp and a new pirate stole Gage's attention for a moment as he exchanged several sword thrusts. He disarmed the man quickly and swiveled back to the first, burly man.

Crack.

His head. It hurt like nothing he'd known before.

He lifted his sword, but black swirled before his eyes.

He tumbled to the ground.

⚓

Adam saw his captain crumble. He had to get him out of the way of the mess that filled the entire main deck, or something could injure him even further. If he even *was* alive, for that matter. Dread clenched his stomach. James's visage flitted in front of his face. James...

No. He would not allow what happened with James repeat itself. He would save Gage's life even if he could not save James's.

He forged his way through the battle to his captain's side. A man's boot squashed his hand. Adam waited for the man to nudge away before he forced himself forward and hefted Captain Thompson's body in his arms. With a grip under his armpits, he could drag him below to his cabin. Then, maybe Lady Shaw would be able to assist him.

Please, Lord, do not let her be afraid of blood.

⚓

Ivy's hand hovered over the doorknob. Should she really open the door in the midst of the battle? Should she even acknowledge her presence?

"This is Mr. Douglas, milady. It is urgent that you open the door." His voice held a rushed, almost panicked tone.

She unlatched and flung open the door.

"It's the captain. He's been injured badly. I need you to take Emma and go to his cabin immediately—then bolt the door behind you. Please tend to him, if you feel you're capable. If not, stay by his side and comfort him until we can get a surgeon to him. All right?"

Dread surged through her body. What had happened to the poor man? "Of course I'll go." She reached for Emma and stepped out the door. "Will... will he live?"

Adam stopped still in his tracks for a moment. The pause alone was answer enough for Ivy. He didn't know. His eyes searched hers beseechingly. After a second, he grabbed her arm and pulled her to the captain's cabin.

The screams of the battle were even louder here. They seemed to be magnified and multiplied. Clinking swords cut the air. Ivy gladly stepped into the captain's cabin—she did not want to get caught outside in the battle. Mr. Douglas didn't follow her. Instead, he went straight to the men on the main deck.

The sounds of the battle were muffled when she shut the door, thankfully. She scanned the room and blinked her eyes to adjust to the dim light. Was the sun setting already?

Finally, she located Gage, sprawled halfway on his bed, a hand pressed against his left side. He was in a swoon. Half of his body rested on the ground. Immediately, Ivy set Emma on a chair and sped to the man's side. His hands were cold. Almost like ice. Panic filled her. Was he even alive? *Please, God. Please.*

Frantically, she gripped at his wrists and laid her ear against his chest. Good. He was still breathing. Now she had to get him all the way onto his bed. She grabbed his legs and tried to heft him up. "Ooof." She might as well have tried to lift the ship they were on. Would he wake up if she stirred him? She hadn't checked his injuries yet. He needed to be on a stable platform for her to look at them.

"Gage? Gage? I really need you to get yourself onto the bed, sir." He stirred but didn't respond. She was almost tempted to kiss him to see if that would wake him up, like in a fairytale, but she knew that would be ridiculous. "Gage!" She squeezed his hand. A groan filled the room, and she realized it was hers. *Please.*

Ivy hefted his legs up and with all her might hurled them towards the top of the bed. Her back ached, but she had succeeded. He was completely on the bed. *Thank you, God.*

Now, to inspect his injuries.

CHAPTER 17

Ivy pushed loose hair from her face. His side seemed all right. He had lost a lot of blood, but it was only a stab wound, and whatever had cut him had not touched any major body parts. She hoped.

Ivy chewed on her lip. She highly doubted her abilities as a nurse, but she was the only person available to help Gage.

The blood flowing from his side had slowed nearly to a stop. Unfortunately, the red liquid had stained all of his sheets and his coverlet. These were probably his only bed things, but there was nothing she could do about it. His safety was far more important. Now, she was left to determine the state of his unconsciousness. True, he had lost a large quantity of blood, but... oh, yes. Mr. Douglas had said Gage hit his head.

She ran her fingers through his hairline, checking for bumps. A round area protruded from the surface of his scalp like a chicken egg. Some blood pooled around it. The poor man. That surely felt terrible.

She ran over to the table in the cabin and snatched the pitcher of water from it. He could get an infection if she didn't clean his stab wound. A doctor who had treated little William after he had scraped his arms and legs up playing outside had told her as much as that. So many terrible things could happen to him if she did not tend to him properly. God help her, she needed to stop thinking about that and get to work.

Ivy tore off a strip of the coverlet and dipped it in the water. She gingerly dabbed at the wound on his side. A wave of nausea washed over her when the sharp smell of blood bit her nose. Her hand shook. Her vision doubled. *Give me strength, Lord.* The cloth jerked in her hand and bumped into his wound much harder than she intended. Still, he didn't stir.

Ivy let out a sharp hiss of breath and gritted her teeth. The poor, dear man. She cleaned the rest of the wound and wrapped it with the cleanest bit of cloth she could find.

She glanced around the room for something that could further cleanse the gap in his flesh. No alcohol in sight. She would have to ask for some when he woke. If he did wake. *Please, God, let him wake up.*

The bump on his head was just that—a bump. What could she do to treat it? She supposed the most she could do was to sit here and wait with him until the horrible battle outside the cabin door quieted. An agonizing scream pierced through the thick oak door. Panic tore through Ivy. People were being *murdered* just feet away from her.

Ivy buried her face in her hands. If something happened to Gage... if he...

She could not think of it. She would not think of it.

Ivy glanced at Emma. She slept soundly. How could the child be so calm in the midst of this horrible battle? Oh, she would give anything to be asleep right now rather than hearing the men screaming, the swords clinking, and the guns shooting. Gage moved slightly, and Ivy's heart leapt. Her hand found his and she held it. It was cold. Oh, that was a terrible feeling. It was unnaturally chilled. His face was pale. Gray-toned and pale.

Ivy bit her lip. Where was Adam? Maybe he would know what to do. It seemed as if the very life was flowing out of Gage, and yet she had no clue what to do to stop it. She brushed a lock of dark hair out of his face. His forehead was cold, too. After a moment's hesitation, she leaned forward to press a kiss against his forehead. He smelled of cedar and salty sweat, but the mixture was a pleasant scent. Her lips lingered against his skin for a moment before his arm snaked around her waist. His grip was loose, but he had moved nonetheless.

Ivy pulled back. His chocolate brown eyes were half open, staring at her face. One side of his mouth tipped upwards in an attempt at a smile. He coughed. "At least kiss me on my lips, milady."

Her face heated, but a chuckle escaped her mouth. His eyes slid closed as she brushed her lips against his. He did not respond. Ivy sighed. The man had slipped back into unconsciousness. But surely it was a good sign he had opened his eyes and teased her.

Something pounded on the door. Ivy shot up from the bed. She prayed it was not one of the pirates, or someone like Rogers.

"Lady Shaw, it is Mr. Douglas. Please grant me entrance for a moment."

Ivy sped to the door and unbolted it. Mr. Douglas shut it behind him before Ivy could see what was going on outside. "How is he?"

"I-I don't know. He woke up for a second and spoke, but his skin is cold to the touch. I cleaned his wounds, but he lost a lot of blood. I-I'm... afraid."

Adam glanced over her shoulder at his captain, his forehead creased. "I fear for him also, milady, but I am afraid there is nothing I can do for him right now. The battle is over—we managed to fend the pirates off."

"Oh, thank God," Ivy sighed.

"However, milady, we face a new issue. That's why I came to you."

Ivy tensed. "What is that?"

"The crew... they are unhappy. They say we should have raided the pirates rather than just fend them off. They feel that right now, while Captain Thompson indisposed, they should take full control."

⚓

Adam fumbled with his hat as he stood before the lady. He noticed a fresh scratch on his hand from which blood trailed down. He did not remember getting scratched. Silence stretched through the room for a moment, and finally Adam glanced up.

Lady Shaw's face had faded to a chalky color. She swayed and then caught her balance on the table beside to her. "M-mutiny, Mr. Douglas?"

"Yes, milady. Mutiny."

"What are we to do?" Her voice emerged from her lips as a whisper.

"I do not know, milady. This is a tricky situation."

"May I go up on the main deck with you?"

Adam glanced at his captain's still body. The man would definitely not approve of him taking the woman up to the crew when they were in such a disagreeable state, but on the other hand, Adam did not want to deal with the riotous crew alone. Captain Thompson seemed to be doing all right. Lady Shaw was a bright woman. He was certain she could help.

"Do not let Captain Thompson know I let you go above. And for goodness' sake, please be careful. But yes. Hurry. I fear we have little time."

Lady Shaw blinked rapidly. Finally, she faced Emma once more, who slept soundly on an armchair. "She should be all right by herself, sleeping. I'm ready."

Adam ran a hand through his hair and prayed he was doing the right thing, before opening the door and motioning for the woman to exit first.

$ $

Addie heaved out a sigh as she sprawled across her cot in the millinery shop. Her back ached. Her fingers ached. Her neck ached. *Everything* ached. Apparently, sewing and mending used different muscles in her body than gardening because this occupation took a toll on her. Her eyes had grown bleary from staring at the tiny needle all day long. All week long. Over and over and over.

Where was Gage? Would he really come to help her, or would her beloved brother prove to be like all the other men in her life? Their father had left them with no prospects. Then her adopted father had sold her to the highest bidder. Her husband had been useless with his constant drinking and gambling and left her deep in debt after he died. And now, would Gage fail her too? If only women could live on their own without relying on men. It was a struggle to purchase even her necessities with the small payments Mr. Faulke gave her.

When would this end?

$

Ivy blinked against the glare of the sun. When her eyes finally adjusted to the light, she wished to close them again. A large majority of the crew was utterly battered. Blood drenched everything, soaked their clothing, and pooled on the wood. The deck seemed divided into two sections, with groups of men standing on either side. They did not look at all pleased with each other.

Rogers stood at the head of the men on the left. Ivy's stomach sank. Of course that wretched man would be leading a mutiny against Gage. *Oh, what were they to do?*

Mr. Douglas stepped with a hand behind his back to keep Ivy a step behind. She liked to think of herself as brave, but she was glad to stay back. These men were vicious and not in a mood to be polite. "Brought the cap'n's little lady friend to protect you, didja?" Rogers sneered.

Indignation shot through Ivy's veins. How dare the man? She lunged forward. "It is not right to speak that way and you will do well to change your tone, mister."

After a moment of painful silence, the majority of the men burst out in laughter.

Heat flooded Ivy's face.

"The little lamb does have a bite!"

"Hey, I didn't know she could speak fer herself!"

"That's just 'cause her girl-friend, the *cap'n,* ain't here."

Ivy's hands balled into fists at her waist.

Adam stepped forward. "Silence!" Ivy had never heard such a sharp tone come from the soft-spoken man. "What is your position, men?"

Voices roared on both sides of the ship.

"Order, please!" Adam proclaimed. After a moment, both sides quieted. "Now, you first. What say you?" He motioned to the right half of the crew.

A man with golden-red hair that glistened with sweat cleared his throat. "We are standin' behind Captain Thompson. He's been fair to us and was good to a lot of us when we was on Captain Archer's ship, too."

"Aye!" Some of the men near him shouted. Ivy's knees nearly buckled. There were more men on that side than on the other side. However, she dreaded to hear what Rogers had to say.

Nonetheless, Mr. Douglas faced the other side of the deck. "And you?"

Rogers jerked forward and jutted his chest out. He spat on the deck, and many of the men on his side of the ship did the same. "That sissy will not be my captain any longer—he never deserved the title and he doesn't now, that's for sure. He can't even command us successfully during a battle. He can't even *survive* a battle—he's hidden away in his little cabin with whate'er injury he claims to 'ave gotten. 'E's like a dog hiding under the table with his tail between its legs."

Ivy clenched her fists tight. Oh, how she wanted to speak her mind and put this horrid man in his place once and for all and somehow remove him from this ship. But that would be a foolish idea. She was a woman. A small woman. Who was she to attack a man? If she did, she would certainly not fare well. However, before Ivy could do anything at all, both groups of men began to roar. They seemed to be having a conversation, but their words sped too fast for Ivy to understand what they said.

Adam's gaze shifted to Ivy. She shrugged and glanced back and forth between the two sides. They would not be silent. A headache pounding at her temples, Ivy stood up straight. "Silence! Everyone be quiet right now!"

To her shock, the men stopped their racket. They all stared at her with their mouths gaping open. Well... she had not expected the men to even hear her, much less obey her. Now what? Ivy's face heated until she was certain it must be vibrant violet color.

She opened and closed her mouth a few times before some noise finally came out. Noise that seemed like stumbling nonsense. But she kept talking. "I-I uh... y-you men are acting ridiculously. H-how can you be so cruel to your own captain? You have barely given Ga—Captain Thompson a chance. Please, remain loyal to this good man, and I guarantee you will be reaping the benefits."

"We've given that jackal time!"

"Aye, an' he sent us straight into a hurricane, he did!"

"And he can't even hold his own in a battle!"

"We won't stand fer it any longer!"

Ivy moved to Adam, but he no longer seemed to be paying the crew any mind. What on earth was the matter with him? She needed his help now, and he seemed to be staring off into nothingness.

⚓

Adam tried to react. But his mind was elsewhere. If these men ended up mutinying, they would either lock Gage up or kill him. And that consequence would largely be his fault. He could not cope with sitting by while something terrible happened to one of his only friends. He had already failed James. He could not fail his current captain.

And yet, somehow, he stood there dumbfounded as the crew insulted Captain Thompson. Finally, Lady Shaw stepped forward, a stern look darkening her face. "How dare you talk like that? Captain Thompson has been good to you. I do not know exactly how this works for you, but I am certain he pays you well, and he has kept you safe despite the hurricane and the pirates. Please, just... leave him be."

"He didn't keep us safe! We've hardly been safe since we set foot on this ship with that man!"

"Yeah, the wench is just confused, that's all!"

Lady Shaw pressed a hand to her forehead. "Please, men. Please."

One of the men—from the side of the deck that supported Gage—nodded. "What state *is* our cap'n in?"

"Yeah, how's he doin'?"

Lady Shaw nibbled on her bottom lip. "He seems to be stable; however, I do not think he will be able to do much on the ship for at least another week. He has been injured fairly badly."

"What a child," sneered one of the men.

Adam sighed. He wondered how these men would react if it were *they* who had sustained the injuries.

"I'm sure it wasn't Captain Thompson's fault, and I am certain he will be back up on his feet as soon as he can be. This could have happened to any one of you. You should be thankful you are well and able to stand on your own feet." The woman's tone sharpened slightly and most of the men fell silent. Their mouths gaped open.

Adam had to hold back a chuckle. She was proving she could hold her own among this group of wild scalawags.

Lady Shaw crossed her arms across her body. "You all should be ashamed of yourselves for your behavior. You are acting quite unreasonably."

Most of the crew grumbled for a few moments. Finally, one stepped up. "Well, even if we want that man to remain our captain, we don't have any leader right now. What if something happens to Cap'n Thompson and he doesn't heal? We need somebody to lead us right now, while our cap'n is indisposed."

The men on the left side of the ship groaned.

"Mr. Douglas would be our reasonable answer," piped up Mr. Francis, a man who still supported Gage.

Adam's blood slowed its journey throughout his body. Was it possible for it to simply inch through his veins, rather than flow? His breathing altered to a shallower intake of air. He did not want to be responsible for the lives of so many men after he had so miserably failed in preserving the life of his closest friend. However, one glance at Lady Shaw restored some strength to his body.

The woman's eyes bore through him, determination lighting a fire behind their gray depths. She stood tall, her head tilted at a confident angle. This woman—an English-bred *lady*—possessed more strength than he did. And yet she did not seem cocky about it. No, instead she grabbed his hand with both of hers and stared straight into his eyes. In a low voice, she whispered, "I'll help you. I'll stand by you. Please. Gage needs this. We must keep everything in order for him."

Adam felt his forehead constrict into a frown. This lady was an angel. Gage should be happy someone as strong and brave and compassionate as her felt so strongly for him. Adam could only hope that someday a woman so resilient and kind would fall for him. Finally, he nodded. "I will step into Captain Thompson's place only until he feels well enough to return to his position."

Half the men groaned.

Ivy held her head high. "And you will respect Mr. Douglas. I do not expect to hear about any unhappiness among you. It would serve you well to be cooperative. If you please."

The men watched her with open jaws and stayed silent.

Adam's eyes widened. What on earth had gotten into the lady? Whatever she was doing, he would not complain. These men obeyed her better than they had obeyed Captain Thompson.

⚓

Gage could make out something pleasant in the midst of all the pain. No, that must have been a dream. Surely there was not a bronze-haired angel hovering over him, tending to him and fussing with his bandages. Surely the angels in heaven did not look exactly like Lady Ivy Shaw. However, it was a pleasant notion, and one he would not give up. Her lemon-tinted scent was almost distinguishable as well. He had not realized how much he thought about the lady until those thoughts were intensified by his pain-fogged mind.

A bump in the mattress inched its way into his back. He tried to roll over, but it was quite difficult to make his muscles obey him. When he finally could move, a radiating pain cut through his left side. It seemed as if his very flesh was being torn open, thread by thread. Suddenly, a soft, warm hand landed on his forehead, brushing away the sweat and soothing him. The angel. What was she doing here again? Not that he would complain. However, he really longed for the angel to kiss him. That would be nice.

Her lips pressed against his skin, searing a hole through his forehead. He tried to raise a hand to pull her closer, but his arm would not obey.

He needed to touch her. To hold her. Even though she wasn't real, he needed to think she was. It was the only thing keeping him sane.

However, after a brief second, a baby's cry rent the air. The noise might as well have split his head in two. To make matters worse, the angel left his side. His eyes, previously opened to slits, now slid closed. It was not worth the effort to keep them open just to see the wood bulkhead.

The angel's voice cooed comforting words to the child. The sound soothed him as much as it soothed the babe. Soon, his mind drifted back into blissful unconsciousness.

CHAPTER 18

Ivy shoved her hair back up into the hat Mr. Douglas had allowed her to borrow. He had loaned it to her when her skin started burning from all the time she now spent in the bright sun. She had new respect for the crew and the work they and Captain Thompson did on the deck. Sweat dripped into her face, stinging her eyes. In reality, she was not doing the same duties as the rest of the crew, but she was pitching in somewhat to help. With the captain hurt and a few other men unable to perform their duties because of their injuries, Ivy had offered to help the men on the deck.

Mr. Douglas made it clear he was uncomfortable taking on the role of captain in Gage's place, so Ivy had decided to help. Although she knew nothing about the world of sailing, she helped Mr. Douglas make certain decisions and perform activities. The job was fulfilling, yes, but quite tiring. Since she was not strong enough to do many of the men's activities, Ivy had agreed to do simple chores around the ship, and right now she was on her hands and knees scrubbing the deck.

Ivy glanced upwards. The sun shone high in the sky. Emma would probably be waking from her nap soon, and it would be time to check on Gage. She threw the piece of canvas she had been using to scrub the deck into a nearby bucket and stood. Her limbs protested. Ivy rubbed her lower back with her hand. The men around her chuckled, but she ignored them. She had already heard enough snide comments from them and had no wish to endure any more.

She made her way down to the captain's cabin, where she had been spending her days and nights ever since the skirmish with the pirates. It was much easier to keep the man and the child she took care of in one place. After a quick glance over her shoulder to make sure no one followed her, Ivy stepped inside.

Sunlight streamed through the large porthole built into the bulkhead, illuminating the cabin and offering an enticing view of the sea. She had grown to love the water after she had gotten over her seasickness. A low groan drew her attention to the left of the room, where Gage rested on his bed. He was still asleep. The poor man had barely been awake the last few days, and when he actually was awake, he was not fully aware of his surroundings. All he did was murmur words like "I'm sorry" or "angel" or "forgive me." Those were certainly an odd array of phrases, but what could be expected from a feverish man? Ivy hurried to his side. His eyes were slit partially open, and he raised his hand to touch her arm. She leaned down close.

The poor man's forehead was all bruised from the nasty hit to the side of his head, and the dark color had spread even to his cheek and temple. It looked too painful to even think about. His stab wound, on the other hand, seemed to be healing as normally as could be expected. She cleaned the bandages every day, but with time, it would heal, and he would be left with merely a scar.

After the battle, the ship's surgeon had offered to see to Gage, but Ivy felt uncomfortable near the man. He seemed to be in cahoots with Johnson, and he was not the type of man she wanted near the injured captain. So Ivy had seen to the man's needs and prayed she had done an adequate job of it.

"Beautiful." Gage reached up and brushed a curl of hair behind her ear. Her cheeks heated, but she knew it was only his delirious state that brought forth such words.

"Gage, I need you to get better, all right? You've been like this for two days. Please. We need you captaining the ship. I cannot be captain with Mr. Douglas for much longer. Please, we need you back to help us." She grabbed his hand with both of hers and pressed a kiss on it.

Emma gurgled, stirring in her slumber. Ivy laughed and scooped the child up off the chair she had been lying on. She could not wait until Gage was well and she could stop working around the ship. Time spent with Emma was precious and far too short these days. The child brought life and light to the entire ship.

Emma smiled sleepily and entangled her little hand in Ivy's hair. Oh, this little one was precious. She made Ivy terribly miss her dear brother back in London. What was William doing now? Was he warm, happy, and well-fed? Did he miss his sister? Ivy gulped. What would he think of her when she finally did return home? Would he ever be able to forgive her for abandoning him?

Ivy sighed. Sometimes she felt as if she did too much to help others, so much so that she was unable to give each person she wanted to help in her life all of her devotion. She had been forced to stop taking care of William when she had chosen to find her best friend, Eden. Now she split her time between caring for Emma and Gage and trying to help Adam run the ship. Although she wanted to give all of these people her best efforts, Ivy had grown mentally and physically exhausted.

Emma giggled as she tugged on a piece of Ivy's hair and watched it spring back into place. The girl's face lit up. "Pretty," Emma chirped.

Ivy beamed. The child had recently begun speaking a few words, and the thought made Ivy's heart sing. Except for when she thought of what would happen when they arrived back home. She had no idea what would become of Emma, but she knew that apart from the girl, her own heart would never be complete again.

Gage groaned from his position on the bed. Ivy smiled tenderly. Her heart might not be complete without her dear man either. But there was absolutely nothing she could do about her heart. It would not be fitting for her to pursue a life with a sailor, captain or not. Eden had promised her life to a sailor, but she had run from everything she once knew to escape a terrible man and had been all alone in the world. Ivy was not in nearly such a desperate situation. Besides, Ivy had promised Aimee she would not let herself grow attached to a pirate. She was a London-bred English lady. Goodness, did that thought sting.

⚓

Eden snuggled Reed close against her chest. She loved days when the boy came into her and her husband's cabin in the early morning. Today, they snuggled on the big bed in the center of the cabin. This time with him was precious, and she was glad Caspian now recognized the fact. Caspian propped himself on one elbow and winked at Eden.

She smiled and ran her finger down the length of his jaw. He stilled her hand and pressed a kiss to her fingertip.

Reed sighed, interrupting their moment. "What's wrong, dear?" Eden nudged the boy forward so she could see his face.

"I hope we find my uncle soon. I don't like going to all these ports all the time." Reed scrubbed a hand across his forehead.

"Oh, we'll find him. Don't worry. I know we will find him." Caspian ruffled Reed's hair.

"Where are we sailing to now, Papa?"

Eden beamed at Reed. Oh, how happy she was to call this fine young lad her son.

"We are going north. Hopefully we can find your mama's brother there."

⚓

Gage groaned as he propped himself up on his elbows. His head spun, but he continued until he had forced himself in a sitting position. Next, he swung his legs over the side of the bed. It felt good to be up again. He turned his head slowly to glance about the room and scan its contents without making himself dizzy.

The cabin was empty, save Emma, who slept soundly on the chair. It must be nap time for her.

Gage gripped the end of his mattress and tried to bolster himself up. The room swayed before him. His knees buckled. The cabin door burst open. The abruptness startled him, and he started to topple over. Ivy entered the cabin and immediately braced an arm around his back, preventing him from crumpling to the floor.

"What were you doing? For heaven's sake, you should see how pale you are right now. Lay back down, lay back down." Her soft voice soothed his nerves and helped steady his vision. He allowed the woman to gently pull him back down onto the mattress until he finally reclined against the pillow. She ran the back of her hand across his forehead. "What were you doing, Gage? Are you well? Did you need something?"

"I... wanted... to stand." Gage winced. *Since when did it take so much breath to speak?*

"Why? Can I get you something?" Her tone was so sweet it almost made him hurt more. And, he needed to stop looking into those gorgeous gray-blue eyes. He could get lost inside of them. "Gage?"

"Hmm?"

"Can I get you something? You should not be getting up on your own."

Oh. Well, if he could remember what in tarnation he had gotten up for, he would not want her to get it for him. His face heated. Weren't men supposed to be strong in the presence of women? He was anything but strong at the moment. "No, miss." His voice came out far more gruffly than he ever intended.

She blinked. "A-all right. Are you sure you are well?"

"Yes, miss..."

She graced him with a small smile. "It's good to see you up, Gage. I was so concerned for you in the last few days."

Gage's eyelids started to weigh down. He struggled to keep them open.

Ivy brushed a lock of his hair from his face. "Sleep well, sir."

His last memory was her lips on his forehead before he drifted back into a deep slumber.

✤

Ivy bounced Emma up and down in her arms as Mr. Douglas spoke to her. They sat in her cabin, mainly because Douglas did not want the crew to hear them, and Ivy did not want to disturb Gage. Emma yanked on a lock of Ivy's hair, and she bit back a grimace. The girl grew more energetic as each day passed.

"They are unhappy with the direction we are sailing. They say it isn't worth it to go find Captain Thompson's sister—that after everything we have been through, they do not want to do it."

"What should we do? I know how important this is to Gage. We *have* to get his sister. I understand his need because of how much I need to see my brother."

Mr. Douglas rested his elbows on his knees and his forehead on his hands. "I don't know, milady. I was never meant to be a leader. I love sailing, but I am much better at following under someone else's command. I don't know how to lead them. Perhaps you could speak to them? That worked well last time."

Emma settled in Ivy's arms, nestling her head in the crook of her elbow. Ivy snuggled the girl closer as she contemplated what Mr. Douglas said. "I-I could say something to them. Or I could try."

✤

Adam had to stop himself from squeezing his eyes shut. This discussion was not going quite as they had planned.

"What do we care?" Someone heckled.

"Please, men. Please listen to me for a few moments' time."

After a minute—and some shushing from Adam and a few others still loyal to the captain—the men silenced their protesting to the point where Lady Shaw could actually be heard above them.

She started out timidly. The poor woman had probably not spoken in front of so many people in her life before the speech she had given them two days ago. "Can you please just take a moment and think as if you were Captain Thompson?"

"I ain't that much of a ninny!"

"I beg you, gentlemen. Let me speak. Just please, think of your own families. Think of how much you love them. Do you have a sister at home? A daughter? A mother?"

"I don't have no family!" Another man yelled.

Adam struggled to stop himself from growling. "Silence!"

"Why should we listen t' you?" The man glared pointedly at the left side of Adam's face and Adam felt it like a fresh burn to the spot.

He had always been uncomfortable with the injury to his face, and when people mocked it, he felt sick. Adam clenched his eyes shut, lest the men see the emotion running across his features.

"Don't you understand? Please think back to your childhood. I'm sure there is someone who loved you, who cared for you enough to make sure you were always safe. And even if you didn't have someone like that, surely you felt that way for someone at some point!" Lady Shaw bit her lip, and then moved around the deck. She stopped at one man and rested her hand gently on his arm for a moment. "Sir, what is your name?"

He looked to the left, before finally facing Lady Shaw. "Todd, ma'am."

Lady Shaw nodded sweetly. "Now, Todd, please tell me, do you have someone at home? Someone who you have known at any time, who depended on you?"

Todd fixed his gaze on the wooden planks of the deck. "Yes," he mumbled. Adam had to strain to hear him.

"What, sir?" Lady Shaw planted her hands on her hips.

"I said... yes, I have a wife, an' a little girl back home. They need me."

A grin split across Lady Shaw's face, lighting up her expression. "I understand, sir. So do you realize why we need to help Captain Thompson take one short side trip to get his sister?"

"Yes."

"Good. Now, the rest of you men..."

CHAPTER 19

Gage rubbed his temples. Ever since the battle and his injuries, he suffered terrible headaches. However, it was a joy to be sitting in an upright position with his mind in a mostly clear state. Ivy had refused to allow him to do much standing or walking so far, but during the times she was absent from the cabin, he would rise and pace back and forth. It was a strange feeling, walking after being bed-ridden for so many days. His legs felt as if they belonged to someone else. He had been doing a lot of practicing, too, because Ivy was away from the cabin fairly often.

It still shocked him that the little woman had practically taken over his role as captain of the ship while he was indisposed. He had no idea how she had garnered the respect of his crew, but apparently she had. The lady was a complete mystery to him at times. His thoughts slowed as a child's giggle filled the air. Emma. The sweet girl sat in the corner of the cabin, playing with his sextant. She practically grew more each minute of the day.

He crouched beside the child and squeezed his eyes shut for a moment. At times, he forgot that sudden movements disoriented him. A tiny hand wrapped around his wrist. Gage smiled. "Hello, sweetie."

"Hello, Papa!" Her youthful chatter filled the cabin with warmth.

"Oh, sweetheart..." Gage couldn't bring himself to correct the child. Of course, he should have long ago. He was not the girl's father, and unlikely he ever would be. However, Emma calling him "Papa" tugged at a bit of his heart. He'd never actually taken care of someone this dependent on him before. The responsibility of caring for his sister had fallen on his young shoulders, but in all reality, they were close in age, and once they had joined Caspian's family, she was not entirely his anymore. Emma was so special to him... she seemed like... well, she seemed like she truly *was* his own child. It only seemed right for her to call him her father. Then again, the fact that the child called Ivy her "Mama" only added to the pleasure of the situation.

Emma launched herself into Gage's arms, causing him to reel to catch his balance. His side still throbbed, but the pain was not the child's fault by any means. Gasping for breath, he set the girl aside gently. Her face puckered up and a low whine emanated from her throat. Finally, just as she opened her mouth to produce a full wail, the door burst open.

Ivy stumbled in, yanking off a tri-corn hat and wiping sweat from her brow. That was *his* hat. The little thief. He grinned. Her copper hair tumbled over her shoulders in waves. Sunlight sprinkled in from the porthole of his cabin and reflected off her tresses. He wanted to touch them.

She blinked. He had been caught staring. Heat rushed to his cheeks. He had to distract her. "H-how are things going, Miss Captain? Is my crew treating you well?"

His comment elicited a curve of her lips. "I'm not even remotely a captain, Gage. You are being silly."

Gage rose, stretching out his shoulders. It felt good to be standing on his own two feet once more. "Well, you have been doing much of my job these past few days. I would say that makes you a captain. Faith, how did you manage to control my band of ruffians?"

"I've no idea, Captain. I suppose God helped me through it. The men still do not seem pleased, but they are sailing us to Charles Town with nary a complaint." She reached a hand up to tuck an errant strand of hair behind her ear. The woman performed the simple act with such grace that he had to blink to be sure he was seeing correctly. Yes, she was a true lady, that much was certain. One a pirate like him did not deserve, but one a pirate like him desperately wanted to keep.

He needed to stop thinking like that. Surely she didn't truly care about him anyway. "How long until we reach Charles Town, Miss Captain?"

"I asked Mr. Douglas yesterday. He says the men believe we will reach the port by tomorrow afternoon if the winds are in our favor."

A grin tugged at his lips in anticipation of seeing Addie. Oh, how he missed her. "Do you have any siblings other than your little William?" He suddenly felt incessantly curious about this lady.

She gave him a small, sad quirk of her lips. "No, sir. I wish I did. Then mayhap someone else could help me make sure he was safe. I grew up as an only child for most of my life."

"Ah, miss. I know your young brother is very precious to you. I assure you he must be safe, though. I know God would not let anything happen to him."

She blew out a breath, sitting down on the chair next to his bed. "You must be right. However, I find myself struggling to trust. I have always been one to want to control my own destiny, to do everything I needed done by myself. I suppose I have trouble trusting others." Her shoulders shook.

Gage's mind refused to help him determine a reply. He needed to comfort her. He felt like a big, bumbling idiot. How dare he bring up a topic like this when it obviously pained her to think about it?

"Oh, you must think me a ninny." She swiped at her eyes with the backs of her hands. "I am sorry, Captain. I need to go do something... outside. Good day." She spun around and headed for the door.

"Ivy, wait!" Gage braced his arms on the bed, trying to rise. His head spun, but he jumped to his feet anyway.

Her face crumpled. "I am fine, Captain. Please don't follow me. I need some time to myself." She swung herself out of the cabin and banged the door behind her.

Gage lowered himself back down onto the bed and covered his face with his hands. Egad, he had not meant to upset her. *Please, God, help me understand how to help this lady. She needs to trust in You. I need to trust in You as well.*

He uncovered his face and surveyed the cabin. His gaze halted on his desk, where his Bible sat. An idea formed in his mind. *Thank You, Father.*

⚓

Ivy cringed at the way the cabin door slammed behind her. She glanced to her left, down the companionway. It would probably be a good idea to run to the privacy of her cabin, but she could not bear to be confined in that tiny place. In fact, being stuck on this cramped ship had begun to grate on her nerves. She needed air.

She swung to the left, towards the main deck. The cool sea breeze slapped her face. Her hair loosened from its coiffure and whipped around her face. *God, help me. Help me.* But her prayer seemed empty, and lacking in conviction. Since when had she been so poor at praying?

Mayhap always. It seemed as if she only prayed to God when she needed something. When was the last time she had read a Bible?

Ivy made her way to the bow, absently nodding at Gage's men as they hailed her.

The ship dipped, causing sea foam to mingle with the tears on her cheeks.

What is wrong with me?

Could she not simply trust in God to take care of her brother as Gage had insisted? And what about Emma? What would become of her? The thought caused fresh moisture to run out of her eyes.

No... no...

Could a Lord who allowed Emma to be abandoned by her own mother care enough about the child to provide a home for her? What about the Lord who allowed her best friend Eden to be repeatedly abused by her own fiancé?

Ivy cringed at these extreme thoughts. Her faith had certainly deteriorated from what it had once been.

Shock struck her body, making her feel almost as if she could not move. What a terrible person she had become.

However, despite all of the tragedies that had befallen her and her friends, good things occurred as well. Ivy had met wonderful people like Gage and Emma. The crew had begun to obey her orders as if she truly was their captain, and they were finally back on track after all of the struggles they had seen. Nausea bubbled in the pit of her stomach.

The ship dipped again. Ivy swung her arms about to keep her balance. She leaned down to a crouch and stared at the water swirling below her. A wave of nausea swept through her body, and before she could calm herself, she spilled the contents of her stomach into the sea.

A hand rested on her shoulder in a brotherly manner. A glance over her shoulder revealed the half-gnarled face of Adam.

How could God allow this man to lose so much, to even lose his handsome face? Adam was a good man. He did not deserve the cards he had been dealt.

"Ivy, calm down."

She inhaled deeply. It was hard to take a full breath. Her heart pounded violently against her chest. Her head swung back and forth. She could not breathe.

"Ivy, your face is bright red. You've been crying!" His arm circled around her and he helped her up from her crouching position on the deck.

"Lady Ivy Shaw, you need to breathe. Come here. Let's get to your cabin."

Tears sprung from her eyes yet again. She let him help her across the deck, down the companionway, to her cabin, and onto her bed. Her head was light. Everything spun.

Adam leaned over her, a furrow in his brow. "Ivy, I need you to calm down. You are fine. Everything is fine." He held her hand in his, and with his other, wiped at her forehead.

"No... it is not okay. I'm beginning to think God does not care about any of us."

His hand stilled. "Ivy, you should never say such things."

"I don't care." Finally, her breathing stilled to a normal pace. She glanced around the cabin before her gaze rested on Adam once again. He seemed truly concerned. She could not stand it. "Please leave, Adam. I need to rest."

He grimaced as he straightened to his full height. "Yes, milady." Adam left the cabin, silently shutting the door behind him.

Ivy rolled on her side, buried her face into her pillow, and sobbed herself to sleep.

A shiver iced down Addie's spine as she sat in the dining room of a local tavern. She had been eating here for weeks—Mr. Faulke did not provide her meals nor a place to cook them—and she felt uncomfortable at every meal. This tavern was far too close to the docks for her liking, and it was a long walk from the milliner's shop. The customers were mostly unruly sailors. The men eyed her like she was a piece of meat.

Addie bit into her spoonful of stew and glanced out the side of her eye at the man to her right. He stared at her.

"M-may I help you, sir?"

The man was a pirate, by the looks of it. An intimidating one, possessing a long, scraggly beard, earring, colorfully mismatched outfit, and horrible stench. She inched away from him until she was sitting on the far side of her seat.

He grunted and lowered his gaze for a moment. The second she looked away, she could feel his eyes on her again. "Please, sir, I must ask that you leave me alone. You are making me uncomfortable."

That elicited a rude chuckle, revealing a mouthful of rotting teeth. "I'm makin' ye uncomfortable, wench? No worries, I can easily show ye how t' be very comfortable." He reached for her, and she rose abruptly. The dishes on the table jingled.

"You are overly forward, sir. I must demand you leave me alone."

He laughed and rose as well, lurching toward her. His steel hand gripped her shoulder. She jerked from his grasp, but his strength sent her tumbling over her chair. The wretched man caught her with a better grip. Addie attempted to butt at him with her head, but his hands held her at arm's length. "Release me at once, sir!"

"Nay, milady, methinks ye just need to cooperate an' you'll be very happy."

Her pulse rose. She needed to escape this man at once.

Her eyes scanned the room for a weapon, anything she could use to defend herself.

Some men in the room observed her situation with mild interest or boredom. Others ignored her completely. Violently, the man tugged on her shoulder, drawing her closer. He leaned near her neck and inhaled deeply. The women in the room, barmaids, eyed her with pity, but did nothing to interfere.

"Let! Me! Go!" Yet again, Addie tried to free herself from his grasp. Her struggles were met with a laugh as he pulled her closer yet.

He swung her around and leaned down, eyeing her lips. She spat in his face. As the saliva in his eyes disoriented him, she braced herself and jerked her knee upwards. A low moan and her sudden release told her she had met her target. Addie did not stay to observe the consequences. She flung a coin on the table for her meal and sped out of the tavern. This was the last time she would be dining in this *fine establishment.*

⚓

Adam pounded on his captain's door.

"Who is it?" The man's voice sounded as barely a whisper above Emma's soft snoring.

"Adam, sir."

"Come in. It's unlocked."

Adam let himself in. The cabin was gloomy in the light of the setting sun. Captain Thompson sat at his desk, his Bible in front of him. He held a quill in one hand and was steadying a piece of parchment with the other. After a moment, the man glanced up from his work. "Yes, Mr. Douglas?"

"I-I am concerned, Captain."

Gage stopped his work and set his quill down. "Concerned? About what, my good man?"

Adam tore his hat from his head and passed it back and forth between his hands. "Lady Shaw, sir. She does not seem well."

Gage's face darkened immediately. "Aye? What do you mean?"

"I found her on the bow, sobbing. She seemed to be in great turmoil, and I am concerned for her. If anyone could do her good, I believe it would be you, Captain."

The captain rose. "Where is she now? I must make sure she is all right."

"She is in her cabin, but she practically fell asleep while I was there. She should not take a visitor right now."

CHAPTER 20

Something cold twisted around Gage's heart and tugged. What had he done? First, she became upset and stormed from the room, and now, Adam was concerned for her?

"Did... did she tell you at all what was bothering her? I was just going to give her this—" he motioned to the Bible sitting on his desk "—but if there is something else I can do for her..."

Adam's face tightened. "Before I left her, sir..." His voice trailed off.

Gage glanced at Emma to make certain she was sleeping peacefully. "Yes, Mr. Douglas? What happened?" His pulse sped up.

"She said God doesn't care about anyone. I... I do not hold a very strong faith myself, but that declaration from a lady like her was quite unsettling. I do not know what she is going through, but she seems quite tortured."

The coldness around Gage's heart plummeted even further. "I must see her."

§

Captain Caspian Archer stood on the foredeck of the *Dawn's Mist* and stared out at the night sky. Stars twinkled white against the black of the never-ending span above him. That expanse was just as glorious and infinite as the sea around him. He sighed. Here he felt true peace. True freedom. This was where he belonged.

A soft arm slipped across his back and he grinned. *This* was where he belonged. "Good evening, my darling."

Eden stretched up on her tiptoes and planted a kiss on his cheek. "Good evening."

Caspian circled his arms around her waist and drew her close. "We should reach Charles Town in two days, my sweet."

Her face lit up. "Do you really think we will find him there?"

"I pray so. That's where Gage was sailing, and I would think he would stay there for a while." Caspian hugged his wife to his chest. "We will find your brother. I am absolutely certain of it."

She leaned back and wrinkled her nose. "How can you be so sure?"

He smiled and placed a hand to her chest, above her heart. "I can feel it in here, milady. And I know it will happen. I can feel that God wants you to find your brother."

Eden rested her hand atop his. "I do not know what I will do *if* we find him. I am not sure if I will hug him or beat him over the head for all of the fear he has caused me."

Caspian chuckled. "You always were a feisty one, were you not, my wife?"

She gave him a saucy grin.

"It might be a shock to him when he learns his baby sister married a pirate."

Eden lowered her lashes. "He will have to grow accustomed to it quickly. I'm not leaving you any time soon."

"I have never known more comforting words, my sweet." Caspian raised her hand to his lips. "Now, shall we retire to bed? It has grown quite late."

"Aye, Captain." Eden giggled as Caspian swept her into his arms and to their cabin.

Gage rose early that morning after not having slept a wink. Ivy had never come to retrieve Emma, so he had kept her in his cabin throughout the night.

Ivy must have been too exhausted to think about the little one. The child had whimpered and inquired as to where "Mama" was, but he told her she had spent the night by herself. The toddler woke up repeatedly during the night. Not that he was sleeping, however. Fear, regret, and pity for Ivy coursed through his veins and made each breath painful.

God, please. I know not what is hurting Ivy so, but please allow her to see the error of her thoughts. Please have her come back to You. For her sake, for Emma's sake, for her brother's sake, and for mine, too. Please, Father.

Gage paced to the other side of the cabin and peered out his porthole. The sun was beginning to rise. He rubbed his eyes. They itched from unshed tears. Although he felt awful, he had not wished to frighten Emma by crying. He glanced at the girl now. She slept peacefully.

He should go check on Ivy. Surely she felt better now that the night had passed and she had spent time reflecting on her thoughts alone. Before he left the cabin, he glanced in his tiny shaving mirror. Dark circles pooled beneath his eyes. Whiskers had sprouted across his chin and cheeks after going days without seeing a razor to trim them. Why, he looked terrible. But he didn't have time to freshen up. He needed to see Ivy.

Gage ran a hand through his hair, trying to tame it to some extent. He didn't want to *scare* the woman, for heaven's sake. A few paces down the companionway brought him to her cabin door. He hovered outside, suddenly nervous. What should he say?

Bah! He'd left the Bible in his cabin.

Gage spun around, retrieved the Bible, and returned to his place in front of the door. Should he knock? If he knocked, the lady would probably refuse him entrance. But just attempting to open the door would be rude. He knocked. Cleared his throat. "Miss?"

No answer.

"Miss?"

Silence.

"Ivy? Lady Shaw? Are you in there? Please tell me if you are in there." Gage tried to mask the panic in his voice as he pounded his fist on the door. Had something terrible happened to her? *Oh, God, please, no. No, no, no.*

Dread sank to the bottom of his gut like a stone thrown into the deep recesses of the ocean.

A muffled noise came from behind the door. "Who is it?"

Hope sprung into his heart, lightening the fear resting on his shoulders. "'Tis Captain Thompson, milady."

"Oh. The door is locked, Captain."

Captain? He was back to "Captain" to her? *Lord, please help me get through to this woman.*

"I have a key, milady."

She groaned. Seconds passed. The door creaked open an inch at a time. Gage squeezed his way in and shut the door behind him. Lady Shaw retreated to the cot on the left side of her cabin. Her eyes were red and swollen, her fragile skin splotchy. Golden-orange hair ran loose down her back and over her shoulders in a tangled mass.

"Ivy, we need to talk."

"That is Lady Shaw, sir. I loathe saying it, but I fear we must spend less time together for both of our sakes and for the sake of Emma. You are naught but my voyage home." She bit her bottom lip and refused to meet his gaze.

Her words cut like a knife through his heart. His knees wobbled. Gage sank down on the cot next to her. "Ivy..."

Her chin quivered. Gage pulled her into an embrace and urged her to rest her head against his chest. She sat there stiffly, but did not attempt to leave. Wet tears streamed from her face onto his chest.

"Ivy—Lady Shaw—I apologize for upsetting you yesterday evening. It hurts me to see you like this."

"It was not anything you did, Gage. You have been so kind to me. I have just been struggling with... my faith, I suppose. I do not wish to speak about it right now."

Gage ran a hand down her arm. His hand wrapped around hers. "I am going to leave you for now, miss. But I have a gift for you, first."

A frown creased her forehead. "A gift? Captain, I do not deserve a gift."

"Shush, miss. Do not be silly." He reached over to the table where he had set her gift and presented it to her.

Her face remained stoic as she studied the Bible, and then him. "I... I don't understand, sir."

Gage felt his lips tug upward in a small smile. "Flip through it when you have some spare time. I feel well enough to resume the duties as captain once more, so you may have some extra moments to spend in your cabin. I pray it helps you."

"Oh... I suppose I will give it a try, Captain."

"Gage?" He squeezed her hand.

She smiled timidly. "Gage."

⚓

Ivy glanced down at the Bible that Gage had presented her. What was wrong with her? She had always been the strong one. Whenever Eden or Aimee had a doubt or a concern, they went straight to her. Now, she was so unstable she would not be able to help anyone else, let alone herself. And now, a pirate was helping her glue her spiritual welfare back together.

The man had certainly survived a hard life. And he still held strong to his faith, it would seem. Ivy glanced down at the Bible in her lap. What kind of pirate kept a Bible in his cabin? Nonetheless, the book was a nice amenity. Heaven knew Ivy could use it right now.

God, please forgive me for my rash words last night. I did not understand what I was thinking.

Ivy flipped the heavy book open. The pages fell to a certain spot. A small piece of parchment lay there, marking the page. She lifted it to the light drifting in from the porthole. Neat, basic handwriting scrawled across the scrap. "Trust in

God to care for William. He knows what is best for both of you, sweetheart. See Psalm 40:4. Gage."

Ivy frowned. The note had marked that page. She read the verse. "Blessed is that man that maketh the LORD his trust, and respecteth not the proud, nor such as turn aside to lies."

She had not given God her trust. No, she had been proud and had trusted in herself and her own abilities to take care of William, not God's. Had she really believed those lies?

What was going on, anyway? Gage put this marker here. Why did a pirate like him know so much about the Bible? For heaven's sake, had he spent all of last night preparing this for her?

Ivy flipped to another page, where there was yet another piece of parchment. How baffling. "Psalm 118:8. Gage." Her eyes moved further down the page to the verse. "It is better to trust in the LORD than to put confidence in man." Tears welled up in Ivy's eyes and threatened to spill onto her cheeks. Of course it was better to trust in the Lord than in herself. God would always be there. *I'm sorry, God. I have just been so afraid for him...*

Ivy flipped through a few more pages, curious about how many excerpts Gage had shared with her. She stopped on another note. Her eyes scanned the verse. "What time I am afraid, I will trust in thee." Ivy's heart warmed.

She paged to yet another verse. "When thou liest down, thou shalt not be afraid: yea, thou shalt lie down, and thy sleep shall be sweet."

Ivy flipped through each verse, and felt comfort embrace her and loosen her tense muscles at each one. Gage had proven himself to be such a sweet man to think about her and go through the entire Bible just to comfort her. She owed him so much. Ivy flipped to the final page of the book. There was another note. "I realize you must not feel comfortable talking to me about your fears and your problem with trusting. That is all right. I understand. I simply want you to understand that if you ever do want someone to talk to, or if you want help with anything, I will always be here. Affectionately, Gage."

Tears slipped down her face. The sweet man!

God, I am sorry about all of the doubts I allowed to taint my mind yesterday. Please forgive me. Also, please, if there is some way...

No. There was no way. Her thought was so foolish, Ivy let out a rueful chuckle. There was no way at all for her to be with this man. He was a pirate, she was a lady.

CHAPTER 21

Gage paced back and forth in his cabin that evening. He had not visited Ivy since he had given her the Bible. What did she think of him? Did she find his efforts foolhardy, or did she appreciate them? Had she even *looked* at the book or his notes inside? Mayhap not. The thoughts shooting through his head were about to turn him mad.

Gage ran a hand through his hair. He had been worrying about the woman so much throughout the day that he had barely had the concentration to focus on his work. In fact, the men had teased him again. Many had seen Ivy run from his cabin, sobbing, the night before, and they did not miss the chance to poke fun at him. A sigh escaped his lips. No, he did not care what the men said at all. All he cared about was if the woman fared well. He feared a visit to her side might trigger her to cry again.

"Captain, you are bound to pound a hole through your deck and crash down to the hold below." He had almost forgotten about Adam, who was with him, helping him chart their course.

"I apologize. I'm simply concerned, 'tis all. Surely you understand."

Adam chuckled. "Of course I do, sir. I am concerned for her as well."

"D-do you think I should pay her a visit? I want to make sure she has everything she needs."

"No, sir. I believe what she wants right now is solitude." Adam hefted Emma up in his arms and swung her high above his head. Her playful giggles sweetened the air. Gage smiled, despite his tortured mood. Ah, but it was pleasant to have a young child in their midst. He could really grow accustomed to having the tyke around.

A soft tap on the door interrupted his thoughts. "State your business," he called.

"Captain?" A feminine voice replied.

Ivy. Ivy. She had come. And she sounded happy. Gage glanced at Adam excitedly.

"You might do well to let the woman in your cabin, sir." Adam smiled.

Gage chuckled. "Aye." He pulled the door open. Ivy nudged her way inside the cabin and wrapped her arms around him in a sudden embrace. Over his shoulder, Gage noticed Adam's eyebrows rise nearly to his hairline.

"I'll be going now, Captain. I wish you a good evening. You as well, Lady Shaw." He made his way around Gage and Ivy and shut the cabin door behind him.

Ivy pulled away from Gage, her face stained bright red. "I-I am sorry, sir. I had thought you were alone."

Gage flashed a grin. "Believe me, milady, there is no need to apologize. In fact, I would be pleased if you did that much more often."

The woman's face heated to a deeper shade of red.

"You enchant me, my good woman. Now, to what do I owe the pleasure of your company?"

"You, Captain—Gage."

His heart skipped a beat.

"I read your notes in the Bible you gave me. That was the sweetest thing anyone has ever done for me. It aided me, as well. I feel much better than I did last night."

Gage pressed a kiss to her hand before entangling both her hands in his. "That is a true honor for me, Ivy."

She smiled, stood on her tiptoes, and hesitated. After what seemed like an eternity, she leaned forward and pressed a kiss to his cheek. Gage felt his eyes widen. Was she just expressing her thankfulness to him, or did she perhaps harbor some deeper feelings for him?

Please let it be the latter.

He pulled away from her slightly, only to allow himself a better view of her beautiful face. His gaze halted on her lips. They were pink and moist. Oh, he was sure they were very soft, too. Memories of their last kiss in the jungle inundated his mind. Had it been a mistake, or a boon? Whatever it was, Gage wanted to relive it. He closed his eyes, leaned close, and touched his lips to hers, gently. Heavens, he did not want to frighten her away.

She gasped. Gage cupped her cheek with one hand and angled her body closer to his with the other. Her pulse accelerated under his hand. His own coursed faster than he could recall it ever moving before. The woman wrapped her arms around his neck. He tilted her head to the side to deepen the kiss. She moaned.

Gage pulled away to catch his breath and press some kisses to her cheek, her jaw, her forehead. Her hands entangled themselves in his hair. He leaned back in for another kiss. She tasted sweet, like honey and tea. Oh, what was he to do? She was perfect.

⚓

This man was perfect. Ivy did not care if he was a pirate. He was perfect, and he was kissing her. And it felt like heaven. In fact, he chased all thoughts from her head and all she was left with was the pleasure of his company. A sigh escaped her lips as he deposited a kiss on her throat.

A toddler's cry rent the air. Ivy pulled away immediately and backed up a few steps. Her back slammed against the door. Gage swung away as well, putting just about as many feet between them as he could in this tiny cabin. After a few moments of staring at her, he finally looked to his left, where Emma lay on the bed, squalling.

Ivy pressed her hands to her burning cheeks. Gage leaned down and scooped the child in his arms. 'Twas a good thing he was minding Emma, because Ivy was unsure if she was steady enough on her feet at the moment to do so. She leaned back against the sturdy oak door. A glance in the small shaving mirror on the captain's desk told her that not only were her cheeks bright red and her lips swollen, but her hair had come almost completely down from its up-do. She groaned and bent down to the floor, searching for lost hair pins. *How long have I been kissing the scamp?*

The scamp cast a sidelong glance as he scooped Emma in his arms. He winked at her. "What, do you miss me already, milady? I would be happy to kiss you again as soon as I've tended to the babe."

Ivy raised a hand to her throat. Of all the... "Sir, I *do not* ask you to kiss me again. I will... admit the kiss we shared was enjoyable. However..."

He cradled the child in his arms. Oh, were his arms muscular. "However, what, miss?" The man flashed her a charming grin as he bounced Emma in his arms. The description for this pirate was dashing. Her mind went a little fuzzy. Had he asked her a question?

"What, Ivy? You were explaining to me why I should not kiss you again."

Oh, right. "Yes, sir. You should not kiss me again because... because..." The scoundrel balanced Emma in the crook of his arm and took a few steps closer to her again. He knew the effect he had on her.

"You were saying, miss?"

"Oh, you big bully! I insist you step back. I have no room to breathe."

He obliged, smirking.

"I was saying you should not kiss me. You do realize we have no future together, right, sir? You are a sailor and I am a lady. Society would shun me if they found out I had connected myself with a man such as you... no matter how I felt about you myself." The very thought pained Ivy. But someone had to voice it. They would have to part ways eventually, and when they did, it would only be harder if they had grown accustomed to each other's company throughout the voyage. Aye, it would be best if there was no more kissing.

§

Gage's eyes flicked down to her lips, unbidden as she spoke. How was he supposed to stop kissing the woman when her lips were so pretty and inviting? *Focus, Gage.* He shifted Emma to his other arm as he studied Ivy. She did have a point, after all. They needed to decide what to do when they reached London.

He did not want to lead her on by offering sweet kisses and words without honorable intentions. But how could he have honorable intentions? She was far above him in station. There was no doubt about that. And although he could keep her well fed and cared for, he could not provide her a title the many earls of England could. *I am an awful man. What am I doing to this woman?*

"Ivy..."

"Let me talk, Captain. Please." She squeezed her eyes shut and inhaled deeply.

"Aye, miss. Anything you wish."

Her lips twitched upwards ever so slightly as she opened her eyes. Turmoil swirled in their gray-blue depths. "Sir, I... I must admit I do care for you. I would be a fool to deny that. And I realize you seem to have feelings for me as well. But what will become of us? I am a lady. You are a pirate."

"I'm a privateer, actually, milady. Commissioned—or soon to be commissioned by the king to do his work on the seas." Gage ran a hand through his hair. He did not wish to hear where Ivy's speech was taking them. He wanted her. He wanted her to be his wife.

"Either way, sir, our marriage would lower my status considerably."

He should let her go. He should let her marry some rich, fat earl who would probably be unfaithful to her. But that outcome was not fair. It was not fair to either of them, or to Emma. No earl would take Emma. What would become of the child?

"Ivy, I understand you have a reputation to uphold. But I will work hard. I-I believe I can become well-respected in this business. Caspian has taught me well. I will do all I can to make you proud."

A tear slid down her cheek. "You already have done me proud, Gage. You really have."

"Then I beg of you, miss. Give me an opportunity. I want a chance to prove myself to you. To win your favor."

Her eyebrows drew close together.

"Land ho!" A cry drifted down from the main deck. Gage transferred Emma to Ivy's arms and sped up the companion-way, with Ivy following. He pulled out his spyglass and, sure enough, there lay the city of Charles Town, her lights shining bright against the sky.

Gage snagged Ivy's hand in his and squeezed it. His sister was somewhere in that city.

⚓

Addie ignored the tears that streamed down her face as she made the finishing stitches on the hem of a gown she had received yesterday. She must not allow herself to get so emotional. So what if Gage never came? Why, she was just fine by herself. The past few months, she had been getting along just fine on her own. Of course, she had received some charity from the kind souls in town, but she had worked for most of her money. So who cared if yet another man in her life failed her? Nothing was new.

She had not seen her brother in several years. What did he look like now? Was he still the clean-shaven, polite young man she knew and loved? What had the sea done to him over time? A stab of pain shot through her heart. What if he was hurt? Injuries and death at sea were common. Was she to lose him, too? First her birth parents, and then her adopted mother. Finally her husband. No, she could not allow the thought to pass through her mind. Surely Gage was fine.

Addie glanced out the window of her room at the top of the milliner's shop. The ocean glistened a few streets down, just barely in her view. Surely Gage was out there, sailing towards her. *Please let it be so. I am not certain how much longer I can live like this.*

§

Addie. He would see his little sister within the next day! Oh, but God was good. A grin stretched across his face as he remembered the "lavender lawn" fabric, as Ivy had called it, stashed away in the hold. Addie would love the gift. Gage was certain of that.

Ivy. That woman was an entirely different concern. He frowned, remembering her declaration stating they may not allow any further affections to grow between them. But he would win her. He would. For he needed her in order to be happy.

Gage would provide for her and give her the best life he could. Sure, he did not have the title of an earl, but from what he had heard from his friends, those men were naught but cruel imposters anyway. Caspian's wife had been promised to an earl who regularly beat her. No, Gage would not allow Ivy to face some dismal fate simply because she wanted a respectable title. He would win her heart even if it was the last thing he did. Heaven knew, she already had his.

§

Ivy buried her face in her hands. What had she said to Gage? The man already had her heart. He had no business trying to win her favor. He already had it. No, there was naught she could do. She had fallen thoroughly in love with this privateer captain and she had no idea what to do to rectify the situation.

Shouts from the deck roused her from her position on the bed and made her wander outside to find the source. The men milled about on deck, some swinging back and forth on the ropes in the rigging, others adjusting the width of the sails. She gazed upward in awe. The crew was certainly fearless when it came to heights. Just looking up at them made her dizzy.

Adam spotted her and jogged to her side. "What brings you up here on this fine day, milady?"

"What is going on, Mr. Douglas?"

"The men are preparing the ship to make port. We must adjust the sails and be careful when we dock her."

Ivy's gaze moved to the land. Since it had been spotted last night, it grew closer by the hour. Now, they sailed near enough for her to see the faces of the men milling about on the docks. Few people were outside this early in the morning, but those who were focused on their business. Ivy almost jumped up and down in excitement like a child. Although this stop slowed their trip back home, it would be nice to spend a few days on solid ground.

Her thoughts darkened when she spotted Gage on the forecastle, staring at her. How long had he been there? *Oh Lord, please help me. I do not know what to do about this man.*

What is it you want to do about him?

Ivy cringed. Gage bounded down the forecastle steps and approached her. Adam gave her a short bow and strolled away.

"Good morning, miss." Gage sent her a charming grin. "How did you sleep last night?"

Ivy lowered her gaze. *Not very well, thanks to your statement last night.*

He chucked her underneath the chin with his forefinger and thumb. "Come, come, now, precious one. What ails you?"

His eyes met hers. "I believe you know, sir, what ails me, unless you are that oblivious."

"Ah, miss, I suspected what ailed you. I feel like a scoundrel to admit this, but while I do not wish to see you ailing, I am pleased your feelings about me meant enough to cause you ailment." He sighed. "Ah, I am bumbling like a fool. I do not mean that I wish to see you ailing, but that I am pleased you have thought of me."

Ivy almost smiled at him. It was endearing to see him like this, fumbling over words as he wrung his hands together and sweated profusely. She could let him suffer further, but that would make her feel too cruel. "Aye, sir, I understand what you mean."

His face brightened. "Ah, that is a comfort, miss." He paused, suddenly appearing self-conscious. "Have you decided, miss, if you will give me an opportunity to win your favor?"

Ivy hesitated. She wanted with all of her heart to affirm his hopes. So why should she not give him a chance? "Yes, Gage. I will give you a chance while I think about our future."

He lifted her hands to his lips and pressed a kiss to her knuckles. "Ah, bless you, Ivy. You have made my heart happy today. Is there anything I can help you with, mayhap? Or did you just come up here to watch?"

"I just came up here to watch. I wanted fresh air and a chance to see solid land. I have missed it so."

He chuckled. "Well, you are in luck, miss. We should be able to get you off this ship before fifteen minutes have passed."

CHAPTER 22

Gage's chest puffed out in pride as he strolled through the streets of Charles Town with the beautiful, graceful Ivy on his arm. No matter how disheveled they might have looked from their weeks-long journey, Ivy still held herself as a true English lady.

Now, where had Mr. Poole's house been? He knew he had been told, but his last visit to Charles Town had been many, many years ago. It was easy for him to become disoriented.

After much searching, he stopped at a house that seemed to fit the description and address Addie had given him. Bright yellow paint stained the outer walls. Gage frowned. Addie had hated that color. His hand hovered over the door, but he could not bring himself to knock. What made him suddenly fearful? Addie had told him in her letter only basic details: where to find her, that her husband had died, and she barely had enough money to live on. How had she fared in the time he had not been able to reach her?

Ivy nudged him with her elbow. "What is wrong, Gage?"

He shook his head. "Nothing. I just... I feel something is off." After a moment, however, he raised his hand and knocked on the door.

The butler, a middle-aged man, opened the door. He studied them with curiosity and inspected them up and down, no doubt considering their somewhat ragged attire. "How may I help you... sir? Ma'am?"

"I am here to see Mrs. Poole, sir." Saying his sister's married name did not sit well with Gage. He had never approved of the marriage, although he supposed he may never approve of his sister being given off to some other man.

"Mrs. Poole? No Mrs. Poole lives here, sir." He began to pull the door shut.

Gage spared a glance at Ivy before he spun back to the man and stopped the door from closing. "Perhaps she goes by Miss Thompson nowadays?"

"No, sir. No one by that name here." The man frowned.

The blood drained from Gage's head slowly, making him feel faint. Where was his sister? Ivy squeezed his arm comfortingly. "Do you happen to know of a Mrs. Poole or Miss Thompson? I am a stranger to this town. Perhaps I have the wrong address."

"Now that you mention it, sir, this home was newly purchased. Sold along with everything in it, I believe. Someone died in debt, and his widow couldn't keep up with what he owed."

Gage had known Addie's husband had died and left her with almost nothing. He had not known the man's death had left her in debt. In fact, if the man weren't dead, Gage would find him and make sure he became dead. Slowly and painfully. "Do you know where this man's wife went to live after her house was sold?"

"Not for certain, sir. I heard she was out on the streets. Don't know what happened to her after that. Probably ended up in a brothel, poor thing."

Anger coursed through Gage's veins. His sister? On the streets? *In a brothel?*

That was not good. Gage clenched his fists. "Thank you, sir. I appreciate your help."

The man nodded and shut the door. Gage walked away from the house to the sidewalk, and then leaned against the fence lining the sidewalk. Ivy stopped before him. She rested a hand on his forearm. Concern lined her face. "Where can we find your sister now, Gage?"

"I-I have no idea, Ivy. I was not aware her fool husband left her in debt. I certainly never knew she had been forced to sell her house and everything in it." Gage glanced at the front lawn of the impressive home. The huge garden in the front of it appeared to have once flourished but now seemed in desperate need of care.

Addie had adored gardening. She had no doubt been gone a long time, then. Months, perhaps. The dear girl could be anywhere now. Why had she not sent word to him? How had he not heard about this?

Oh no. Since he had not received any word telling him her current location, she could be lost... living in some gutter... Heaven forbid, living and working in a brothel of some sort. Gage would never forgive himself if the latter was the outcome. Nevertheless, he would search everywhere. Everywhere. No, there was no way he would give up the search for his Addie.

⚓

Ivy clung to Gage's hand as they shoved their way into the crowded shop. He asked the shop owner the same question he had asked at the five or so shops they had already visited. "Excuse me, mister; may I take a moment of your time? I am searching for my sister, Addie Thompson Poole. She is about this tall," he gestured with his hand, "and she has dark, curly hair and green eyes. Please tell me you have seen her."

And they got relatively the same reply. How had no one seen this young woman? Ivy was really feeling concerned for her, and she had never met the lady. As they walked out of the crowded shop, Ivy stopped to face Gage. "Is there somewhere else we can search for her? It does not seem like we are getting anywhere inquiring in these shops."

Gage sighed. "Aye, but the only other locations I can think of are taverns and other places no lady should ever go. I could never bring myself to take you with me there."

Ivy let out a noisy sigh. "How are you going to find her, then?"

"I don't know, milady. We simply must continue trying."

Ivy's mind brightened with an idea. "What if we ask at some of the local churches in this area? Maybe, if she was in trouble, she would have gone to them for help. She could even be staying in one."

"'Tis possible, milady. Let us attempt that. We have nothing to lose."

⚓

Ivy inhaled deeply as they walked into the third church they had tried. So far, no one knew anything about Addie. She was beginning to believe this woman had vanished into thin air. A glance upwards told Ivy it was well past noon already. They had spent most of the day searching for Gage's sister.

As they neared one more church, Gage slowed. His face tightened.

"What is wrong?" Ivy whirled to see him face-to-face and shielded her eyes from the glare of the afternoon sun.

Gage let out a long breath. It hurt Ivy to see him like this. The man had not smiled all day, and smiles were something he distributed regularly. His eyes were lined with dark circles underneath, and they lacked their usual sparkle. "What if I don't find her, Ivy? What then?" His voice emerged from his throat, choked and pitiful. "Or worse? What if someone informs me she died? What do I do then?"

Ivy felt tears pool in her eyes. The poor man was heartbroken. She glanced about the empty street before enclosing him in a hug. He needed every bit of comfort he could get. Gage wrapped his arms around her and leaned his face against the top of her head. Wetness hit her hair, and she realized he was crying. "Gage... it's all right. Addie is safe. Trust God. Pray. Ask him to help us find her. I know I will." Realization hit Ivy like a blow to the stomach. Even if Addie, or William— she cringed at the thought—was not safe in an earthly sense, they could trust God to care for them in a heavenly sense.

Gage pulled away from her after a pause, sniffed, wiped at his eyes, and grinned. "Aye. You are correct, milady. Now, let's see about this church, shall we? I have a good feeling about this one."

⚓

Well, it was not right to describe the feeling he had right now as *good*, but it was the closest thing to *good* he had felt all day. He stared up at the immense door, heavy with wooden carvings. A stained glass window perched high atop the building, directly above the door. He blinked. This church covered an immense stretch of ground. St. Paul's Church, one of the few places of worship in Port Royal, was not nearly this large or ornate.

A feeling of dread washed over him as he strode halfway up the stairs. What was he doing? It was highly unlikely Addie was here. She was never fond of accepting charity from others. There was no way she would be inside this church.

Ivy squeezed his hand. The tingling sensation from her warm fingers was almost enough to ease the sick feeling that had plagued him, but not quite. He shook his head at her and began to turn away, when the church door burst open.

A middle-aged woman offered him a sweet smile. Her graying brown hair was pulled up into a mob cab, and she wore plain clothes but possessed a pleasant disposition. "How may I help ya, sir?" She wiped her hands off on her apron as she noticed Ivy. "Good afternoon, missy."

Gage stared at the lady, dumbfounded. Ivy nudged him in the ribs with her elbow. He blinked. "Miss, I apologize for interrupting you. I am searching for a young woman, my little sister. Her name is Addie Thompson Poole and..." Gage recited his description of Addie. This church would be no different than the three others they had visited. Or the eight shops. Next, he would try some taverns. He could take Ivy back to the ship, or find a reputable place for her to stay, and then he would spend the night questioning the town's many taverns and... brothels.

"Addie? Addie Thompson? You know her?"

Gage's heart leapt into his throat. *His* Addie?

"Oh, bless the Lord! I've been prayin' she'd find her brother! The poor, sweet child! Do you realize how happy she will be?"

She *knew* Addie? Gage could not believe his ears. Ivy grinned and squeezed his hand. He returned the favor. "Where is Addie, miss? Are you keeping her in here, in the church? Is she safe?"

"Oh, sir, yes, she is safe. And no, she's not stayin' here, she never did, just stopped by for one afternoon and my husband and I did as any Good Samaritans would and helped her get back on her feet." The woman fussed with her hair, shoving a few wispy strands behind her ear.

"I thank you for that, my good woman, but do you know where she is right now?"

The woman giggled. "Oh, forgive me, sir! Addie took up a job at the milliner's shop down the street in the city square."

A *milliner's* shop? Addie could never sew. She had tried to pick up the hobby, but she could never concentrate enough or have a hand steady enough. But he did not care. Addie was safe! Gage leaned forward and hugged the woman. She tittered. "Thank you for the help, miss. I truly appreciate it."

Before the woman had time to respond, Gage grabbed Ivy by the hand and dashed down the stairs towards the town square. Now to find this milliner's shop...

$

Addie grimaced and pulled her thumb into her mouth. How many weeks had she been working at this job? It did not matter how many. She still jabbed herself with the needle more times than she could count in one day. A sigh escaped her lips. A hopeless cause, she was. Ah, well. It was time for her day to end anyway.

Time had managed to pass quickly for once. Addie packed away the pair of trousers she was working on repairing and climbed up the stairs to her small room. She let out an exasperated sigh. Her fingers ached. They were used to different movements than sewing. She loved working in the garden and watching her plants grow. There was no better feeling than sitting out in the sun and tending to plants. Why, Addie could almost taste the sunshine on her lips, see the vivid blue sky. She had never cared if the sun baked her skin to a brown color, despite the glares she often got from other ladies. Green grass surrounded her, and colorful flowers painted the lawn. She could smell the fragrant blooms, the fresh air...

"Miss Thompson!"

Why was Mr. Faulke summoning her? He never did that. Oh no. Had she made an error in a customer's order? Mr. Faulke had warned her what would happen if she made another mistake. *No, no, no. I cannot lose this job. It's all I have.*

"Yes, sir?" Addie leaned her head outside her doorframe to be better heard. Maybe he had just forgotten to tell her something before he closed up the shop for the night. *Please let that be it.*

"There is a man... and a uh... a lady here to see you, miss. I suggest you come down here at once."

Addie frowned. A man? Why would there be a man here to see her? She did not know any men... or any lady. Nonetheless, Addie walked to the landing and treaded down the narrow, steep staircase in the back of the shop. Maybe it was the reverend and his wife. She made her way to the front of the store and almost screamed.

Gage. Gage! Addie squealed. She ran to her brother and he collected her in his arms, twirling her in the air. Addie fell against his chest and inhaled her brother's familiar scent. Oh, how she had missed this man. The one man who had not failed her. The one man who actually cared about her. "Oh, Gage."

He chuckled. "It's good to see you, too, sister."

A wink creased his chocolate brown eye for a moment. He looked hardly the worse for the wear. Brown waves of hair fell to his chin, and he had the same dashing smile and dimples. His cheeks were scruffy with a beard, and his clothes a little wrinkled, but he was the same Gage she had always known.

Mr. Faulke stepped into the back room, claiming to allow them all a moment of privacy.

176

A soft cough came from Gage's left. Addie shifted her gaze and noticed a beautiful young woman standing to his side. Her orange hair was pulled back in a simple bun, and she had a sweet disposition. What was Gage doing with her?

Her brother's gaze seemed to follow hers. He grinned. "May I introduce you, Addie Thompson Poole, to my... to Lady Ivy Shaw."

Lady Shaw offered a kind smile. "It is a pleasure to meet you, Mrs. Poole."

Addie shook her head. "Please, call me Addie. I never want to go by that man's name again."

⚓

Something tugged at Ivy's heart. The poor woman appeared quite hostile towards her deceased husband. She prayed he had not been abusive towards her. Ivy had seen the effects of an abusive man on her dear friend Eden, and she did not want anyone else to have to deal with that turmoil.

Ivy cast a sideways glance at Gage. His jaw and fists were tight and his eyes narrow. "We'll talk about Mr. Poole at a later time, shall we? Now, I want to hear how you are and what you have been doing." Gage offered her his arm. "May I take you on a stroll to my ship?"

"You have a ship, brother? Or do you mean Caspian's ship?"

"Ah, but I never told you! I am a captain now. I have my own ship, the *Siren's Call.*"

A crease formed between her eyebrows. "Is Caspian all right? Did you two get in a disagreement?"

Gage chuckled. "Nay! We captured this ship and he decided to give me the authority he thought I deserved."

"Oh, how kind of him!"

"I think so, too. Caspian is married again now, as well."

Addie's bronze eyebrows shot up, nearly meeting her hairline. "I thought the man would never remarry after Isabelle... passed away."

Gage lifted his shoulders in a shrug. "He met a special woman—Ivy's close friend, in fact." He nodded at Ivy and offered her a wink. "They are quite happily wed." Gage's gaze drifted off, and his eyes seemed to glaze over as he thought of something.

"And how is Reed? Oh, how I miss that dear child!" Addie clapped her hands together as she spoke, her face a canvas painted with excitement.

"Reed is well. I miss him also."

Addie giggled. She wrapped her arms around Gage once more. "Oh, how good it is to see you again!"

A throat cleared behind them. Ivy spun around and noticed the same middle-aged man who had let them in and called Addie down to meet them. "I'm sorry folks, but we can't use this space as some reunion location. Can you do your visiting elsewhere?"

Gage stood up to his full height. "Yes, sir. And Addie will be staying with us tonight—maybe even for the rest of her life."

"What are you saying, sir?"

Gage glanced at his sister, who nodded, before he spoke. "I think Addie will no longer need employment here. I truly appreciate the help you have given her, but I think it is time for her to move on."

The man frowned.

Addie stepped forward, bowing her head shyly. "I can work until you find someone to replace me, sir."

He burst into laughter. "I'm sorry, miss, but I have actually been looking to employ another young woman. I meant no offense to you, but I felt another individual could do the job in a more efficient manner."

Relief etched across the woman's face. "Oh, thank you, sir!"

Gage lifted his eyebrows. Ivy could tell they were siblings. They moved their faces in a similar fashion. "Shall we leave, then?"

"Yes. Oh, I suppose I should pack up my things. Can you wait here just for a moment please?"

Gage nodded his acquiescence and she bounded up the stairs. Ivy nudged him with her elbow. He looked at her and grinned. "I praise God that she is safe, my dear."

A smile tugged on Ivy's lips. "Indeed, Captain."

He leaned back, away from her. "Back to calling me 'Captain' again, milady?"

Ivy put her hands on her hips. "Nay, Gage. The title just seems to fit you."

To her surprise, Gage did not reply with some amusing quip. He maintained a serious expression, and muttered, "I'm pleased to hear *you* at least think so."

Ivy wound her hand around his and tugged him towards herself until he met her eyes. "Gage, you are a great captain, and I do not understand why you fail to realize that. You got your crew safely through that hurricane and then through a battle with those horrible pirates."

"You are mistaken, my sweet. I did not make it through that battle in one piece. I was knocked out cold before it was even finished." His chocolate brown eyes held a hint of sadness.

Ivy reached up on her tiptoes and pressed her lips to his cheek. An afternoon's growth of stubble tickled her nose, and she giggled.

"What?" he inquired.

"Your face is itchy."

He laughed and shook his head. Addie bounded down the stairs, two steps at a time. She held a grin on her face and a small bag on her shoulder.

"Are you ready?"

"Yes!" Addie turned and said her farewells to the owner of the shop and they were on their way.

Chapter 23

As Adam bounded up the companionway, young Emma nestled in his arms, he heard a clamor on the main deck. Although most of the men had left for town to spend their shares of the treasure from the one ship they had gone against, a few remained. And they were shouting.

Emma whimpered and Adam bounced her in his arms. She stretched her little arm up to his face, and he tweaked her nose with his fingers. The babe giggled. This tyke's innocence was refreshing. Not once had she ever seemed to notice or care about his scarred face. That was unlike any other person he had met since the accident had scarred him. Even if those seeing him tried to mask their shock, or disgust, or even pity, he could tell. But to Emma, he was just the same as everyone else.

He had once been what most considered handsome. Yes, he missed those days, the days when a look at him did not send ladies running, but he could manage. It was not worth anything to be friends with people who only cared about how nice his face looked anyway. No, and that was just what the society he had been raised in was like. And he never wanted to return to that. This accident was one of the best things that had happened to him.

Adam made his way onto the main deck and chuckled, pushing aside his dark thoughts. Of course Captain Thompson and Lady Shaw had returned. With this crew, only one thing could cause them to make so much noise: a woman. But had they not grown to respect the woman more? Well, they were pirates. And a woman was a woman to them no matter how well she was at helping control a ship full of unruly men, he supposed.

As Adam approached the two, he realized it was not Lady Shaw the men were making catcalls at. No, it was a young woman who braced her hands on pleasantly round hips. Her golden tan skin was flushed red, and her brilliant sea-green eyes narrowed in anger. Dark, curly hair fell loose from a bun high atop her head and billowed in the sea breeze. Adam felt certain he had never seen anything so pretty. And her attitude. Her spunk. She seemed just about ready to slap the face of every man on this deck. Quite viciously, in fact.

And if Adam didn't stop ogling her himself, he might very well be the first to be introduced to the palm of her hand. He averted his gaze to his captain, who stood with his fists and jaw clenched. Mayhap Gage would hit the men after she slapped him down, as well. This was his sister? Hmm. They shared many characteristics.

Adam shook his head, blinked, and continued toward the trio, focusing his gaze on Lady Shaw. She wouldn't hurt him. She was too sweet... Most of the time. He remembered her expression when she had scolded the crew, but then her face lit up when she saw Emma. The little girl reached her arms out and practically jumped into the woman's arms.

Gage cleared his throat. "Adam, would you please show *Miss Thompson* to her cabin? She will be joining Ivy."

Spend some more time with this ever-interesting creature? "Aye, sir."

Adam offered her his arm.

Miss Thompson looked at it, up at him, back at his arm, and stood up straight. "No, thank you, sir. I can manage." With her nose in the air, she started across the deck.

Adam sped to catch up with her. He snagged her elbow. She jerked away.

"Excuse me, Miss Thompson, but I am guessing you do not know the way to your cabin."

"I've been on my share of ships before, sir, so I do not think it will be too difficult to find. I used to sail on Gage and

Caspian's ship many times. You need not be concerned." Her sea-foam green eyes flashed as she stared at him.

Why was he so entranced by this woman? His captain's sister? Why, he had only known her for a grand total of five minutes at the most. Maybe it was because she looked him straight in the eye, not off to the side, or straight at his scars. She made him feel like a normal person again. That must be it.

"Miss Thompson, if you would just allow me the honor of escorting you to your cabin. Your brother asked me to." Adam nodded at his captain, who leaned against the forecastle railing, chatting with Ivy. A grin stretched across his face as he spoke to the woman.

A sudden longing filled Adam. Wouldn't it be wonderful to care for a woman as much as Gage did for Ivy, and to feel that emotion returned?

A sigh escaped his lips.

"As you wish," Miss Thompson muttered. She followed him down the companionway, past the door to the captain's cabin, down a ways further, to the cabin Ivy had been staying in. He opened the door and motioned for her to enter.

She did, and set her small bag on the cot.

"Is that all you have with you, Miss Thompson?" He nodded to the bag.

A frown creased her forehead. "Aye. 'Tis all I have."

"You will need to discuss the... sleeping arrangements of this room with Lady Shaw. There is only one cot, but you will need to share the room with her."

"If you could have someone set up a hammock for me, I would be happy to sleep there."

Adam raised his eyebrows. "Are you certain?" He knew many men who had fallen out of their hammocks their first nights at sea.

The woman crossed her arms across her chest. "Like I said, sir, I have enjoyed my share of voyages with Gage." She moved about the room and glanced out the tiny porthole at the far end. After a moment, she came back towards him. "Who are you, anyway? I do not recognize you from Caspian's ship."

"Ah, yes. Gage allowed me to join starting this voyage."
Adam bowed at the waist. "First mate, Adam Douglas at your
service, miss."

She nodded.

"And may I ask you your full name, miss? I don't believe
Gage told me."

Fire flashed in her eyes. She was getting annoyed with
him. Rather quickly. "Addie Thompson Poole, but please call
me Miss Thompson."

Adam raised his eyebrows. Why would she not want to be
called by her married name? In fact, she did not appear to be
very mournful to have lost her husband only a few weeks ago.
No, the only thing she appeared to be was quite annoyed.

"Please, sir, I do not want you to think I am angry with
you. I am just not in a mood to talk to a man. I mean you no
offense, but the only man in my life who has not lied to me or
treated me rudely is my brother. So I have no interest in further associating myself with any others."

Before Adam knew it, the little spitfire had tossed him out
of the cabin.

⚓

Addie squeezed her eyes shut as she leaned against the door
she had just slammed in the man's face. What was wrong with
her? She had obviously hurt his feelings, and he had seemed nice
enough. But she was in no mood to deal with men and their lies.

First, her father. He had left before she was even born.
Then, her adopted father. The man sold her off to the highest
bidder, just to get her out of the house. And the highest bidder
had whisked her away to another town and left her in debt.
And then there was Mr. Faulke. When had he planned on telling her he was seeking out someone to replace her?

What is wrong with everyone?

Addie grimaced at the memory of the sadness in Mr.
Douglas's eyes when she had shooed him out of the cabin. He
truly had not done anything to her. A terrible feeling sank to
the pit of her stomach. How cruel of her.

And he had... seemed different than most of the other men. Sure, he had stared at her. But he seemed to notice *her*, and not just how she looked.

Addie, on the other hand, *had* noticed his features. The whole left side of his face was scarred like melted wax. It was a pity, for the right side was quite handsome. Poor man. But someone must love him, for he had been cradling a baby in his arms when she had first arrived. Where was the man's wife?

$$\clubsuit$$

Gage laughed as Emma babbled a story in baby gibberish to him and Ivy. Ivy grinned at him from over the child's head. He planted a kiss on Ivy's cheek and tousled the tiny ringlets of fuzz on Emma's head. "You're a sweetheart, you know that?"

Ivy leaned close to him. "She likes you. A lot. You know that, right?" Her eyes twinkled as she spoke. Gage could not resist a smile. Aye, he knew the babe liked him. It was the woman's favor he was trying to win.

He glanced at her from the side of his eye. Her gaze was focused only on the child. Only a handful of her copper locks had remained restrained in the coiffure she had stuffed them in earlier in the day. Their trek through the town had loosened them, and Gage had to admit, he much preferred her hair this way. Her cheeks were flushed, highlighting her tiny freckles. Her lips... her lips were pink and perfect. And he longed to kiss them again.

Gage glanced about the deck. No. His men were watching. And if his men were watching, they would lose whatever trace of respect they had developed for her when she had been their captain.

Ivy pulled away from Gage, and twisted to face the other direction. Frowning, Gage followed her gaze. Oh, Adam. Why was his face tightened in displeasure? "Is all well, my man?" He asked as Adam approached.

"Yes... yes, Captain."

Gage raised his eyebrows.

"Your sister has requested for a hammock to be strung in her cabin. She said you may continue to sleep on the cot if you wish." He nodded to Ivy.

"Very well. If you please, get one of the men to hang a hammock in the ladies' cabin." Gage rested a hand on Ivy's arm as he addressed Adam.

Adam nodded and left.

"Why did he look so flustered, Gage?"

Gage rotated to Ivy. Her forehead was furrowed with concern. "Oh, 'twas nothing, I am sure. He must simply be wondering how Addie could sleep in a hammock when many men on their first voyages fall out of those contraptions. Addie has been on a few voyages on Caspian's ship, and she had to sleep in a hammock. She has grown accustomed to it now."

"Well, your sister seems to be a nice lady." Ivy played with a lock of Emma's fuzzy hair.

"Aye, that she is, milady. I am pleased to have found her. I have missed her so. For a long time, she was all the family I had, so she means a lot to me."

Ivy's eyes brightened. "When are you going to give her the lavender lawn we purchased in Port Royal?"

"Lavender lawn... ah, the fabric! Yes, I will give that to her tonight. I want her to join us for dinner in my cabin. Tomorrow, I promise we will go out and stroll through the town. I know you enjoyed the chance to be back on dry land, and since my men will still be carousing about the wharves, we should have time to do so."

"Oh, thank you, sir! I appreciate that. I really do."

Gage chuckled. "It's entirely worth it to see you happy, my sweet."

Emma let out a happy squeal and stretched her arms out toward Gage. "Papa!"

Ivy cringed.

Gage felt it like a knife through his heart. It seemed as if he was winning her over, yet she cringed at the thought of Emma being their daughter together. Mayhap she would never come to love him or actually accept his suit.

§

Why did the babe continue to call Gage "Papa" and Ivy "Mama"? And yet... the sound grew more and more pleasing to Ivy's ears every time she heard it. In fact, it made her smile inwardly. Ivy would give almost anything to be Gage's wife and Emma's mama. But would she give up her place in society, her reputation?

Giving everything up was worth the struggle. Heaven knows, it was worth it. Why had she not realized so before?

Since the day Ivy had vowed to stay away from Gage, he had seemed to push himself closer to her than ever. And she had loved it. Instead of growing to dislike him, it had only served to strengthen her love of the man. What was wrong with her? There was no way she could ever leave him without her heart breaking. It was an unavoidable fact.

So what was there to do? Nothing. Because, this man, this captain, was hers. And she was not going to lose him.

"Mama!" Emma seemed to voice Ivy's thoughts. She was made for this family. This man and this toddler were hers. And she could never leave them.

"Gage, are we staying on your ship tonight?"

Ivy blinked. Oh. When had Addie come to stand in front of them? She hadn't even noticed the girl come up on the deck.

"Yes, we are, Addie. I feel safer with you and Ivy—Lady Shaw here with me, other than in some place in the city."

Addie's stomach grumbled and she pressed a hand against it, her tan face growing red.

Gage chuckled. "Are you hungry, my pet?"

She laughed, flashing a set of perfect white teeth. The girl was like her brother in many ways. "Yes, I am. I've been avoiding eating in the town's taverns at all costs. I would thoroughly enjoy a nice full meal."

"Why were you avoiding taverns?"

"Oh, 'twas nothing to concern you. Shall we eat something now?"

Gage frowned. "Aye. A meal should be arriving at my cabin in a few minutes. We can wait there." He offered his arms to both ladies, who accepted his offer and allowed him to escort them to his cabin.

Ivy balanced Emma on her hip as she walked. Once they arrived at Gage's cabin, she settled the child on the bed.

Addie stepped forward as Ivy nestled Emma in a cocoon of blankets. "Why doesn't Mr. Douglas take care of his own child?"

"Excuse me?" Ivy tucked the blankets around Emma as Gage rearranged the furniture of his cabin to accommodate the three of them dining.

"Why doesn't Mr. Douglas take care of his child? And where is her mother?" Addie gestured to Emma. "Except for when I first came aboard, I have only seen you and Gage caring for her. That's incredibly selfish of the man."

Ivy laughed. "Oh, no, Emma isn't Adam's baby! She's mine. And Gage's."

Silence stretched across the cabin.

Gage stopped fumbling with his desk immediately.

Addie choked.

Ivy gasped.

"I-I didn't realize..."

"No! I did not mean it like that!" Ivy clapped a hand over her mouth.

"Emma is not our actual daughter, Addie. We found her on the streets of Port Royal, being abandoned by her own mother. So we took her in, and she is ours now." Gage shared a secret smile with Ivy. The action alone sent warm butterflies speeding from her belly to every direction of her body. A connection seemed to pass to her from his body, although they did not even touch. Aye, this man was special.

"That was kind of both of you." Addie raised her eyebrows.

Gage shrugged. "It seemed to be the only decent thing to do." He moved over to a trunk on the far side of the cabin. "Ah, how could I have nearly forgotten? I have something I wanted to give you today."

"Really?" Addie followed Gage.

He opened the trunk and pulled out the bolt of lavender lawn. Her face brightened, and she emitted a high-pitched noise. "Oh, Gage, it is simply gorgeous! Whatever is this for?" She wrapped her arms around her brother's neck in a hug.

He chuckled as she loosened her grip. "Whatever you want, sister. When I caught word your husband had died and you could use my help, I decided to give you a gift when I came to retrieve you. Then I remembered the times when we were young and on the streets and you would want fabric for a new dress so terribly, but the shop owners would always toss us out of their establishments when they noticed we were parentless."

Addie's gaze dropped. "Aye, I remember that. I did not enjoy being treated in that fashion."

"And now, I wanted to give you a new bolt of fabric. I could never buy you one before, and now I can. I wanted to see you happy again."

Addie smiled up at Gage and Ivy suddenly felt like an interloper, intruding on these sibling's private affairs. She wished she knew this woman better.

"I am happy, brother. Not only because of this gift, but because I am back with you." Addie chuckled.

"What's funny, Addie?"

"Well... I adore the fabric. I really do. It's just... I never want to see another needle and thread again, so I fear this gorgeous material will not be made into a gown anytime soon."

"Oh, forgive me, Addie! When I chose the material, I had not realized you had taken a position aiding a milliner."

"No, do not worry; I am very pleased you even remembered those days. I will cherish this, and I'm sure I can get someone to help me sew it into a gown." Addie winked at her brother.

"I would be pleased to sew the gown for you, Addie." Bittersweet tears stung Ivy's eyes. She was truly happy for Gage and Addie, and yet she missed her brother dearly. However, she knew now that she could fully trust God to do whatever was best for the boy. Surely she would see him soon enough. After a moment, Ivy sat on the bed next to Emma. Emma's face brightened and she crawled over the mattress to sit on Ivy's lap. Ivy smiled and bounced the child up and down before cuddling her in her embrace.

CHAPTER 24

Gage beamed as his sister fingered the fresh, bright fabric. Oh, the joy that had brightened her face! His gaze drifted over to the other side of the cabin where Ivy sat on the bed, playing with Emma. The poor thing. There had been a few times this afternoon Ivy had been left looking alone while he and Addie spoke of the past. She no doubt was missing her brother terribly when she saw him reunited with his younger sibling. He moved over to her side and brushed a lock of hair out of her forehead as Emma giggled and played with a piece of lace on Ivy's dress.

Slowly, Ivy's eyes rose up to meet his. They were filled with adoration, confusion, and a hint of sadness. She looked over at Addie, who lounged in one of Gage's armchairs. Addie smiled sweetly in their direction and then stared out the porthole, where the docks were bustling with nighttime activity.

Gage ensnared Ivy's hand in both of his and gave it a reassuring squeeze. He would let her get to know Addie, and they would soon get together like a small family. He hated to see Ivy feel out of place. Maybe after dinner together and they had shared the cabin for a few days, they would feel more at ease near each other. Gage would hate to see the two most important women in his life uncomfortable around each other.

His thoughts were interrupted as one of his men carried in a tray of food and deposited it on the table. Another man trailed in behind him with cups and a pitcher of water . They sent a few long gazes in Addie's direction, but after Gage thanked them, they exited the room.

"Oh, this smells good!" Ivy commented. Her face brightened.

Hunger rumbled in Gage's stomach as he leaned to the table and sniffed. Yes, it did smell good. Platters of rice, poached pears, and roasted chicken and vegetables lined the table. Steam and savory scents wafted towards him. A plate of cheese on the far side of the table completed the menu.

Addie gasped as she took in the wide array.

Ivy's eyes twinkled in appreciation. "Oh, Gage, this is amazing! I was growing so sick of the dried food we were eating during the voyage."

Gage flashed her a wink. "I made sure we would have good food while we were at port." He circled the table, pulling out chairs for the women. Once everyone had settled, he positioned himself between the ladies. He said a blessing, and they began to eat.

"It is nice to eat here without the rest of the crew, Gage. They have become more reasonable, but still... I appreciate the privacy." Ivy cut a small piece of pear off of her plate and popped it into Emma's mouth.

"Aye, miss. I just never thought it was proper for me to invite you here to dine alone with me." He shrugged.

"The food is delicious, brother." Addie sank her teeth into a chunk of chicken. She was eating faster than he had seen anyone eat in a while.

Gage felt a frown crease his forehead. "Have you eaten well since your... since Mr. Poole passed away, Addie?"

She lowered her eyes. "After I secured my position at the milliner's shop, I would dine in a tavern when I had enough money, but I despised being harassed by the other customers. The milliner's shop was too close to the wharves for my liking."

Something sour sank in Gage's stomach. "They didn't... hurt you, did they, Addie?"

"No, no, I got away. There's nothing to worry about. I just taught them to keep their eyes and hands to themselves and I started to limit the times I went there because I did not like the patrons." She nibbled on a chunk of cheese.

Ivy slipped a spoonful of rice into her mouth and then drank a sip of water before speaking. "I am sorry you've had to go through everything that has been thrown your way, Addie. It sounds like you have had an unpleasant life, and you are still quite young."

Addie shrugged. "I know everything that has happened is for a reason. I may not know what it is right now, but I will someday."

A smile tugged Ivy's lips upwards. Gage had trouble tearing his gaze away from those pretty lips. "That is true."

Emma grabbed a chunk of a roasted turnip off of Ivy's plate and tossed it into the air. It landed square on Gage's nose. He raised his eyebrows. Emma giggled and pointed. After a moment, Ivy and Addie shared a look and burst into laughter. Gage joined them as he wiped off his face. He watched Ivy and Addie, who smiled at each other. Finally, they seemed more comfortable together. He released a sigh as he leaned over to poke Emma on the cheek.

⚓

Eden's heart seemed to soar high above, near the stars that glittered in the black sky. In a few hours, they would land in Charles Town. A trace of doubt raced through her body. Would they finally find her brother? Perhaps they were not even following the correct facts. They could be chasing another man. Not her beloved brother. *Oh God, please let it be him this time. Please. I need to know he is okay. I need to hug him again.*

Tears welled up in Eden's eyes and, despite all of her efforts to blink them away, spilled down her cheeks. She quickly batted them away with the palms of her hands. It would not do to have either Reed or Caspian come upon her and see she had been crying. Goodness, she had found herself crying at the drop of a hat in the last few weeks. Perhaps her emotions were running higher than normal because she had recently discovered she may be with child.

A strong hand rested on her waist, and a familiar scent of wood and spice wafted over her. Caspian leaned down and scrutinized her face. His warm breath fanned over her lips. He frowned. "You've been crying, my love."

"No, Caspian, it is nothing to worry about." She reached up on her tiptoes and kissed his cheek.

He gently nudged her back. "My wife was crying. I think that is something to worry about." Caspian gently wiped wetness from her face with the pad of his thumb.

She gave him a weak smile. "Don't fret, dear. I was just thinking about Adam. You know how I fret about him."

He sighed as he cupped her face in his hands. "Sweetheart, we will find him. Your brother will be safe." He brushed his thumb across her lips.

"Mama! Papa!" Reed's tormented voice bounced from the other side of the ship. Eden swung around. The child raced up the companionway and across the deck. He skidded to a stop in front of her and Caspian.

"What is it, my son?" Caspian crouched down to Reed's eye level.

"I had a terrible dream!" He threw himself into his father's open embrace.

"Oh, sweetheart, I am sorry." Eden lowered herself to her knees and rubbed Reed's back. Tears filled her eyes at the fright in her child's voice.

"I... I was so frightened..." Reed hiccupped between breaths.

"Honey, it's all right. You're fine. Everyone is fine."

"What happened in your dream, Reed?" Caspian rested his elbow on his knee as he wiped the tears from his son's face.

The child's face crinkled up. "I don't want to talk about it."

Eden sighed and smoothed sandy curls away from Reed's face. The poor thing. She hated to see him upset. Pulling his head back to rest on her chest, she spoke into his ear, "Reed, darling, everything is all right. It was simply a dream." Sparkling blue-violet eyes gazed back up at her. Something tugged at her heart. She loved this boy so much.

"Now come on, Reed. Let's get you back to your bed." Caspian rose and stretched his arm out to his son, offering to help him up.

"Oh, Papa, please, no!" Reed sniffled. "I am too frightened."

Caspian's eyes met hers. She nodded. "All right, Reed. You may sleep with your mama and me. Just this once."

Eden smiled. Her husband had really become good at understanding their son and what he needed. And when the child had a startling nightmare, it was best he was comforted by his parents.

She squeezed Caspian's hand as they made their way down the companionway to their cabin. "I love you."

He pressed a kiss to the top of her head. "I love you too."

⚓

Addie awoke that morning with a crick in her neck. But she did not care. No, she was safe on Gage's ship. She did not have to worry about sewing nonstop or being harassed at a tavern, or if she would even make enough profit to eat. Even if there was nowhere for her to garden on this vessel, for once in the last two years she was safe. Safe. The feeling warmed her heart.

She found Ivy sitting upright on her cot, still in her nightgown, rocking Emma in her arms. The woman yawned, and then smiled when she noticed Addie. "Good morning."

"Good morning."

"Did you sleep well?" Ivy laid Emma back down on the cot and covered her with a corner of the coverlet.

"Yes, I did. Thank you for asking."

Addie swung her legs out of the hammock and managed to exit the contraption without embarrassing herself. Although she had always slept in the hammocks when she was younger, it had been years since she had done so. It would take her a while to get used to it again.

Addie stretched her arms over her head. "I'm hungry."

Ivy laughed. Her stormy gray eyes twinkled. "Gage usually sends Adam down to give us some fruit and tea, or some biscuits."

Addie cringed. Adam. Wasn't that the man she had treated poorly yesterday? Well, no matter. He was a man. She should not feel guilty for treating him poorly after so many men had treated her poorly. And yet she did. He seemed kind.

"Is something wrong, Addie?"

She blinked. "Oh, no, Ivy. Nothing at all."

"Hmm." Ivy rose and moved to the porthole. Addie joined her. Although it was early in the morning, the town was already bustling at work. The ship gently bobbed up and down against its moorings.

A knock sounded on the door. "It's Mr. Douglas, ladies. I've come to bring you a meal."

"Come in," Ivy called.

Addie turned around as the door opened. Mr. Douglas strolled in and set a tray of fruit on a tiny table next to the bed. He picked up the teapot and began to pour one cup. His gaze reached Addie's. A small smile raised one side of his mouth. "How are you today, milady?"

Why should he smile? Addie had been rather rude to him the day before. She moved towards the table to stand near him. "I am all right, sir."

His eyes met hers and held their gaze. He blinked and then continued pouring tea. His hand shook. She reached out to steady the cup for him, thinking maybe the gentle sway of the ship on the waves was causing him trouble. Hot tea scorched her hand. She yelped and drew back.

Mr. Douglas immediately set the pot back on the table and lifted her hand. He pulled it up to his mouth and blew on it. "I'm sorry. I am so, so sorry, milady."

"You're so clumsy! What are you doing?" Addie pulled her hand away from his grasp. Immediately, she regretted the harsh tone to her voice. It had been an accident.

Ivy sped over to them, concern tightening her eyebrows. She seemed to assess the situation and spun back around fumbling with the washbasin.

"I apologize, Miss Thompson. I was trying to blow on the burn to cool it down. I know burns are terribly painful."

She bit her lip as she studied his face. Had it been burned? Is that what had disfigured the left side of his body? Well, she felt like slapping herself in the face if that was how he had been scarred and she was sitting here whining about a splash of hot tea. "What's done is done, I suppose."

Ivy faced them once more and placed a cool, damp cloth on Addie's hand. Immediately, it soothed the pain of the burn. But it did not soothe the pain coursing through her as she took in the extreme disappointment on Mr. Douglas's face. After a moment, he backed away. "I apologize again, milady. If there is anything you are ever in need of, pray let me know. I am at your service." With that, he turned on his heel and sped from the room.

$$\text{⚓}$$

What was that about? Ivy frowned as she tended to Addie's burn. The man had never been clumsy before, and Addie had certainly acted strangely around him. Odd.

She inspected the platter Adam had left on the table. Croissants, a treat since they were at port! Oh, but those were delicious. Aimee's mother, a Frenchwoman, had ensured that her cook made the French pastries once in a while. They were truly scrumptious.

After Addie had treated her burn, she joined Ivy in nibbling at the croissants. She was quite a change from the ravenous young woman Ivy had seen last night. "Addie?"

The girl's sea-foam green eyes slowly rose from the pastry to Ivy's face.

"Do you feel well?"

"It only hurt for a moment. I am fine." She flaked off a piece of the pastry.

"I am going to be completely honest with you. I was not talking about the tea, Addie."

She remained silent for so long, Ivy had given up all hope of receiving an answer. Finally, she said, "What happened to him?"

Ivy brushed the remaining flakes of the croissant off of her fingers and finished off her tea. "What do you mean, 'what happened to him'?"

"What happened to Mr. Douglas? Why does he look like that?"

"You mean the side of his face?"

Addie gulped. "Yes. What made it look like that?"

Truly, Ivy did not know. She had never felt right to directly ask the man about it. But she had queried Gage on the matter once. "Gage told me he was burned in an unfortunate accident a few years back. It scorched the whole left side of his body, but mainly affected his face. The rest has mostly healed."

"Oh." Addie's face darkened in upset.

Realization hit Ivy. "Oh, Addie, don't worry about that!"

"I was... fussing because he accidentally spilled some warm tea on my hand, and here he was horribly disfigured by a fire. I feel awful."

Ivy laid her hand on the young woman's shoulder. "Sweetheart, it is all right. I'm sure he didn't even think of it. He rarely seems to care about his face. Adam is a kind man. He wouldn't let something like that bother him, especially from someone like you. He knows you weren't acting maliciously."

"I was cruel to him last night, too, Ivy. I do not understand what is wrong with me. I am being so rude when I really am so grateful to finally be safe once again."

Ivy pulled the girl into her arms. "Darling, you have been through a lot during these past few months... or however long since your marriage. It is understandable you are a little jumpy and that would affect how you act around people. Don't worry. It'll pass soon, and I am certain you will go back to feeling like yourself quickly."

Addie pulled away slightly. "Really?"

A smile stretched itself across Ivy's lips. "Really. Now enjoy your meal."

CHAPTER 25

After determining some details for when they would depart with his quartermaster and how to promptly remove Rogers—a deep annoyance—from his crew, Gage sprang down the companionway steps, eager to see his sister and Ivy. He rapped on the door with his knuckles and Ivy almost immediately opened it. Her orange hair was mussed, and the collar of her dress was not lying correctly. Gage immediately realized the source of her dishevelment when he noted Emma propped against her hip, tugging yet another lock of hair out of the woman's coiffure.

Gage chuckled as Ivy blew a curl out of her face and grinned at the tot. "I like her hair better down too, Emma. Smart thinking." He winked.

Ivy's face immediately reddened. "Really, Gage, you mustn't say such things." But he could tell she was pleased by his compliment.

"What do you say to a nice stroll about the town, ladies?" Gage stepped inside so he could see his sister, who was lounging on the cot.

"Oh, that sounds lovely! But I fear it is time for this little one's nap." Ivy pressed a kiss to the top of Emma's head.

Oh, how could Gage have forgotten?

Addie rose and stepped over to him. "I'll stay with Emma. You two go ahead and enjoy your stroll. I would appreciate to get better acquainted with my 'niece.'" She reached to take Emma from Ivy's arms.

Ivy bounced Emma, who leaned against her shoulder and yawned. "Are you sure, sweetheart? It might do you good to get some fresh air."

"I am certain. I don't feel a burning need to ever see that town again, anyway."

Gage frowned. "I will miss you, Addie."

"I will be all right, brother."

He sighed. "I suppose. You aren't a little girl anymore. We will not take long, either, so we can come back to see you."

Ivy handed Emma over to Addie and then met Gage. He offered her his arm. "Shall we?"

Gage gloried in the feel of Ivy's hand on his arm, and he relished the split-second moments when her curves brushed against his side as they walked through the town. He truly could get used to this. When they strolled side by side, arm in arm, through the center of the town, it made him really feel like they were together. And the bystanders on the street who probably assumed they were married? Gage didn't mind them one bit. In fact, he cherished the idea. He needed to find out where her thoughts were on the idea. Because, heaven help him, he could not wait to have some sort of promise from the delightful woman.

Gage had stopped in with the local silversmith early in the morning, who had promised to find a beautiful ring for the lady by evening. If it didn't fit her properly, then the silversmith had agreed to adjust it free of charge. Unfortunately, Gage did not have one in his own possession already. His father had never given his mother a ring, and she had been forced to sell her grandmother's long ago to provide for herself. So Gage had to purchase a new one. And if he were to propose to Ivy, he would not do so without a ring. She deserved one. She was a special lady and she deserved the best.

Ivy's steps slowed as they moved outside the edge of town, near a beautiful beach. They were the sole visitors.

"Do you want to walk on the sand, my dear?"

Pink flushed her cheeks. "Oh, yes I would."

He smiled and took her hand. "Why don't you take your shoes and stockings off? I personally know it is irksome to get sand in your shoes."

She hesitated and glanced around, but found they were completely alone. Surely it would be fine to just take her shoes off. Her skirt would cover them mostly anyway. She bent down to untie her boots. Gage crouched at her feet and stayed her hands. "I'll help." The woman had tiny feet. Tiny, adorable feet. The second his hand touched the laces, heat radiated through him. He was so close to her. She smelled good. Like citrus. Gage made quick work of loosening the laces and sliding the shoe off. Ivy wiggled her toes in her stockings.

Gage glanced up at her. Her face was red, but she gave no indication she was uncomfortable with his hands on her. He was tempted to also remove her stockings, but he felt that would be too personal. So, he moved on and removed her other boot.

"Thank you for helping me," she breathed.

He rose and met her gaze with his. Intensity passed between them. "It was my pleasure."

Her gray-blue eyes widened. Her lips parted. He needed to kiss her. It had been far too long since he had done so.

Gage slowly lowered his mouth to hers, giving her plenty of a chance to turn away, to reject his advance. But she didn't.

⚓

Ivy felt her toes curl up in their stockings as Gage kissed her. Her eyes drifted shut. He cupped her face in his hand, and he drew her close with his other. A moan escaped her throat as his lips moved to her cheek, to the pulse at her neck. His mouth moved back to her cheek, and then to her lips. Oh, it was heaven to kiss this man. Pure heaven.

His hand at her waist roamed across her back, gently caressing. She reached up and entangled her fingers in his chocolate brown hair. It felt soft, and smelled of pleasant spices. After a moment, his hand moved from her cheek down around her waist.

Ivy wanted to get closer to him. Needed to. She wound her arms around his neck and pulled his body against hers more tightly. Her hands moved to his shoulders and worked their way to his chest. He pulled away. Confusion swept some of the heat away from her. She opened her eyes. Gage stood with his hands on her waist, his chest working double time to catch his breath. She stood on her tiptoes, intending to kiss him again, but he moved his hands to her shoulders with a chuckle and kept her down. "Believe me, milady, I would love to continue kissing you, but it is not proper." He nodded to a gathering of townspeople standing a few yards away, gawking at them. He shook his head at them and they scrambled away.

"Oh." Her face heated. "Let's get to the beach." She tugged her stockings off, placed them on a rock next to her boots, and surged forward, her feet meeting the rocky sand.

He sped to catch up to her and kept a hand at her elbow, steadying her as she marched across the sand to the ocean. Finally, she stopped to enjoy the view. Behind them, tufts of tall grass grew abundantly, only parting to offer a small path from the town to the beach. To their left, a set of rocks jutted out from the ocean. Waves rushed around it, their white froth slapping the base of the forms. Mud swirled around in little eddies. Soon, they were covered completely but for their skinny tips. Gage slipped an arm around Ivy's waist. "The tide must have just come in. Too bad. I was hoping to catch it before it came in to show you the tide pools."

"Tide pools?" She leaned her head against his shoulder.

"Yes. When the tide goes out, some water rests in holes in the ground. Little sea creatures live in them, and I was going to see if I could find some to show you."

"Oh, that sounds delightful."

"We will have to come back another time, when the tide is out."

"Yes." She squinted against the bright, mid-morning sun. Although she enjoyed resting on solid ground once again, she hoped they would not spend an unreasonable amount of time in Charles Town. She missed her brother terribly.

"Would you like to sit down?" He gestured to the rocky beach. "I think it would be nice to just watch the waves. Or... or would that soil your dress? That wasn't very thoughtful of me—"

He was babbling. It was quite endearing. "I will sit."

Gage flashed a relieved grin. He shrugged out of his waistcoat and set it on the ground as a sort of blanket to protect her gown from the sand. How sweet. After he ensured she had settled comfortably, he sank down beside her, propping himself by stretching an arm out next to her. He cradled her hand in his as they stared out at the ocean.

"We need to talk, Ivy darling."

She sat up a little straighter. He pressed a kiss to the palm of her hand. The act sent tingles up her arm and down her spine. "Mmm-hmm?"

"Ivy... what are we going to do?"

She remained silent, for she had no idea how to answer the beloved man.

$

"What do you plan on doing about Emma, Ivy?"

She hesitated. "I... I want to keep her. I couldn't bear to give her to someone else. Why, she might as well be my own child."

That's what Gage had thought. Hoped for. Prayed for. "The child needs a father as well as a mother, Ivy."

Ivy's chest rose sharply as she inhaled. She did not respond.

"Don't you think? I believe every child deserves both a male and a female parent. Emma doesn't deserve to be raised alone."

"Yes. I think so."

"If you want to keep her, then who should be her father?" He leaned closer as she pulled her face slightly away. She sucked in another breath, and he put his finger underneath her chin until her eyes had no choice but to meet his.

"I... I suppose—"

"Gage? Gage, is that you?"

Reluctantly, he released her and pulled back. "We will talk about this later, darling."

He stood and faced the direction the voice had come from. "Caspian!" Gage lurched forward and met his friend halfway across the beach in an embrace. Eden stood at his side, holding Reed's hand. Gage hadn't realized how much he had missed all three!

"Eden!"

"Ivy! What on earth are you doing here?" The women sprang toward each other and hugged. Tears sprang from Eden's eyes. "Why are you with Gage?"

"He offered to take me home. We thought we would reach England before Captain Emery, but now I am not sure. But... it's all right. I know William is safe. He is in God's care." Ivy brushed some tears from her own eyes.

Gage smiled inwardly. Ivy had really grown to trust in God during the past few weeks. In fact, he was proud of her. He slid closer to her and slipped an arm around her waist in a supportive gesture. Bad idea. Eden's eyes widened in shock. She glanced back and forth between him and Ivy.

"Papa! May I go by the ocean?" Reed's exuberant voice brought a laugh to everyone.

"Reed, don't you want to say hello to your Uncle Gage?" Caspian leaned down and ruffled his son's hair.

"Hello, Gage. You seemed busy talking to the adults, so I was gonna go look at the ocean and then come back and say hello to you."

Gage grinned and launched the boy up in his arms. "I missed you, little man." He pressed a kiss to the child's forehead. Reed giggled. "Now, go ahead and look at the ocean. I'm sure we'll be able to talk soon enough."

Reed ran off across the beach, squealing in delight.

"What brings you to Charles Town, Caspian? Why did I find you out here on the beach?" He clapped his friend on the shoulder.

"Well, I am glad we found you, because you are what we were here for. I asked the men at the docks where to find you, and they directed me to your quartermaster, who directed me to you. He said you had some plans to spend the day on the shore side." Caspian tucked Eden against him, his hand resting on her hip. She tilted her head towards her husband.

A pang of jealousy smacked Gage straight across the jaw. What he wouldn't give to have Ivy look at him in such adoration...

He shook the feeling. Caspian was a talented captain. He deserved to have a devoted wife. Gage, on the other hand, wasn't such a great example.

"After inquiring at many ports, we heard you had signed on a fair amount of men to balance out your crew when you reached Port Royal."

"Yes." Gage wasn't sure what this had to do with anything. Maybe Caspian had doubted in his abilities as a captain and had decided to check up on him. But would he really spend so much time traveling across the sea to find him just for that? Oh well. No matter what they discussed, he was just glad to see Caspian again. The man had been his best friend since childhood and the best captain a man could ask for.

"Did you come across a man by the name of Adam Trenton?"

Trenton... "That's Eden's last name."

"Of course it is Archer now, but yes. This man is her brother. Do you know him?"

"Adam... an Adam Douglas is my first mate."

Eden's eyes brightened. "May we see this man? Please, Mr. Thompson?"

⚓

Adam sat on the forecastle deck and rested his forehead on his hands. They were coming back. The horrible memories he had tried to suppress. They had all come rushing back the second he had seen Miss Thompson's burn. He had not meant to hurt her. But she *had* hurt him. Now, he supposed, they were even.

He rubbed his temples and squeezed his eyes shut.

First, the trembling. It had seemed as if the entire world was crashing down around him. If he recalled correctly, he had believed it was the end of the world. But it wasn't. No, it was an earthquake, and an awful one at that. The force had knocked him right on his back. Port Royal had experienced small earthquakes before, he had been told, but nothing of this caliber. And Adam supposed he could consider himself a lucky man because he had been on the outskirts of the town, away from the ocean. Away from the mass destruction.

But when he had gone back toward the center of the town to see if he could help anyone, everything had changed. He could still hear the people's cries, see the dead bodies. And that was when the building he stood next to seemed to explode. It must have been on fire before Adam had reached it, he reasoned, but he had not noticed.

At first, he didn't feel anything. He didn't even notice the flames climbing up his shoulder, or the smoke circling him. He didn't notice any of it. After a moment though, the pain hit him. Like a boulder. His skin was melting. The earthquake must have truly been the end of the world as he had suspected, and he had been sent straight to hell. Hell looked a lot like Port Royal, he thought. The flames licked at his face, jumping higher, singing his hair. It hurt. It hurt like the dickens.

He remembered doubling over.

The smoke bit his throat.

His mouth was too dry to allow him to cry out, and even if he had any saliva, he suspected no one would help him in hell. The fire crawled around him. He batted it away, desperate to keep it from scorching his skin. His bones ached. Everything ached. Sweat evaporated as soon as it left his body. Tears wetted his eyes, and the smoke coaxed them out.

Help me. Help me.

And then a young man stepped out of the smoke to his rescue, dragging him away from the doomed town and helping him heal. James. The very man Adam later failed to save during the terrible storm. Adam buried his face in his hands and let a sob escape. There was nothing he could do to save him. Nothing he could do to bring him back. Nothing he could do to help James' now fatherless and husbandless child and wife.

It was all Adam's fault. He knew the feeling well. When would he ever be able to escape from the past?

He rubbed his hands against his face and felt the uneven skin on the left half, the area with the severe burns. Never. He would never be able to get away from the past, because he bore a piece of it every day. He could never get rid of these burns. He would never forget, and he would never forgive himself. And he would never find happiness.

"Mr. Douglas? Someone wants to speak to you for a moment."

Adam groaned inwardly. Why had his captain chosen this moment to speak to him? He wiped the tears from his face, stood, and spun around.

Adam resisted the urge to rub his eyes in an attempt to rid them of the mirage before him. Next to Gage and Ivy stood another man and a child, but Adam didn't pay them any attention. For there, at the man's side, was a young woman.

There was no mistaking her. She was years older, and she had grown into a beautiful lady, but of course Adam had never expected anything else of her. She had always been pretty. But he had never expected to see her again. When their father had told him that if he left on a sailing trip one more time, he would never be welcome home again, Adam had never believed the man would stick to his word. But he did, and Adam soon realized he would never see his sister again. She never replied to his letters, and Adam had assumed either she was angry with him, or their father had intercepted the correspondences. So Adam left for good and never glanced back. Changed his surname to that of James to honor the man who had given him a second chance at life, and gave up all hope of seeing the beloved girl.

Her brow crinkled. "Adam... what happened to you?"

He let out a rueful laugh and swung her into an embrace. "It doesn't matter, Ed honey." He swooped down and kissed her forehead. "My, have you grown up."

The man next to her stood up taller. "Aye, she's a married woman, now, as well."

Adam leaned back and studied her husband. He was a sailing captain, there was no doubt of that. Most likely a pirate or a privateer. What on earth was his Eden doing married to a man like this? Why, before Adam had even left, their father had been exploring the young lords who lived around them and might be a good suit for his daughter.

Eden smiled sweetly at the man. "This is my husband, Captain Caspian Archer. And this is our son, Reed."

Reed offered a darling smile. Adam felt his eyes widen. The boy must be six years old. How long had Eden been married? Adam raked his mind... Eden would be nineteen or twenty years old now.

Caspian offered his hand to Adam. He shook it. "Nice to meet you, sir. I have heard all kind stories about you. In fact, I can probably thank you for leading Eden to meet me."

"What do you mean?"

Eden laid a hand on Adam's arm. "I left England to... to go to the Caribbean, because you loved it so much. I thought it must be better than London. Anything would be better than London." A shadow crossed her face before her voice grew cheerful once more. "So, I stowed away on Caspian's ship and we ended up... married." Her cheeks flushed.

Captain Archer drew Eden close.

"Why were you leaving London, Ed? Is Father all right?"

⚓

Eden chuckled at her brother's nickname for her. "Oh, Adam, that is a story meant for another time. But Father is well, I believe." At least she knew he wouldn't be looking for her. After she had disobeyed him so defiantly by running away, and with the fiancé out of the way, the whole situation had been fixed. She was certain he would not send anyone after her. In fact, he had probably told London society she had died. No daughter of his would defy him, run away, and marry a pirate.

"Why didn't you write to me?" Eden's hands clawed into her brother's arms without her bidding. She had worried about his safety for years. Many had assumed him dead.

"I did, Ed. Although I began to suspect Father was intercepting my letters because I never received a reply."

"How could he do that to us?" Tears stung Eden's eyes. All this time, she could have been corresponding with her beloved brother, her only sibling.

"You know he was dead-set against any son of his being a sailor. He feared it would tarnish our reputation."

"Would you like to sit down in my captain's cabin and visit?" Gage gestured to the other side of the ship.

"You would allow us to?"

"Of course I would. You four go along. I am so happy for all of you. I'm going to stay up here for now and speak with Lady Shaw."

Ivy raised her chin. "But Gage, I would prefer to stay with my best friend. I have missed her so." She paused, her eyes lowered. "You could come along as well."

Eden paused. What had passed between these two? Why had Gage acted so possessively of her earlier? Hmm. She eyed the couple suspiciously. They would make a good match, really. Gage was a sweet man, and Ivy, a caring person.

"Very well." Gage led them to his cabin and made sure they were all settled comfortably before he left the room, declaring he had some business to tend to.

Adam ran a hand through his hair and twisted to face Ivy. "Lady Shaw... Lady Ivy Shaw. I knew I recognized your name. You were naught but a little tyke when I last saw you, playing with my Eden. When I first met you on this ship, I had supposed I may have known you from my days in London, making your name sound familiar, but I never remembered for certain. I had tried to block those days out of my memory. But, my, what a bright lady you have become in the years since."

Ivy smiled at Adam. "Thank you, Mr. Dou—sir."

"Adam, what... what happened to you? What hurt you?"

A shadow crossed over his face. "In '92, there was an earthquake in Port Royal, and I stupidly stood next to a building that exploded. I got caught in the fire and it singed my left side."

Eden swallowed hard as tears welled up in her eyes. "Adam, that must have been terrible."

A shrug rolled across his shoulders. "Tell me more about your husband, Ed." He nodded towards Caspian.

"Oh. Well, Father lost a lot of money in a poor investment. So he soon decided it was time for me to marry."

He raised his right brow. "He married you to a pirate? Now, I suppose it can be a lucrative business, but... he has always been so against sailing."

Caspian chortled from his position in the chair on the other side of the room.

"No, not at all. He announced my betrothal to Lord Clive Rutger." Eden's nose crinkled up at just the mention of the awful man's name. But he was gone now. And she had Caspian. There was nothing to concern herself about. "Do you remember Lord Rutger? He may have not been in town yet while you were there."

Adam shook his head. "I don't remember him, but just by the way you said his name I have a feeling I know what kind of man he was." He clenched his fists. "What was Father thinking? He has always been more concerned with money and status than either of our happiness or well-being."

Eden nodded. It was true. Their father had not cared one bit that Adam had always longed for the freedom of the sea, just as he had not cared one bit that she did not want to marry a man who abused her. She recounted the tale of how her horrible fiancé had beaten her, how she had run away. How she had met Caspian and little Reed and never wanted to turn back.

Chapter 26

Ivy remembered Adam now. How could she not have realized he was Eden's brother before today? Sure, he was quite a bit older than when she had last seen him. And, of course, the entire left side of his face was unfortunately marred. And he had changed his last name. However, now that she knew who he was, there was no mistaking it. He was certainly Eden's brother.

She smiled when she recalled all of the fun times Eden had told her and Aimee about. Why, she remembered stories of them gallivanting about at the docks of London and sneaking out their windows after bedtime. Eden had loved this man very much, and was devastated when she had believed she had lost him forever.

A knock sounded, then the door scraped open. Gage closed it behind him as he balanced Emma on his hip. It was a charming sight. He was the perfect father. Why, he cared about Emma deeply. She could tell. And he cut a handsome figure. *And* he seemed to only have eyes for Ivy as he entered the cabin.

Ivy bit her lip. Why did things have to be so complicated? And yet, she knew despite all of her original objections, Gage was made for her and Emma. In the deepest part of her heart she knew they would all end up together. It was inevitable. They would be a family someday. And what a pleasant thought that was.

Gage crossed the room, stopping next to Ivy and crouching next to her, Emma balanced in his lap. There were no other chairs in the room, and he, the captain of the ship, seemed content with sitting on the floor. That made her... love him even more.

She loved him. There was no denying it.

The warmth of his near body and his cedar scent wafted around, enveloping her.

"Who's this beautiful little girl?" Eden leaned forward and smiled.

Ivy beamed with pride. She thought her Emma was beautiful, too. "Our darling little Emma." A copper curl danced across the little darling's forehead before Ivy brushed it away. They shared the same hair color. Maybe in the future everyone would believe she was truly her own child if she so wished.

"Our?" Eden's voice rang with the question.

Heat flooded Ivy's face.

Gage leaned so close his breath tickled her ear. "If you insist on not allowing me to be this angel's father, mayhap you should refrain from referring to her as 'ours.' Repeatedly." His chuckle rustled the hair at the nape of her neck.

"She's not... ours. I mean... she is, but... Gage?" Her voice was reduced to a squeak.

His laugh reverberated across the room. "We found little Emma being abandoned by her mother, who could no longer risk caring for her. So we took her in and now she's... *ours*." He sent Ivy a wicked grin.

"Oh..." Eden eyed them suspiciously. Ivy wished she could sink into the floor boards and into the bay below. This was horrifying. Gage was a rogue.

"May I hold the baby?" Reed shot up from his chair.

Ivy chuckled. This boy was really sweet.

Eden sent a questioning glance to Ivy, who offered a shrug.

"If you are very careful, you may hold her. But make sure you sit on the bed. I don't want you to drop her, all right, sweetheart?"

"Yes, Mama. I wouldn't drop a *baby*."

Gage walked with the boy over to the bed and gently handed Emma to him. They watched silently as the children played together for a few moments.

Adam and Eden picked up a conversation about their past, recalling one of their childhood adventures.

Ivy asked Gage about his sister. She had told him she would prefer to remain in her cabin for the evening rather than joining them.

Caspian reported to Gage about his ship and how they were faring. Gage talked about the struggles of learning how to be a good captain, and how Ivy had even taken over for him for a while.

Reed returned Emma to Gage as she began to fall asleep, then he bounded off to his father. "Papa, can Mama have a baby soon? I love babies."

Eden's face blossomed to red at her child's comment. The entire room was silent before they all burst into laughter.

"What? Are you laughing at *me?*" Reed frowned.

"Shush, sweetie." Eden rested a hand on her son's as a smile perked up the corners of her mouth.

Caspian chuckled and ruffled the boy's hair.

After a few moments, the group went back to talking and filling each other in on details they had missed. Ivy loved watching Eden. In the past few months she had known her, her cheeks had lost their pretty color, and her eyes, their sparkle. Now she realized the prospect of marriage to that horrible Lord Rutger had tortured her day and night. But now it seemed as if married life agreed with her very well. She was ready with a smile and a laugh. She was happy. And that made Ivy happy.

Soon, the night grew old. Caspian sat up straight and nudged his wife with his elbow. "Sweetheart, I know this is the first time you have seen your brother in years, but we should probably be leaving soon. Reed is practically asleep and the sun has already set."

Ivy glanced down at her friend's son. Sure enough, he had dozed off against his father's leg, and a look out the porthole told her the sky had darkened considerably.

"Can we come back tomorrow?" Eden's forehead creased.

"When were you planning on setting sail, Gage?" Caspian turned to his friend.

Gage stood and stretched his legs out as he rocked a sleeping Emma in his embrace. "Tomorrow afternoon. But I am certain the men wouldn't mind waiting until the day after that. We garnered some treasure from another ship on the way out here, and they are probably itching to spend all of their money and sleep off their alcohol. We should be able to convince Ivy to delay her journey to get to her little brother by a day as well."

"Could we meet tomorrow afternoon, then? Maybe your sister would feel like joining us. Perhaps, at the beach we found each other at today?"

Gage grinned. "That sounds wonderful. I will see if Addie wants to join us as well."

⚓

"Oh, you will adore Eden! I really hope you decide to come. She is one of my best friends." Ivy smoothed out her hair with a brush as she sat in the cabin that night talking to Addie.

Addie rested her chin on her hands. "How do you know these people?"

"Eden has been my best friend practically since I was born. We grew up together in London. She recently married Captain Archer, who used to be Gage's captain."

"I know Captain Archer. He was like a brother to me for many years."

Hmm. Ivy had not known that. "What do you mean?"

Addie cocked a golden-brown eyebrow. "Gage hasn't told you?"

"Told me what?"

"When I was around four years old, after our mother had died and our father left us, Caspian's family took Gage and me in as their own and raised us. Caspian is like my brother."

"I didn't know that." Ivy finished brushing her hair and began gathering it together in one long braid. "So do you suppose you would enjoy joining us tomorrow? Gage said we could stroll through the city, and maybe stop to eat something at a nicer tavern. I think it will be pleasant."

A frown formed on Addie's face. "I don't know... did you say Mr. Douglas is coming, too?"

Well, he was Mr. Trenton now. "Yes. I still cannot believe I didn't realize he was Eden's brother. It seems so obvious now that I know he is."

"I... I will think about it. I will let you all know tomorrow. I am just not certain."

&

The deck of the *Siren's Call* wobbled over a wave the next morning, but Gage stood tall, a grin on his face. The day was going to be perfect. He could feel it. Earlier, he had stopped by the silversmith's, who had given him the ring. For Ivy. On top of that, his sister had agreed to go along with him, Ivy, Adam, Caspian, and Eden for a walk about the town.

Gage patted his pocket to make sure the ring was still there and couldn't resist the temptation to take it out and look at it again. He rolled the smooth piece of silver over in his hand and rubbed his thumb across the small bits of blue and crystal gems circling the top. It would look positively lovely on Ivy's finger. There was no doubt of that. After pressing a kiss to the trinket, Gage gently tucked it back in his pocket.

He needed to find a time to propose to the little lady this afternoon. He wanted to make sure the ring fit her properly while they were still in Charles Town, so the silversmith could adjust it if need be. Not that adjusting the ring was his only reason to hurry. Giddy excitement and nervousness raced through him. When he asked her to be his wife, what would she do? Oh, how he wished she would smile and throw her arms around him and assure him she would love to be his wife. And oh, after he made her his...

"Gage?"

Her copper hair had been braided and then wound into a low knot at the back of her neck. Gage longed to run his hands through that silken hair and let it fall from its confines. She held Emma in her left arm, the child's legs balancing her against the woman. The child leaned against her chest, eyes closed in sleep. And, oh, the pleasure that filled Gage when he caught the expression on Ivy's face. She was happy to see him. And that made him incredibly happy. Her blue-gray eyes lit up and her pink lips curved into a smile. Why, if Addie wasn't standing right there next to her and she wasn't holding Emma, he would have taken her into his arms and...

"Is something wrong?"

Blast it all, she had caught him staring at her. His face heated. "No, no." He glanced about the deck. "Nothing's wrong. Where is Adam?"

"Right here, sir." Adam stepped out from somewhere behind Gage.

"Ah. Shall we head out, then?" Gage offered his elbow to Ivy out of habit, and then realized that that left his sister out. He flicked his gaze to Adam and nodded his head at Addie. If Adam would escort Addie, then Gage would be left with Ivy. Which he would not mind at all.

Adam offered his arm to Addie. She looked at it, then at Gage. He nodded. After exhaling loudly, she reluctantly placed her hand on his arm and allowed him to escort her. Gage took Ivy's hand and tucked it against his side, and the four began their journey to the beach.

By the time they made it there, Eden and Caspian were already perched on some rocks, waiting. Reed played in the sand with a piece of driftwood. Immediately, Eden ran to hug her brother and Ivy. Gage shook hands with Caspian.

"Oh, you brought precious little Emma!" Eden rubbed the little one on the back, adoration filling her eyes.

"There's no one back on my ship I trust her with." Gage fingered a tuft of Emma's hair. Really, it was so much like Ivy's. When he made them all officially a family, it would look just like Emma had really been born to him and Ivy. He glanced at the woman out of the corner of his eye. Once he made her his wife, they would have lots of beautiful orange-haired babies.

Reed bounced up from his position on the sand. "May I please hold the baby?"

Ivy's face brightened. "Of course you can, sweetheart." Ever so gently, the woman lowered their baby into Reed's arms until she was certain the boy had a good grip on the toddler. Emma wrapped her chubby arms around his neck and giggled.

"The beach here is beautiful." Caspian nodded at the tall grasses that made up a large portion of their view. The sand was of a fine texture, but it seemed more like dusty dirt than the grainy sand that populated most of the Caribbean. Although it was still late summer, the water was colder by far.

Eden moved to Caspian's side and wrapped an arm around her husband's waist. "Yes, it is."

Adam stood next to Eden and she laid a hand on his arm. Gage glanced at Addie. She scowled at Adam.

What had his first mate done to his sister? Or was it simply that Addie had always been feisty around any man, and he just noticed her attitude toward Adam? He glanced over at Caspian. No. She had never been impolite to Caspian. The man had been like an adopted brother to her, and she had treated him as such.

Gage's thoughts were broken when a soft hand landed on his wrist. He squeezed Ivy's fingers. This was a good sign. This meant she was still thinking the way he was. Now if he could only find a chance to get her alone so he could officially claim her as his own...

"So, are we ready to go?" Caspian spun around but kept Eden's hand on him.

"Father, I can stay here and watch Emma. So you all can go through the town while we play here."

The corners of Caspian's mouth lifted. Gage had seen him smile more since he had found Eden than he had in years. "Reed, I don't know if you're old enough to stay here by yourself." He looked to his wife.

"I know Reed. He's responsible." Eden glanced up at Ivy. "If it is all right with Ivy and Gage, I think Reed and Emma will be fine. We are just going to be in town for a little while, and it doesn't seem like many people come through this area to bother them." She indicated the empty beach surrounding them.

Gage clenched his jaw. Of course he trusted Reed. But that didn't mean the two of them would be safe all alone out here.

"I... I suppose they would be fine," Caspian offered.

⚓

Ivy paused. Were these people, her friends, truly considering leaving her baby alone with a boy who had probably only seen five years since he was that age himself? She sank her fingernails into Gage's arm, hoping to give him the impression she did not adore this idea.

He flashed her a grin.

Fool man.

"Excuse me. Would you all mind if I had a private word with *Captain Thompson* here?"

"Of course not," Eden replied pleasantly. Ivy could always count on that woman.

Ivy grabbed Gage by the forearm and marched him across the beach, stopping only when they were well out of earshot and well hidden from view by craggy rocks and tall grass.

Another grin lit the man's face. My, but he was charming. If she was not careful around him, he could get whatever he wanted whenever he wanted with a grin like that.

Suddenly, he was leaning forward, and he was kissing her. She almost gave in. Almost. But Ivy forced herself to pull away.

"What do you think you are doing?"

He leaned his head back and let out a ruthless chuckle. Why, she could just...

"I believe that is called kissing, my dear. And it is quite the pleasant pastime. Isn't that why you dragged me back here, out of view?" He winked.

Her face heated. *Wicked man.*

"You know full well that is not why I *invited* you over here. I wanted to have a word with you."

"Yes, dear?"

Ivy was going to hit him over the head if he called her one of those endearing terms one more time. This was not the time or place for such things. "Are you really planning on leaving Emma alone with the child? Why, he can only be five years old."

Gage shrugged, but she saw a shadow pass over his face before he answered. "I believe Reed turned six recently, actually." Ivy had to restrain herself from making a horrifyingly unladylike snorting sound. "Ah, don't worry, dear one. Reed has been practically taking care of himself the last few years. Before Eden came, Caspian didn't know what to do with him. He can certainly take care of himself. He's a good boy. Besides, we will only be gone for a short amount of time. It is not like it is overnight or anything." He offered her a reassuring smile.

Never in her entire time of knowing this man had she ever wanted to smack that smile off his face. Until today. She loved Gage, but what on earth was he thinking?

"Gage, he may be capable of taking care of himself, but certainly not himself and a baby!"

He squeezed her hand. "Caspian and Eden seem to think he will be fine. Listen, sweetheart, this should not take a long time for us to decide. Reed will be all right with Emma."

Ivy knitted her eyebrows together. "Fine then. You and Eden and your sister and everyone can go. I will stay here with the children."

※

That would never work. When would he get a chance to propose to her if he left her here with the children? Besides, he couldn't bear to part with her. No, she would be with him and he would be with his friends. And the children would be all right staying at the beach alone. Especially if Caspian and Eden believed they would be safe. There was really no questioning that.

"Ivy, you are coming with me whether you come along peacefully or if I have to carry you like a parcel."

A frown line formed on her forehead. Her steel gray eyes shot fire at him. A becoming blush painted her cheeks pink. Her lips were scrunched together. She was cute when she was angry. "Gage, if I come with you, then who will take care of Emma and Reed?"

He heaved out a sigh. "Reed can take care of himself and Emma. Really, we should hurry up and decide what we are going to do. The others are waiting for us."

Her little hands curved into balls. He couldn't hold back a chuckle. Maybe Ivy had spent too much time with Addie already. She was turning out to be quite the little spitfire, not the meek caretaker she had appeared to be the first time he had met her.

"All right. But if anything happens to them..." She raised a copper eyebrow in defiance.

He grinned. "Nothing will happen to them, milady. Besides, don't forget about God. He will watch over them."

She offered him a small smile. "That is true. Sometimes it is hard for me to remember I am not responsible for everything and everyone."

Gage laughed and gathered her into his arms, stealing one last quick kiss.

Well, he had intended for the kiss to be quick, but by the time they stopped, a large amount of time seemed to have passed. With flushed cheeks, they peeked around the tall grasses they had stepped behind to find the rest of the group waiting and staring at them. Ivy pressed her fingers to her cheeks to cool them off. Gage groaned inwardly. His friends probably all knew what he and Ivy had been doing while out of their view.

Gage cleared his throat. "The children can stay here."

Reed let out a joyous cry.

Caspian patted his son on the shoulder. "Reed, just be careful not to go into the water. Emma doesn't know how to swim, and you are not big enough to save her if she accidentally falls in."

Ivy's hand gripped Gage's. My, but the woman had a strong grip. And sharp nails. He winced.

"Of course, Papa." Reed smiled up at the adults.

"Very good. Well, shall we get going then?" Caspian took his wife's arm.

Gage needed a chance to talk to Ivy alone. "Yes. But why don't you all go on ahead? Ivy wants to say something to Emma before we go. It should only take a few moments. We can catch up."

Her nails dug deeper into his arm. He almost allowed a yelp to escape his throat.

"We can wait. I don't mind at all." Eden smiled up at Gage, and then darted a questioning look at her friend, Ivy. Gage glanced at the woman out of the side of his eye for himself. She was staring at him, dumbfounded. And she was angry. And beautiful.

"No, no. She said she would rather do it privately. I will wait here for her. You all go on ahead."

Something hard ran into the side of his ankle, almost causing it to buckle. He glanced down. The blasted woman had kicked him!

"Oh... all right. We will head towards town, then." The group set off in the other direction. After they were out of earshot, Ivy tugged him down closer to her level.

He laughed. "It is not nice to kick people, my sweet."

Fury flashed in her eyes as she raised her little foot once more. He jumped out of the way. She huffed. "What was it that I 'wanted to say' to the children, anyway?"

Gage scanned the beach for the little ones. Reed was sitting a few feet away from the water's reach, digging in the sand with Emma. Just like Caspian had said, they would be all right.

"I apologize, milady, but I cannot seem to remember what you were going to say to them." He winked and flashed her a grin.

Her lips set into a firm line. "This is not amusing, Captain. What was it you wanted?" She raised an eyebrow.

"This." He leaned down and planted a kiss on a tender spot of her neck. Immediately at his touch, she relaxed. And then grew angry again.

"This is not the time or place for you to... to waste time... *kissing me.*" She whispered the last two words.

"You enjoy it, though."

She crossed her arms across her chest and mumbled something he could not understand.

"What's that, darling?" He drew her close with an arm at her waist. He needed to stop teasing her. That was not why he had stayed behind with her.

"I may enjoy it, but we must catch up with our friends."

Ha! She had admitted she enjoyed it. Gage dipped his face down and kissed her once more. The woman pulled away. "Gage..."

"Hmm?"

Egad, but she was beautiful. The wind had battered her hair, allowing some glorious strands of orange to fall loose around her pretty face. Her cheeks were perfectly pink, and her lips swollen from his kiss.

She leaned down and grabbed something, but Gage could not keep his head clear enough to see it. Oh well. It didn't matter. He ran a hand along the length of her waist.

Suddenly, a fistful of sand hit him in the stomach. Ivy's eyes widened in... amusement? He glanced down. The little rascal of a woman had thrown it at him herself! Well, he could throw sand, too.

Determined, Gage stooped down low, scooped up a handful of sand, and flung it at Ivy. She stared at him in shock before bursting out in laughter. Gage laughed, too. The woman dove downwards to grab more sand. Smack! It hit him square in the chest. He dodged her next assault, and got some sand in her hair on his next attempt.

After a few more turns, he caught her by shoulder. She fell into his arms, giggling uncontrollably. Gage loved the sound more than anything he had ever heard in his entire life. Finally, she sighed and leaned her head against his chest. He glanced down at her. They were both filthy. "I'm sorry I got your dress dirty."

She pulled back and looked him in the eyes. "I don't care, Gage." She reached up on the tops of her toes and pressed a kiss against his cheek. He looped an arm around her waist once more and softly kissed her pink lips.

"Ivy, my dear... I have been meaning to ask you a question for a few days now." He pulled away a fraction of an inch, enough to feel in his pocket. Yes, the ring was still there. Nervous excitement bubbled in his stomach.

Her eyes widened in... hope? Something warm spread throughout his body.

"Oh? What did you want to ask me, Gage?"

"Uncle Gage! You had better hurry. Mama and Papa and the rest are probably missing you." Gage swung his gaze to Reed, who still sat with Emma.

Had the child been watching them this whole time? He prayed not.

Gage groaned. The little guy was right, though. He had no idea how long they had been gone. He squeezed Ivy's hand. "We had better get going. You are right."

Ivy moved toward town with him, but stopped and faced the children. "You two take care of yourselves, all right? I trust you with Emma, Reed."

"Of course!" Came Reed's cheery reply.

CHAPTER 27

It took Ivy and Gage nearly a quarter of an hour to catch up with the rest of their group—and that was after walking the entire time at a breakneck pace. How long had they been missing? Why, it was all that stupid, charming, sweet man's fault. Before they were in sight of their friends, Ivy stopped to brush sand from the dress Eden had loaned her. The woman had taken pity on her and offered her a few gowns, and here Ivy was, ruining them with sand.

Gage's eyebrows shot up, nearly to his hairline, before he did the same. After a moment, he paused and inspected her. "You've got some here..." His hand reached out toward her head and gently brushed sand away from her hair. Ivy's cheeks heated. She was the one who had started their little sand fight. Why, she should be embarrassed. It was utterly unladylike. A glance out of the corner of her eye told her Gage didn't care she had acted out of hand. In fact, he looked quite pleased.

What was it he was going to ask her earlier at the beach? It was probably nothing important, yet Ivy was desperate to find out. His gaze met hers and his eyes darkened. He reached out and took her hand in his. "I think we are mostly free of the sand now, my dear."

"There you are!"

Ivy squinted against the sunlight. Eden and the rest of the group had spun around and were heading towards her and Gage.

"We were wondering what had kept you," Caspian said.

"Oh, nothing. We just took the wrong street and had to turn around after a while when we were looking for you." Ivy bit her tongue. She had not meant to lie, but she certainly did not want her friends to know she had been kissing Gage and getting into a sand-throwing fight with him!

Gage squeezed her hand. She tugged away. Had the others not noticed how much hand-holding was happening between her and this charming man?

"We decided to walk near the docks. I wanted to look at all of the ships there," Eden explained as they continued their way further down the street towards the bay.

Charles Town was certainly no match for London, but it seemed to be slightly larger than Port Royal and somewhat more civilized. Of course, that could be because they were visiting in the late morning hours. Most of the ruffians were probably still abed, sleeping off last night's escapades.

Eden slowed until she walked at Ivy's side. The boardwalk they were on was too narrow for three to walk side by side, so Gage was forced behind them. That was probably a good thing. Knowing him, he would find a way to brush his hand against hers until he held it. Not that she would stop him, though. Oh, what was she going to do about this man? And Emma? Gage was certainly correct when he said Emma needed a father. And truly, she wanted him to be that man. Wanted them to be a family. Wanted it more than anything.

"So, how have you enjoyed your voyage with Captain Thompson so far?" Eden sidled closer to Ivy. Had she been able to tell what Ivy was thinking? Surely not...

"Oh... it was as good as can be expected. I did not enjoy the storm we sailed through one bit, or when I helped take over command of the ship... or any of the other troubles we ran into along the way."

"A storm? You had to *command* the ship?" Eden tugged on Ivy's arm.

"Yes, those are stories meant for another day. But I have dearly appreciated the company throughout the voyage." She glanced over her shoulder at Gage. He was listening to their conversation. His gaze warmed as it caught hers, and he winked. That alone sent her heart rapidly fluttering.

Eden also glanced backwards and realized they had an audience. She blushed and squeezed Ivy's arm. "Sorry. We will talk about that another time," she whispered.

§

Gage stepped ahead of the ladies in front of him so he walked next to Caspian. His friend thumped him on the shoulder. Gage grinned. "How is married life treating you, Captain?"

The man's face brightened. "Perfectly, I must say. Eden has been a blessing to me in many ways. To Reed, as well. I had never realized how desperately my child needed a mother in his life."

Something tugged on Gage's heart. He had never had a true father as he was growing up, so he knew what it was like to be missing a parent. In fact, he knew what it was like to be missing both parents ever since his mother died, leaving him and Addie to fend for themselves.

Of course, Caspian's parents had taken them in, but that family had never felt like a complete family. Now, Reed had a mother. And Emma needed a complete family herself. The weight of the ring in his pocket suddenly seemed like a boulder. He needed to ask Ivy to be his wife. By the stars, they might as well get married while they were here in town. As a captain, Caspian could even perform the ceremony.

"How is commanding a crew treating you, my man?" Caspian bumped Gage with his elbow.

"I have to admit, when I first began, I did not have what it takes to be a good captain. But so many things have happened since then, I think I may just get used to it. Even though I liked serving under you, I always dreamed of having my own ship. Something to call my own." Maybe it was because he had always felt like he and Addie were a burden to whomever they stayed with. His only memories of Father were the tales his mother had told him, and she had never been pleased with the man. According to her, Father had never planned on having either of his children. They were a burden. Something he was forced to take care of. So, when Addie came along, he left without another word. After that, Gage was old enough to be able to tell that Mother struggled to feed them. When she died, they were a problem to everyone around them. Two orphans scrounging the streets of New Providence for food. Annoying shopkeepers. Getting in the way. Scouring the city for a dry place to sleep at night. And then when Caspian's parents had taken them in, they were yet again an encumbrance to the family. Gage had loved life on Caspian's ship, but yet again he was being taken care of by someone else. It felt good to have his own ship, to be in command of his life for once. Even if his abilities as a captain weren't nearly as accomplished as his friend's had been. He shook his head, trying to jostle those thoughts from it. A change of subject might help. "Ivy... Lady Shaw proved to be a nice captain, though."

Gage turned his head to wink at the precious woman. She was too deep in conversation with her friend to notice.

"Oh?" Caspian's eyebrows rose.

Gage chuckled. "Aye, she is. When I was too injured to even hold a conscious thought, she was not only mending me, but also taking charge of my rebellious crew with your brother-in-law."

The corners of Caspian's mouth tipped upwards in a smile. "Of course a woman like that would be my Eden's friend."

Gage leaned back his head and laughed. The man was correct. Now that he thought about it, he could easily see what characteristics had drawn Ivy and Eden together. And Ivy was—or soon would be, God-willing—his. Excitement coursed through his veins, tickling his insides. For the longest time, he had wanted nothing more than to have a wife and a family. Now, that goal was so close to his grasp. Yet another reason to get the precious woman alone with him for just a few minutes.

⚓

Reed Archer walked alongside Emma as she crawled through the sand. A seagull swooped down near them, but he batted it away with his hand. It wouldn't do for the creature to land on Emma. Then Mama and Papa might not ever trust him with a baby again. He wanted a baby sister or brother badly, so he guessed it would be wise to take good care of this baby. Maybe if he was really good with her, Mama and Papa would think about getting one for themselves.

Emma slowed down to poke at a shell. Reed stopped next to her, picked up the piece, and handed it to her. A smile stretched across her face. She only had a few teeth, but it was really cute on her. He leaned over and kissed her on the forehead, like Mama did to him before she tucked him into bed. The little girl was fixated on the shell. "You like that shell, huh, Emma?"

Reed glanced about the sand until he found another one. This one's insides were shiny. Emma giggled and pointed at the shell. After a few minutes, she set it down and continued crawling along the edge of the shore. Babies didn't seem to pay much attention to anything for a long time. Reed hurried to follow her. He glanced in the direction they had come from. The town wasn't visible from here anymore. All he could see was sand, the ocean, the tall grass that lined the shore, and the craggy pieces of rock that jutted into the sea.

Reed scrunched his face up in thought. Maybe he should stop Emma and turn her the other way. He had never been somewhere like this before, especially not alone. All of his life he had been on Papa's ship, or walking through town next to Papa, or on the beach with Papa. There did not seem to be any sign of any other people near him now. But he did not want to stop Emma and turn her around. She might get upset and start to cry. If he made Emma cry, then maybe Mama and Papa would think he was not ready to have a brother or sister.

Emma plopped down where she was. Good. If he could just trick her into turning around while she was sitting down, then she might not even know she was not crawling in the same direction when she started up again. She babbled something Reed couldn't understand. Reed had found could not understand most of what she said. Her little hand reached towards something that was moving behind him. What would be moving when he and Emma were the only people out here?

Reed spun around. Something made gurgling, grunting noises. Something that sounded like an animal. With a gasp, Reed nudged Emma behind him. The creature, whatever it was, pushed through the grasses, making them move as if wind swept around them. Emma grabbed onto Reed's leg. She seemed to sense the danger, also.

"You stay here, Emma," Reed whispered, gently removing the girl's hand from his leg. He moved forward and pushed aside some of the grass before poking his head through the opening. Three tiny animals sat on a mound of dirt, grunting. Their tiny tawny-brown bodies were striped with white and gray, and their little brown eyes barely opened. Reed laughed. That was what he was afraid of? Why, they were almost as cute as Emma!

If he was by himself, Reed would stoop down to pet the little critters. But he was with the baby, and he didn't want anything to happen to her, so he moved away. Just as something else rustled the tall grasses. Reed whipped back around and found himself face-to-face with a much bigger, much angrier, much less peaceful-looking version of the little creatures. One that bared its long, sharp teeth at him. It looked like a pig he had once seen at a plantation. Papa had told him about wild boars once, and Reed was afraid he stood right in front of one.

A tiny hand squeezed his leg. Emma. She whimpered. Reed felt like doing some whimpering of his own, but big boys didn't whimper. He would call out for help, but if he was too loud, maybe the boar would come charge at him. Maybe if he and Emma stood still long enough, it would leave them alone.

No. The creature roared, and then charged straight toward them, teeth bared. Sharp teeth.

As fast as he could, Reed bent down, grabbed Emma, and ran down the beach. My, but the little baby was heavy. He had held her before on Mr. Thompson's ship, but he had been sitting down then. Now, he was picking her up and moving as fast as he could. A glance over his shoulder told Reed the wild boar was still in pursuit. Practically on his heels.

"Emma, hold on tight."

She babbled something back but Reed felt her grip tighten. Something sharp slashed at his legs. Reed cried out. He stumbled and almost fell smack on his face in the sand. Hot tears trailed down his cheeks. He couldn't help it if he wasn't a big boy. This *hurt.*

Something thick and warm slid down his legs from the place the animal's teeth had struck. Blood. Despite the stinging, Reed surged forward. The shore sped by in a blur.

Where could he go? The animal continued to follow him at a breakneck pace.

"Papa! Mama! Uncle Gage!" His voice cracked on a sob. "Please help us!"

Reed's foot caught on a large piece of rock, and this time he lost his balance. He crashed onto the sand. Luckily, Emma landed on top of him so he didn't crush her. The boar approached quickly. He needed to think fast.

A large piece of driftwood rested near his head. Reed frantically grasped for it, but his hand only hit the empty sand. The boar was practically right behind them. "Help!" Reed got ahold of the driftwood and hefted it over his head as he struggled to a sitting position. He whacked the boar square on the snout with the chunk of brittle wood.

The blow did little to thwart the beast, but at least it slowed its pace a little. Reed surged to his feet as he tried his hardest to balance Emma in his arms. He shot forward and scanned the beach for a way out, for any way to get away from this animal that seemed intent on killing him and the baby.

The creature whirled back to her babies, but then continued towards Reed and Emma again. She seemed to be going even faster now than she had been before.

The rocks. The craggy rocks that jutted out into the ocean, high above the water. Reed sped to them. In fact, they seemed to be made like a staircase, the highest point stopping a far distance out into the ocean. Maybe it was a staircase built by God just for him and Emma. But the tide was coming in, and already some of the lowest sections were covered with water. Maybe Reed could run through it, though. He glanced behind. The boar still followed closely, but twisted back to her piglets once more. The rocks were his only hope.

Reed leapt straight into the ocean. The saltwater stung the scratches on his legs. He couldn't help but cry out again. Emma's tiny, chubby arms wrapped around his neck. Her little blue eyes were large with terror as Reed threw out a hand to grab onto the next piece of rock. Water lapped at his waist. It was moving so fast, it threatened to pull Reed and Emma out into the ocean. Papa had taught him about currents. The waves were deadly when the tide came in.

Reed hefted all of his weight forward and pulled himself out of the water, up onto the next layer of rock. Emma began to wail loudly. Reed paused to catch his breath, but not for long. The water swirled at his feet, further soaking his boots. A glance forward told him he had a long way to climb before getting to the highest point of this outcropping. A sharp piece of rock slashed his hand. After a few more steps, his right foot landed in a puddle that grew deeper by the second. He slipped and almost plummeted straight into the swirling water.

Tears streamed down his face. He had tried to behave like a big boy. He had tried his hardest. And now his legs hurt. More badly than anything had ever hurt before. And he and Emma might not live. A sob tore from his throat. Reed had promised his parents and Mr. Thompson and Mr. Thompson's lady friend he would take care of Emma. That he and Emma would be safe.

Reed glanced behind him. The wild boar had stopped at the water, and now looked a thousand times more disinterested in him and the baby. Good. A sigh of relief heaved from his lungs.

Fierce water swirled about his ankles. Reed bit his lip and continued climbing upward, seeking safety. He prayed the water wouldn't cover the highest point of the rock staircase.

CHAPTER 28

Addie studied Mr. Douglas, or Lord Trenton, as she supposed his real name was, through lowered lashes. She regretted nothing more than their last conversation, when she had been terribly rude and he had been terribly polite, considering the thoughtless things she had said to him. What did he think of her? Most likely nothing well.

She was also incredibly aware of how close he was as they strolled down the narrow sidewalk. Their shoulders occasionally bumped, sending sparks flying through Addie's body. She wondered if Adam felt the same sensation.

What was she thinking? She had no desire to bring another man into her life. Ever. It was out of the question. Even recently, she had been betrayed by her former employer, Mr. Faulke, when he had planned to hire another woman to replace her at her job. Men had a long history of being useless to her. There was no way she wanted to deal with another one of the inadequate species.

"Mrs. Poole?"

Addie's face heated. Now he was *talking* to her? *And* he was calling her by her married name. She was not certain she could handle that. A groan escaped her lips. "Yes, mister?"

"I am really, truly sorry for spilling the tea on you. It was an accident." He reached out and grabbed her hand in a gentle gesture. "I hope your hand is healing well." Addie glanced down, where his hand still held hers. Her skin was slightly pink, but there was hardly even a mark left from the hot liquid.

"Mr. Douglas, I know it was an accident. I wanted to apologize for how poorly I treated you." The words were hard for her to admit, but it was right of her to apologize.

He swallowed hard. "Mrs. Poole..." Then cleared his throat. "Do you prefer to be called Mrs. Poole or Miss Thompson, milady?"

"Miss Thompson, I beg you, sir."

He nodded. "Miss Thompson, you did not treat me poorly."

Addie clenched her hands into fists. Only then did she realize Mr. Douglas still held her hand in his. She jerked it away. "I did treat you poorly. I was sitting there whining about hot tea spilling on my hand, when you... when you..." A sob in her throat tore her voice away. This poor man. She could not imagine what it would be like to be so scarred for the rest of her life.

"When I what, Miss Thompson?" He straightened to his full height. His voice rose. "When I was burned? When I was foolish enough to stand next to a building that exploded right at me? When my entire left side was scarred?" He gestured wildly to his face. "No, milady. It was not fair you complained about the tea to me. But *I don't care.* So stop worrying about me."

Tears wetted Addie's eyes. She felt her chin quiver. A deep breath failed to steady her.

"Mr. Douglas?" Gage's voice sliced through the air.

Addie brushed the tears from her eyes with the backs of her hands and spun to face her brother. Captain Thompson, Captain Archer and his wife, and Ivy had all stopped and were staring at Addie and Mr. Douglas. Heat crept up her neck.

Gage stepped between Addie and Mr. Douglas, nudging her behind him. "What is going on here?"

"I-I apologize, sir." Adam ducked his head.

"Nothing is going on, Gage." Addie grabbed her brother from behind. He shrugged off her arm gently.

"Then why are you crying, sister? I trust Adam... he has been my closest friend on my ship since he signed on, but if he made you cry..." Gage's jaw clenched. Ivy came up and rested a hand on Gage's arm. His body loosened, but he still was as angry as Addie had ever seen him.

"Gage, this is not anything to worry about. Please do not concern yourself." Addie tapped her foot on the ground.

Gage stepped closer to Mr. Douglas. Although Douglas was a tall man, Gage still was taller than him by an inch or two. Panic swept through Addie. Her brother would not punch a man, would he? "Why did you make my sister cry?"

"I am sorry, Captain. I was careless in what I said." He nodded to Addie. "I hope you will accept my most sincere apology, Miss Thompson."

"Mr. Douglas, you did not say anything that upset me. I don't know why I started crying. I have not cried in years. If anything, I was just upset with myself." Addie laid a hand on Mr. Douglas's arm. He nodded and offered her a half smile.

"Well, I do not want to see you upset her ever again."

"Gage!" Addie swung her fist into her brother's arm. He yelped, and caught her fist in his hand.

Adam offered her brother a friendly smile, but his gaze seemed fixated on nothing but Addie. "I will not, Captain. You have my word."

§

Gage felt like punching the man square across the jaw. Addie had always been the one person that made him feel at home his entire life. She was his only true family left. And when he saw she had been hurt, he certainly wanted to hurt the man who made her feel that way, even if that man had been his closest confidant for the past few weeks. Adam may be a friend, but hurting his sister was not a thing for a friend to do.

He shook his head. Really, he was overreacting. Addie was fine. Adam had not done anything to hurt her. There was nothing wrong.

Caspian clapped Gage on the back, and then slung an arm around his wife's waist and continued forward down the sidewalk. Gage sped to catch up with them.

Ivy's hand landed on his elbow and slid down to his hand. Gage took a deep breath. The side of her skirt brushed against his trouser leg, making him even more aware of the ring in his pocket. He needed to get this woman alone for once so he could propose.

For a few moments, they walked forward in silence.

"The weather is lovely today, is it not?" Eden murmured, glancing back at the rest of the group.

Gage grunted.

Addie mumbled some pleasantry.

"Yes, it is. And I love the chance to walk on land again. I have been on a ship far too long in the recent past," Ivy spoke up.

Gage furrowed his brow. He hoped she did not dislike sailing too much. Of course, once they were married, they would settle somewhere so they had a house to live in, but Gage needed to continue his privateering if they wanted any money to live off of. And he was not about to leave his wife home alone while he was out sailing. No, she would go on his voyages with him like Eden did with Caspian. If she wanted to. Hopefully she did not mind. He really needed to hurry up and propose to her so they could actually discuss all of this. They would probably need to take regular trips to London so she could see her family, but that was not a problem for Gage as long as she was happy.

He stopped in his tracks so suddenly that Addie bumped into his back in an effort to slow down. "Ivy and I are going to go check on the children. We can meet you all at the docks. I think I know of a shorter way to get there from the beach, so we can easily get back to you in time."

"What?"

Gage gently nudged Ivy in the side before she could say she had never discussed going back to check on the children. She seemed to take the hint and closed her mouth.

Caspian and Eden turned around. "If it will make you feel better, you can. But I am certain they are all right."

Eden smiled. "Reed is a good, smart boy. He will be able to take care of himself and little Emma."

"Thank you, but I think we will check on them. Just to be sure."

Ivy gazed up at him prettily, her stone-gray eyes wide in question. He offered her a wink.

⚓

"I never said we needed to go back and check on the children. Granted, I was worried about Emma, but as you and so many people have told me, Eden's son is responsible enough to handle the situation." Ivy picked up the powder-blue skirt she had borrowed from Eden and sped up to catch up with Gage as he charged through the streets of Charles Town.

The man let out a long, low groan, whirled around, and grabbed her around the waist. He lowered his mouth to hers and suddenly he was kissing her there, right in the middle of the town. Ivy's arm made its way up to his shoulder and rested against his chest. She only pulled away when some bystanders whistled. She had not realized there were people watching. Ivy gently slapped the side of his arm. "You cannot keep kissing me like that when people are watching!"

He chuckled and tucked her hand in his elbow. "I needed some way to stop you from babbling and babbling on, my dear."

Ivy resisted the urge to roll her eyes. He had dragged her away from her friends yet again, and for what? Why did he keep doing this to her?

They walked a ways out of town, toward the beach. There was no sign of Reed and Emma nearby, but they had probably just wandered off to the other side of the grasses. Gage halted in his tracks and faced her.

"What is it you wanted, Gage?"

He opened his mouth as if he intended to speak, and then closed it. Then he scrubbed his hands over his face. Shoved a hand in his pocket. Took a deep breath. "Ivy... I've been trying to ask you this question for a long time."

Her breath halted in her throat.

"And I figured it is about time I finally go about doing it."

"Yes?"

His face bloomed red. He opened his mouth and closed it again. "Ivy, I feel like I am bumbling like an idiot in front of you, but I don't know what exactly to say. I never seem to have the right words to use when I am around you."

"Oh, Gage... you do not bumble around me." She laid a hand on his arm. The poor man. He was really endearing when he got embarrassed like this.

"Well, I do sometimes. But what I am trying to say is—"

"Papa! Help!" The voice garbled. "Mama!" A cry rent the air.

⚓

Shock sucked the breath from Gage's lungs. That was Reed's voice. Reed was in trouble, and if Reed was in trouble, then where was Emma?

"Reed? Where are you?"

"Help me!"

Gage sprang forward, jogging across the beach. Ivy followed right on his heels. If he had time to think, he would have admired how quickly she could move in all those skirts.

His gaze landed on the ocean. The water was moving rapidly.

The tide was coming in.

Dread raced through his heart. "Reed! Are you in the water? Can you hear me?"

"Mr. Thompson?" The child's voice sounded ragged, as if he were gasping for breath. *Please, Lord, don't let him be in the water. Not with Emma, too.*

Oh Lord, where is Emma?

With the strength of the tide, there would be almost no chance of locating them and bringing them back to safety.

"Reed, answer me right now! Where are you?"

"Emma!" Gage spared a second to look at his woman. She was sobbing, her voice raw. He did not have a moment to spare to comfort her, or he would. Truth was, he was pretty near sobbing himself.

"Mr. Thompson? I'm out on these rocks. The water keeps coming faster and faster. I can't hold Emma this high much longer, Mr. Thompson. You need to come save us."

You need to come save us. Worry nibbled at Gage. He had never been the one to save someone. Caspian had always been the stronger man. The better captain. Well, now Caspian was not here. It was quite possible Reed and Emma's lives rested in his hands.

"Gage. Go!" Ivy shoved him from behind. He surged forward once more. The tall grasses of the beach blurred by as he ran. How far had the children gotten?

Ivy let out a horrified screech. "Stop!"

Gage strained against her grip on his arm. What on earth was the woman thinking? Reed had said he needed help, now.

He shook his arm. "What is wrong with you?" He hadn't intended for that to sound like a growl.

She pointed straight ahead of them. A wild boar faced them with bared fangs.

"Mr. Thompson!" Reed might as well have been in the middle of the ocean, perched on a jagged rock, Emma balanced in his arms. The moment Emma saw him and Ivy, she wiggled, kicked her legs, reached her arms out, and wailed as Reed screamed once more, "Mr. Thompson, please help us!"

The child must have run off onto the jagged bar of land to escape the boar, and the tide had come in behind him and was still rising. Well, Gage could try to go out and rescue them, but he was not about to leave Ivy alone on the beach with an angry wild animal. Maybe if he just waited for Caspian to come, everything would be all right.

"Gage, you need to do something. Now. The water is rising. I don't know if Reed can stay there much longer with the waves crashing against his legs. Go save them!" Ivy shoved him forward.

God, help me. I am not going to abandon my woman on this shore without any protection from that beast. But I cannot leave the children to get carried off by the current of the ocean. I don't trust myself to save them on my own. I'm never good enough. Never strong enough. Let Caspian come. Adam, even. I don't trust myself.

Tears sprang into his eyes, but he quickly battled them back. What kind of man was he?

You are good enough for me. Trust me.

Gage sucked in a deep breath. He had been telling Ivy this whole voyage to place her trust in God. Maybe it was about time he trusted God enough to give him the strength to do what he needed to do.

His gun. His gun! Why had he not thought of that before? He knew why, though. Because he had been too paralyzed with fear to even hold a rational thought.

"Gage, you need to *help them!*"

Gage drew the pistol from his waistband. Caspian and common sense had taught him to carry the firearm with him nearly everywhere he went, and he was certainly glad he had today. He aimed at the sand next to the boar, and fired a shot.

The animal let out a roar and leapt closer to him. Panic surged through his veins. He did not want to kill the creature. It might have piglets, and the little ones could not go without a parent.

Still, the boar charged straight at him. Ivy screeched. It shoved at her legs with its head, and caught her skirt between its teeth. "Gage!"

The boar's piglets would have to do without their mother if it intended to hurt Ivy.

Gage reloaded his pistol with wavering hands, but quickly tried to steady himself as he aimed far away enough from the boar to not kill it, and fired. It hit the animal in the hoof. The creature let out a cry and jerked backwards. After a moment, it ran until it was completely out of view, yelping with each step. Ivy struggled to her feet and appeared unharmed. Gage's legs nearly collapsed out from underneath him with the relief that coursed through his body. But that quickly faded when he heard the children's whimpering. He longed to take Ivy in his arms and comfort her, to make sure she was not injured, but he needed to go out there and save Reed and Emma.

"Stay here, Ivy."

CHAPTER 29

The second Gage faced away from her, Ivy sank down onto the sand. Her head hurt. She had been so terrified when the boar had charged straight at her. And it was not over by any means. No, now she was terrified for Emma and Gage and Reed.

God, please help him. Please let him save my child. Our child. Even though Emma had not been born to her and Gage, she was still every bit theirs.

Gage strode into the water as if the waves crashing against his legs did not affect him one bit. He continued at an angle toward the raised strip of boulders where Reed had perched himself with Emma.

The water reached Gage's waist, and soon his body tugged back and forth with the force of the current. He must have lost his footing, for he suddenly slipped to the side and his head almost went under. Gage quickly righted himself and spun around. "Reed? I'm going to have to go back and take my boots off. They're getting in the way. I will be right back and I promise I will get you and Emma down, all right?"

Reed whimpered, and Ivy felt like doing the same. She would help Gage, but she had never been in the water before. She had no idea how to swim. Her help would probably only cause more trouble. Although her body itched to go take the situation into her own hands, common sense told her to stay back and trust God and Gage to save Emma and Reed.

Gage made it back to shore and shucked his boots and his weapons. Ivy cringed. He must have not been thinking when he charged straight into the water. His gunpowder was probably wet now and they had nothing to defend themselves with if the wild boar came back. Soon he was back in the ocean, heading towards Reed and Emma with a determined look on his face.

He met a wave head-on, lunging forward to break some of its force.

"Mr. Thompson! I don't know if I can stay up here much longer. I-I'm just so tired."

It hurt Ivy's heart to see the poor dear so upset. Her little Emma was crying, too. *Oh God, please help Gage. Please let him get those children safely back here soon.* Ivy wished she had paid more attention when they were out on the beach yesterday. Had the tide completely covered the rock Reed was perched on, or did it stop short of it? If the tide reached Reed and Emma before Gage did, they could be swept away and it would be far more difficult to rescue them.

"Hang in there, little man. I'll get to you in just a moment." Gage had made it to the wall of rocks. He reached up and grabbed a rock that jutted out, and then propelled himself upward. A wave crashed against his body, but he shook off the water and continued on, scaling the wall. The water rapidly filled up the narrow strip of rock that led to the children.

Gage finally made it to the top of the stack of boulders. He crouched at the summit and carefully stood up, keeping his balance against the surging water. "Reed, can you move over to me very slowly?"

"N-no. I'm afraid. I know I should be a big boy, but I'm not. I'm afraid, Uncle Gage."

"Reed, I know you are afraid. It's all right to be afraid, little man. You just stay right where you are, then, and I will come get you." Gage moved forward with agonizingly slow speed.

He was just feet away from the children now. Only a few more steps.

Please.

A huge wave surged up from behind the rocks. Reed swung an arm out, blindly grasping for something to hold onto. Something to catch him. In his other hand, he clutched little Emma against his chest.

Ivy could not hold back a cry. Gage froze in his path.

Reed fell backward into the swirling water.

"Reed!" Gage jumped forward, straight into the ocean. Reed went under with a wave. Gage's body lurched to the side. Soon, his head disappeared under the surf also.

Panic surged through Ivy. Her heart seemed to stop. "Gage!" She pitched forward, straight into an incoming wave. Ivy didn't care. Gage, her child, and Eden's child were all underwater, battling the violent waves.

The water rose around her at an alarming rate as she made her way toward Gage. His head had not surfaced yet. Shouldn't he have come up already?

Oh God.

"Gage!"

Her boot caught on something under the water. She kicked it free and continued on. The water reached her waist and the current tugged at her, but she continued. Maybe if she could get up to the rocks, Gage would be able to grab ahold of her hand and pull himself back up to safety.

"Gage!" Her throat was raw from tears.

A dark mass moved toward her from under the water. She could not quite make it out underneath the froth of the ever-moving waves, but she knew enough about the sea to guess it was a shark. *Oh no. It probably killed the children or Gage. Or both.*

Tears blurring her eyes, she dodged to the side. "Someone help me!"

She almost made it to the slippery wall of rocks. Something grabbed her ankle. A... hand. Well, sharks didn't have hands.

Gage's head popped above the water, followed by his shoulders and... Reed and Emma, circled in his arms.

Ivy nearly collapsed with relief, but she forced herself to remain standing. She was not about to give poor Gage yet another person to go rescuing. "Oh, thank God, you are all right."

But his face was grim.

"What's wrong, Gage?"

He nodded down at Reed and pushed past her, straight to the beach. "He's not all right, Ivy." Although he tried to steady his voice, Ivy could sense the tremor of terror in it.

Gage reached the shore with Ivy close on his heels. Ivy squeezed her eyes shut against a wave of nausea. Reed was not okay. Eden's son was not okay.

"Take Emma."

Ivy grabbed the child and held her soaking wet body tight against hers in an effort to keep her warm. She checked to make certain the girl was breathing properly. The little one seemed frightened, but all right. There were no visible injuries or setbacks. Not so for Reed. Gage gingerly set the boy down on the dry sand.

Reed's face was washed over with a bluish tint. Ivy sucked in a breath of shock. Would... would he be all right?

"Can you hear me, little man?" Gage shook the child's shoulders. He failed to respond.

Gage leaned down and put his mouth to Reed's, breathing air into his lungs. He pulled back after a long stretch. "Come on, little man."

Nothing happened. Ivy's heart sank.

Gage moved to face her. Tears streamed down his face, mingling with the ocean water. He shook his head. *No! God, please. This child means everything to Eden and her husband. Please.*

Ivy fell into Gage's arms.

A scratching sound met her ears. Coughing. *Coughing?* She glanced down at Reed's limp little body. He was coughing!

Gage, hope lighting his chocolate brown eyes, rotated the child onto his side. Water poured out of his mouth. After another fit of coughing, his violet-blue eyes opened. Ivy had never been happier to see someone's eyes in her entire life.

"I kept Emma above the water." Concern drew tight lines on Reed's small face.

"Aye, that you did, little man. That you did. Emma is all right." Gage drew the boy into his arms, laughing in relief.

Ivy wrapped her hand around the child's small hand. "Reed, we were so worried about you."

He pushed himself until he was sitting up, facing the two adults. "I am all right. Where are Mama and Papa?"

"They are still in town. Did you want to see them?" Gage brushed a wet lock of hair off of the boy's forehead.

"Oh, I can wait. I don't want them to worry about me or think I can't take care of a little sibling."

"All right, little man. I'm proud of you, do you know that?"

Reed's face brightened into a smile as Gage hugged him.

After a moment, Gage leaned backwards and pulled Ivy and Emma with him until they were lying back against the sand. He slung an arm around Ivy's shoulders. She leaned her head against his chest. "Ivy?" He trailed a finger along the inside of her arm.

"Yes?" She closed her eyes against the soft glare of the afternoon sun.

"By fire and thunder, what were you doing running out into the ocean?"

"I... I couldn't see you. I was not going to stay safe and dry on the shore while you and Reed and our... Emma drowned."

Gage inhaled a long breath. "How did you expect to save us when you don't even know how to swim?"

Ivy stiffened. "How do you know I do not know how to swim?"

"Because I know you, and if you knew how to swim, you would have run in front of me to go save the children yourself before I even got a chance to do it myself. Besides, I know Eden never used to know how to swim. I figured you would not, either."

"Well, you are correct. But I would have found some way to get to you."

He leaned to the side and pressed a kiss against her nose. "I am glad you did not have to, my dear."

§

Gage twisted his head to the side and kissed Ivy's cheek. The freshness of citrus engulfed him like a pleasant, heady sort of perfume. He smiled. Oh, how he loved this woman. Emma crawled over from Ivy's arms until she rested on his stomach. He patted the dripping wet tyke on the back. They all were in desperate need of some towels and a change of clothes, but that would have to wait.

Ivy's soft hand wrapped around his. The dear woman was soaked from head to toe as well. He twisted a lock of her copper hair around his finger. Most of it had tumbled down from the blasted bun she always tied it up in. Well, he would not get caught complaining about that.

Her stormy gray eyes met his and they were filled with such admiration that his heart seemed to cease beating altogether. He propped himself up with an elbow against the sand, leaned over her, and lowered his lips to hers. She made a soft noise at the back of her throat and tore her hand from his, only to wrap both her arms around his shoulders. Gage took that as an invitation to deepen the kiss and run a hand through her beautiful orange curls. She moved a hand up and down his arm.

He pulled back and rested his forehead against hers. She tasted like salty water, but it was the most pleasant flavor he had ever tasted. Just as he leaned in for another kiss, a small hand landed on his back. "Hey, Uncle Gage? Are you gonna marry Lady Shaw? Because if you are kissing her like that, I think you should marry her. It's what my Mama and Papa did."

Gage immediately pried himself away from Ivy and stood. Why, he had all but forgotten they were not alone while he was busy kissing the woman senseless. He knew his face was turning red, but maybe not as red as Ivy's. She also stood, balancing Emma against her hip as she brushed sand off of her skirts. It was no use, though. They would all have to wait until their clothes were dry to get the sand off of them.

The woman was going to wear a hole in her skirt if he did not stop her soon. "Ivy."

Her hand stilled.

"Look at me."

She looked at his chin.

"Look at me in the eyes, my sweet."

Her gaze made it to the bottom of his nose.

"Ivy."

Finally, her eyes met his.

"I have been meaning to ask you something for a while now."

She swallowed.

"And little Reed here just reminded me what that question is."

⚓

Ivy's heart jumped into her throat. Was Gage really going to ask her what she was thinking he was going to ask her?

The charming man bent down on one knee. The sun brought out the bronze streaks in his hair and the golden flecks in his chocolate brown eyes. Those eyes regarded her with such admiration and adoration that Ivy's stomach twittered with pleasure. This man, this wonderful man, was looking at *her* in such a kind way.

"Ivy, my dear, I love you. I have loved you ever since I first saw you on Captain Emery's ship that day you came running to save your friend. I love you more than I ever thought I would be able to love, and I would be honored to call you my wife." He pulled an engraved silver ring out of his pocket. A small clear gem sat in the center of it.

Excitement coursed through her. "Gage, I love you, too." She crouched down until she was resting on her knees before him. "I want nothing more than to marry you."

His face brightened with a large smile. He winked, and then leaned forward and pressed a soft kiss against her lips. Finally, he pulled back, grabbed her hand, and slipped the ring on her finger. And then burst out in laughter.

Ivy raised an eyebrow. "Is it funny that I agreed to marry you, sir?"

He pulled her against his chest. "Ivy, my beautiful, beautiful betrothed, it does not amuse me that you agreed to marry me. I was laughing because I have spent the entire day desperately trying to propose to you because I was afraid the ring would not fit you properly and we would need to get a silversmith to fit to your size while we were still in Charles Town. But it fits you perfectly."

Ivy pressed a kiss against his jaw. Although he had probably shaved this morning, stubble scratched her lips. "I could not be happier, Gage. And I want our wedding to be soon."

Reed gasped. "My Papa is a captain so he is allowed to marry people. He could marry you both tonight."

Gage beamed, allowing Ivy a glimpse of his charming white teeth. "Why, that is an excellent idea, Reed."

CHAPTER 30

Gage could not stop staring at his soon-to-be wife. After everything had settled back at the beach and Caspian, Eden, Adam, and Addie had returned, the group had moved to the deck of Caspian's ship, the *Dawn's Mist*. Now, they were in the middle of a wedding ceremony. Gage's and Ivy's ceremony. His heart leapt at the thought. This woman was about to officially become his.

Ivy stood across from Gage, and she seemed to only have eyes for him as he only had eyes for her. Caspian was interposed between them, reading from his Bible. Eden stood at Ivy's side, holding a now-sleeping Emma. Reed leaned against his mother, and Adam had a hand on his sister's shoulder. Addie smiled beside Gage, paying a lot more attention to Adam than Gage would have liked. He was tempted to nudge her with his elbow to make her stop her gawking.

But Gage was doing his fair share of gawking himself. Ivy's orange hair was now dried and tucked into a loose, wavy bun. Either her friend Eden had done her hair for her, or she had discovered somehow that Gage did not like it tied back so tightly. Charles Town harbor's wind had pulled a few curls loose, and they danced around her collarbone. Her blue-gray eyes sparkled, and her complexion was lit with a becoming pink tone. She had changed out of Eden's old dress—the one that had grown stiff from its dip into the ocean—and into another of her friend's gowns. This one was a lovely turquoise that hugged her body in all the right places. The neckline scooped low. The sleeves and collar were trimmed with yellow rosebuds and white, frothy lace. She had never been more beautiful.

Gage feared he was doing a terrible job of listening to his wedding vows, but all he really needed to do was say "I do."

Ivy started fussing with the lace on her dress. Gage reached forward and stilled her hand, offering her a grin and a wink. She smiled back at him shyly, and he kept her hand in his.

Caspian closed the Bible and set it aside. He turned to Gage. "Captain Gage Thompson, do you take Lady Ivy Shaw to be your wife?"

Gage squeezed Ivy's hand. "I do."

"And Lady Ivy Shaw, do you take Captain Gage Thompson to be your lawfully wedded husband?"

Ivy beamed up at him. "I do."

"I now pronounce you husband and wife." Caspian clapped Gage on the shoulder. "You may kiss your bride."

Gage grinned and pulled his bride closer to him. He could certainly grow accustomed to calling her his bride.

He thanked God for allowing this to happen as he leaned down and kissed the woman. Gage had certainly kissed her before, but this kiss was special. It was filled with promise and hope and passion and happiness. By the time he remembered to end the kiss because they were not alone, a fair chunk of time had passed. A glance around at his friends told him that the length of their kiss had not gone unnoticed. Eden's face had warmed to a shade of pink, Addie had looked away, and Caspian was laughing silently. Gage squeezed Ivy's hand and glanced down at her. Her face was bright red with a blush. He chuckled, pulled her closer, and kissed her cheek for good measure.

"Congratulations!" Eden rushed forward and hugged Ivy before Gage could kiss her again.

Adam shook Gage's hand, and Addie hugged Gage.

He was certainly glad to have been able to share this day with his friends and his family. Gage silently thanked God for that and for the beautiful, brave, caring woman he was now allowed to call his wife. What had seemed to be one of the most difficult days in his life had turned out to be one of the best.

🔱

Ivy held her husband's hand underneath the table as they dined in Captain Archer's cabin directly following their wedding ceremony. Caspian had worked hard to prepare the cabin to accommodate all of them for a meal of the best food he could gather on short notice.

Gage speared a piece of roasted fish with his fork and popped it into his mouth. Ivy nibbled on a square of cheese contentedly.

The children had fallen asleep after they had eaten only a few bites of food and now rested on one of Caspian's armchairs.

After the dinner was out of the way, Gage rose and helped Ivy up. "Well, I think my wife and I will be heading back to our ship for the night." He ran a hand up and down her arm, shooting tingles across her body. "We truly appreciate all you have done to make this day pleasant for us."

Caspian stood, closely followed by Eden. "Gage, you are like a brother to me, and your wife is like a sister to my Eden. You saved my son's life today. It was no trouble at all for me to have my cook prepare a meal for you and Mrs. Thompson."

Ivy smiled at the name. She adored it.

"I will escort Miss Thompson back to her cabin," Adam offered.

Gage shot a glare at him, but did not refuse.

"Caspian and I can keep Emma with us for the night." Eden smiled at her son and the baby.

Ivy glanced over at the little one. She was sound asleep. The thought of being alone with Gage for the night made her stomach jump in nervous anticipation. "That is kind of you, but—"

Gage squeezed her shoulder, cutting off her sentence. "We appreciate it." Ivy swallowed. "Are you ready, my love?"

"Aye." Ivy patted Emma on the head lightly, and then faced her best friend.

Eden hugged her. "Do not be nervous," she whispered.

After saying goodbye to Caspian, Gage wrapped an arm around Ivy's waist and led her out of the cabin. The sun had fully set now, and twinkling stars lit their path.

They walked together in peaceful silence off of the gangway and onto the still-bustling Charles Town docks. Gage sent one mischievous look her way, and before she knew it, she was in his arms, lifted like a sack of potatoes, and speeding toward his ship.

"Gage, there is no reason for you to carry me!" She squeaked through a fit of laughter.

He pressed a lingering kiss against her earlobe but did not slow his pace by a second. They were now making their way up the gangway to his ship. "I am going to carry you across the threshold, my love."

Goodness, but she could not be happier than she was this instant. This amazing, charming, strong man was hers. And they were about to make their marriage complete. Butterflies raced through her stomach as Gage carried her across the deck of his ship.

None of the crew was up and about on the main deck, a fact that comforted Ivy. She could just imagine their teasing and was glad she did not have to endure it on this happy night.

Her husband balanced her against himself as he used one hand to open their cabin door. He set her down inside the cabin and then kicked the door shut. "I did not get a chance to tell you that you look beautiful." Ivy glanced down at her borrowed turquoise gown. Eden had told her it brought out the blue in her eyes. "Your hair makes me crazy, you know that, sweetheart?" He reached up and pulled the pins out of her hair. Orange ringlets tumbled down to her shoulders. He ran his fingers through them.

"I love you, Gage."

"I love you too, Ivy." He pulled her close for a kiss and Ivy felt all of the nervous tension escape her body. She trusted this man. He was meant for her, and she was meant for him. There was no other place she would rather be than in the arms of her wonderful husband.

🙢

The next afternoon, Ivy stood on the deck of the *Siren's Call* with her child in her arms and her husband at her side as another ship approached at a fast pace. Already an hour away from Charles Town, they had parted ways with Eden and Caspian, who had promised they would all meet in London eventually. Gage made faces at Emma, who giggled uncontrollably. He kissed the side of her neck.

"It's the *Cross's Victory*, Captain." Adam stepped up next to them. "Do you know a ship by that name?"

"That's Captain Emery's ship, Gage!" Ivy frowned. What were he and Aimee doing near Charles Town?

"I see. Hmm."

Ivy held her husband's hand and balanced their daughter against her chest as they waited for her friends to sail nearer.

Finally, they were near enough for Ivy to clearly make out the people on the deck. Aimee stood on one side and Captain Emery just about as far from her as the confined space would allow, with the crew between them. That was typical of them, though. As was the frown on Aimee's pretty face.

"Heave to, gentlemen!" Gage called to his crew. He kissed Ivy on the forehead. "Sorry, my darling, but I will have to see to the crew."

Her husband helped his men bring out ropes to lash the ships together. The second the ships were close enough, Aimee propelled herself over the bulwarks onto Gage's ship. Captain Emery raced over and leapt onto their ship as well.

Gage reached Ivy's side and looped an arm around her waist.

Ivy smiled at her friends as they made their way over to her. But they did not look nearly as pleasant. "What is wrong, Aimee? Are you all right?"

Aimee gestured to Matthew with a look of hatred before turning back to Ivy and Gage. "Ivy, I would like to introduce you to my *husband*, Matthew."

ABOUT THE AUTHOR

Bestselling author **Heather Manning** is a young lady who loves to read—and write. After she won several writing competitions, her first book was professionally published and quickly became an Amazon Bestseller. She is an active member of her local ACFW chapter and lives in Kansas City, Missouri where she attends high school, sees plays, devours donuts, and acts in community theatre. You can find Heather on her blog: heathermauthor.blogspot.com.

CPSIA information can be obtained
at www.ICGtesting.com
Printed in the USA
LVOW07s0034161216
517516LV00001B/194/P